A LE
FROM MARIGOLD

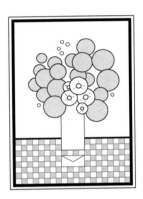

Michael Hill

Matador
9 Priory Business Park,
Wistow Road, Kibworth Beauchamp,
Leicestershire. LE8 0RX
Tel: 0116 279 2299
Email: books@troubador.co.uk
Web: www.troubador.co.uk/matador
Twitter: @matadorbooks

ISBN 978 1800461 000

British Library Cataloguing in Publication Data.
A catalogue record for this book is available from the British Library.

Printed and bound by CPI Group (UK) Ltd, Croydon, CR0 4YY

Matador is an imprint of Troubador Publishing Ltd

I dedicate this book to the forests
I've always loved: to the light and shade,
to the sunshine and shadows
that have fuelled my imagination
for as long as I can remember.

CONTENTS

AN INTRODUCTION

I

In order to widen the scope of this summary, I'd like to begin by quoting from the Introduction to my previous book of short stories 'The First Hints of Purple'. I've adopted this approach not only because it provides for the selective presentation of the lengthier original but also because 'A Letter from Marigold' embodies ideas similar to those on which the earlier book was based. And since it's important for readers to be aware of these ideas, parts of the relevant material are repeated below - *repeated*, I emphasise, rather than *rewritten* because any attempt at greater clarity would be likely to fail.

* * *

Broadly speaking, most of my stories correspond with what 'a story' usually means when the word comes to mind; and, as such, they would survive well enough on their own without the support of the following commentary. On the other hand, I often branch out from that simple definition into what I would describe as short 'literary entities' which, in the majority of cases, retain a beginning, a middle and an end - whilst fighting shy of some of the more predictable features commonly associated with fiction. In this sort of work, the thematic development or storyline may be eventful, tenuous or merely the progression of thought on the part of a character or characters. And occasionally, it may be the narrator alone whose reflections follow a path from a beginning to a conclusion that was by no means always predetermined when the starting pistol fired.

Where the reflective element dominates, the above-mentioned 'literary entities' frequently take the form of what I've described as *Contemplations* in which, with or without an active human participant, the fundamental indeterminacy of the world at large is scrutinised and made manifest. In other words, even if routine in principle, there are many circumstances which, when looked at aslant and with detachment, can also take on the otherness of a reality that cannot be captured by laboratory instruments or deduced from mathematics or philosophy. In these 'Contemplations', I therefore wilfully confuse the distinction between the familiar and the mystical; and I do so because that is the way I see a universe that is by no means fully explained.

* * *

Although I cannot account for it, the present collection (like the last) consists only of *short* stories. This arises from an in-built disinclination on my part to write longer works such as novels - for which the most probable reason is my tendency to reflect the character of poetry or, along the same lines, that of painting. Both of these areas are accessible, more or less, 'at a glance'; which in turn, by reducing the processional emphasis, favours the contemplative content instead. Accordingly, in some cases more than others, there's a creative fusion in my work between event and reflection, between poetic imagination and narrative movement. It's also important to add that, in my own case, this outcome has emerged from gradual self-discovery and definitely *not* from theory-based aspiration.

Just one other matter deserves mention: namely, my previous history and family background. A brief outline can be found on the inside back cover of the present collection. But a great deal more, both about this and other matters, is to be found in the Introduction to 'The First Hints of Purple'. And so, in order to make way for the entirely fresh topic that I wish to pursue next, interested readers are invited to visit my website, *michaelhillinprint.com*, where the above-mentioned Introduction is reproduced in full.

2

Odd though it may at first appear, but for reasons that become obvious later, I'd now like to focus on another author - an author very different from myself: namely, Anita Brookner, whose novels need neither an overview nor even a well deserved word of praise from someone like me. In the present context, however, I'm particularly interested in the two sentences placed ahead of the main text of her novel; 'Strangers' which was first published in 2009.

These sentences boil down to the simple-enough claim that all the characters in her novel are fictitious - to which she adds that, dispersed at random around the globe, there must be real-life characters who closely resemble those in her book. It's a conclusion that can hardly be doubted; and from the statistical angle alone, there's more than ample evidence in the shape of the numberless human beings living at any one time. Further to which, it must also follow that if the 'fictitious characters' in her novel are suitably credible, then her basic proposition gains even greater force.

Naturally enough, I have no means of finding out what prompted Anita Brookner to preface her novel with this statement. At the same time, as an author, I presume I'm not alone in meeting the occasional critic who suspects my stories of being dependent on people I've either read about or known. And it's true, of course, that both for me and for writers in general, 'other people' (as initial reference material) are the only source of information there is.

Having said that, it's important to be more specific about my own particular case; and it's worth emphasising that, when I'm not creating a character or event completely 'out of the blue', my established practice is to alter (rather than disguise) whatever my 'original reference point' may have been. In tandem with this, much time is also spent on devising a set of circumstances that evolve as I go along. The story then takes off on its own - characterised by individuals (often drawn from unconscious or composite sources) who bear no resemblance to anyone I'm acquainted with and involving a wealth of events that never actually happened.

3

It naturally goes without saying that the foregoing notes involve a modus operandi so common that it merits little further attention - although when it comes to the 'contemplative' elements in my work, I acknowledge indebtedness to no one... Indeed, it's the circumstance in which my affinity with poetry is most likely to become evident; and it's also an area in which even I, the originator, may not know exactly where the impulse is coming from. Except to say this: that it's here, at the borderline, where I'm more inclined to paint a picture centred on myself rather than on other people.

Which brings me, somewhat indirectly, to a quite different principle which has lingered in my brain ever since I was a fifteen-year-old schoolboy. And it concerns my old English teacher, Mr Dipstale (*Frank* Dipstale as I've recently found out), who was a man of quiet integrity and wisdom. In those days, I was more concerned with kite-flying than with literature. But even now, when considering some of the stories in this book, readers can still encounter the influence of Mr Dipstale who reminded his young listeners, including me, that it doesn't matter how subjective a piece of writing may be as long as it's sufficiently universal for anyone with an open mind to relate to it.

Michael Hill
1 July 2020

A MAN OF LITTLE ACCOUNT

Now the stallholder herself, whose East End origins went hand in hand with a rather generous self-assessment, was persuaded by Oliver's familiarity to extend to him the privilege of calling her Topsy - an intimacy otherwise restricted to the family. She had not, in fact, made any specific invitation to this effect; but Oliver, having overheard the name on the lips of her sons (and having taken the liberty) was given carte blanche as a reward for his overtures which, it must be emphasised, were entirely innocent of any dark designs. A tacit agreement was therefore established in which Topsy deigned to be amused by Oliver's quips, whilst Oliver (the proud intimate of a Chapel Market stallholder) made ample and loud-mouthed use of Topsy's, Zac's and Benjy's names which he repeated with an absurd degree of pretence and swagger.

From 'The Significance of Oliver Jupp', page 138.

THE HISTORY OF GOTTFRIED EISENSTADT

I

Gottfried Eisenstadt was enigmatic in the eyes of virtually everyone who met him for the first time - most particularly once he'd reached his twenties. To begin with, not only his name but also his accent was plainly of German origin - on top of which (and more to the point) he had a gruff, somewhat staccato manner of speaking. His command of English was extensive; on the other hand, as he grew older, it was blighted by the fact that he spoke it so fast and so breathlessly that, to some, he seemed poised on the brink of a nervous breakdown.

His early years had certainly been spent in Germany - a country to which, with admirable courage, his parents had returned some years after the end of World War II. But to their disappointment, they found that society as it existed before they were obliged to flee the Nazis was gone for good. With the advantage of experience behind them, their former homeland seemed duller - as well as increasingly dangerous, given the Cold War. The result, of course, was that their links with a time of relatively carefree existence had become tenuous. And so, when Gottfried reached the age of twelve, they sent him to an English boarding school because it was in England, during and after the years of conflict, that they'd felt so very much more at home. And now, rather than to their native land, it was to England that they looked for security, dependability and warmth.

It's true to say that no one gets everything right all the time; and Gottfried's parents got it wrong when they sent their son away from home at so young an age. Thus far, he'd developed in such a manner that he carried no baggage from Herr and Frau Eisenstadt's past. All the same, and despite learning the language quite quickly, he was like a fish out of water in an English school which, to him, was an alien institution in an alien land where he was popularly known, amidst the laddish cut and thrust, as 'the Kraut.' He was therefore very ill at ease even though, at the same time, Germany had no particular hold over him. And so, under these conditions, his accumulated experience of life was beginning to turn him into a loner - with the result that he stood apart from the other boys at the Bagshot Academy and did his best to avoid group practices such as sport which was an activity more or less synonymous with being human in the environment of an English private school. The outcome was a proneness to eccentricity: and he was often overheard talking not to others but to himself - from which small beginnings greater outcomes flowed later on.

* * *

In due course, Gottfried's parents received a letter from the Bagshot Academy's headmaster, pointing out that their son's progress was rather slow and that he seemed to be somewhat unhappy. Future support was generously offered; but the headmaster was almost as ingenious as he was generous when he wondered whether a few more years of secure family life might rescue a sensitive child from the consequences of isolation and stress.

This broad hint led to concrete results. Not without relief on their own account and being of dual nationality, Herr Friedrich and Frau Hanna Eisenstadt made immediate arrangements to return to England which enabled them to take their son back under their own wing whilst he attended a highly regarded grammar school. On successfully completing this stage of his education, he then obtained admission to the University of Glasgow where, after three years of effort, he received an upper second-class honours degree in Business Management. Parenthetically, it must also be remarked that his experience of university life produced only three personal involvements which could honestly be described as friendships; and after his studies ended, even these more or less faded away in just over eighteen months.

2

The next stage in Gottfried's career (which brings us closer to the heart of this story) began when he was persuaded to join his father's business as a trainee at the London headquarters - albeit a trainee, given the family association, with brighter prospects than his peers. The business in question, Eisenstadt & Company - with branches in Manchester and Edinburgh - was a specialised, somewhat demanding advisory service, offering guidance and initial financial support to would-be entrepreneurs in various fields. And more to the present point, it called for undeviating loyalty from its employees; it also involved endless meetings and encouraged much out-of-hours, work-centred socialising which soon became irksome as far as Gottfried was concerned. Furthermore, the sort of business specialisms in which he was expected to show an interest increasingly failed to engage his attention. The result was that he was often seen brooding in corners or alone with his notebook on a bench in nearby Bloomsbury Square.

It was the second time in his life that Gottfried began to feel like a fish out of water. To tell the truth, he soon became tired of his job not only for the straightforward reasons just mentioned but also because he'd long ago embraced another interest which had grown exponentially under the oppressive working conditions at Eisenstadt & Company. The plain fact was that he was spending more and more time inventing novel ideas for home entertainment - though only in secret behind the closed doors of his bedroom in the family home (where he still lived) or during his lunch breaks spent scribbling in Bloomsbury Square.

In relation to this unexpected turn of events, we are not talking about naïvely variant forms of 'musical chairs' or 'blind man's buff'. On the contrary, Gottfried was thinking up all sorts of original ideas suitable for children, teenagers or fully fledged adults; and his entire focus was on games that could be played, solo or in groups, at home rather than in a run-down seaside environment along-side the distraction of noisy slot machines. The possible variations seemed endless - some reliant on intellectual skills and ingenuity alone, others based on imaginative versions of what boiled down to betting. And then, of course - at a time long before the invention of the internet - there was a promising future centred on electrical devices: tabletop games with flashing lights; or bells that signalled success, defeat or the need to change tack. Clearly, there were more ways than one of playing snakes and ladders!

Gottfried was nothing if not thorough. He assiduously catalogued, annotated and illustrated his ideas in hard-to-find, rather odd notebooks with their own built-in lock and key. And in a sense, of course, he already had his foot on the first rung of the ladder, having spent quite a lot of time thinking about and sharpening other people's entrepreneurial skills. And so, it was in the world of new ideas for family entertainment that he essentially imagined and to some degree planned his future. Indeed, he thought of little else; and in the end, it began to show.

3

By this time, Herr Friedrich Eisenstadt was getting older and was disinclined to quarrel with his son when he discovered how things stood. Instead, he listened, provided some words of encourage-ment, and agreed (or rather offered) to set him up in business. He also had enough insight to realise that Gottfried could only really function as a one-man band; and so he went further and bought him a flat in a smart Victorian block near Hampstead Heath in North London where he could carry on his business from home. The services of Eisenstadt & Company would be at his disposal, of course; and the support thus offered would be free. Consequently, for a tall and gangly young man who had only just turned twenty six and whose looks were becoming haggard, this was very good news indeed!

* * *

The words 'John Constable Mansions' were inscribed in gold Snell Roundhand script on the door of the block of flats where Gottfried's freshly acquired home was situated. It stood appropriately close to the blue plaque pinpointing the early nineteenth century home of Constable himself whose name added status to any pile of bricks and mortar that borrowed it. And it goes without saying that this particular pile of bricks and mortar housed a selection of wary residents who had their ears to the ground when it came to new-comers. There was therefore immediate alarm when a full week's banging and clattering confirmed the new owner's arrival - especially on the two occasions when the noise continued past midnight.

Eventually, this unwelcome aspect of 'settling in' petered out. Unfortunately, however, it was swiftly followed by lengthy telephone calls featuring contentious issues such as the two phone connections that Gottfried's business would require - not to mention endless (and equally loud) calls to the manufacturers of the various materials needed in relation to his many ambitious ideas. Some of these providers were sited overseas in far-off time zones; and that was the reason why, even at night, the walls and floors of Gottfried's flat transmitted his dealings to all and sundry, obliging them to share his wakefulness.

This not-quite-final stage in the process of nest-building lasted for a further fortnight or thereabouts, during which time the neighbours held their peace in order to strengthen their case with more evidence if the need for action became overwhelming. But luckily, the noisy phone calls gradually became less frequent, although it was clear that, whenever they occurred, Gottfried always shouted rather than talked into the receiver.

In addition to what was actually a change for the better (and all the more surprising, given the involvement of a very young man), there was the welcome, if startling fact that no sound of music was ever heard coming from his apartment. Indeed, between the now moderate number of phone calls, there seemed to be an almost eerie silence. And for long periods, even though the lights in the main reception room regularly remained switched on until the early hours, nothing at all, not even the sound of footsteps, could be heard. It would have been unwise to jump to premature conclusions, of course; and over-optimistic observers were soon to find out that unfounded complacency is a common fault!

In other words, what seemed at first like a genuine improvement had a sting in its tail, for the very good reason that the lengthy silences themselves betrayed evidence of another mystery which to those watching television or trying to get to sleep suggested a darker side to the life and personality of Gottfried Eisenstadt. For example, it was obvious to those who pressed an ear against their bedroom wall that he sometimes talked to himself, because such interludes were brief, involved no voice other than his own and were delivered in a telltale monotone at widely spaced intervals. Odder still were the outbreaks of whistling, very short-lived but piercing, that sounded like a farmer, with his fingers to his lips, directing the manoeuvres of a sheepdog. It all boiled down to an enigma that fascinated but also worried the other residents in the vicinity who, partly out of fear, still hesitated to make a formal complaint to the managing agent.

4

After something like two more months, it became clear that the signs of activity audible from within Gottfried's flat had reached an equilibrium that seldom altered. And for that reason, whilst suspicions persisted, attitudes moderated amidst widespread relief. No further light, however, was ever shed on his ways or on his means of subsistence - other than the fact that the manifestations so far described continued at regular, but not unduly frequent intervals. Questions were still asked, of course: no one really knew what he was up to; many had never even seen him; and the perplexity generated by his long periods of silence was roughly equal to that aroused by the decidedly odd noises that emerged at intervals from his lips.

In the final analysis, the truth about Gottfried Eisenstadt was impenetrable to anyone beyond the confines of his family. Put simply, what it seemingly boiled down to was this: that cocooned in the security provided by others, he had found hope (if not its fulfil-ment) in a world of imagination that promised success of a sort together with a permanent alternative to external governance. At John Constable Mansions, of course, it remained the case that no one knew anything about him. And there was a similar limit to his own self-knowledge - a fact, and very likely a godsend, that saved him from being confronted with yet another challenge from a source far harder to deal with than the faceless manufacturer at the other end of a phone line!

Beyond this bleak set of circumstances, no further information is available. No evidence of sudden tragedy or rejoicing ever reached the ears of neighbours; neither has the local newspaper at any time featured an entrepreneur who made good in the specialised field of home entertainment. Perhaps the heart of the enigma that was Gottfried Eisenstadt struck one observer in particular who noticed, by means of the spyhole in her door, that other than his parents, no one else ever came to visit the young man who was living by himself within the protective envelope of an apartment where his efforts to make good were indiscernible. And that was not the end of it, for as time wore on, his efforts to make good were not only indiscernible but unsuspected - and therefore of no further interest to the world at large.

THE LULL BEFORE THE STORM

I

Matthew Parkinson, a retired academic, was seated on a bench dedicated to the memory of Tim, Nancy and Wilfrid Fuggles who, as the inscription on the back made clear, had once shared his enthusiasm for the same open space where, many years later on, he was following in their footsteps. The day was already hot and humid - conditions that were the main reason why he'd ended up in the shade of an oak tree where he was battling with a book of accomplished but difficult poetry. As if to emphasise the point, his concentration had begun to waver; and the truth of the matter was this: that his problem with the urge to fall asleep was due as much to the poems as it was to the weather.

Hoping for a few snacks (and long familiar with the peculiarities of humans), an audacious, if ominously named 'murder' of crows had just landed a few metres in front of him. To begin with, they kept their distance. At the same time, it's worth mentioning a species-specific trait: namely, that these were urban crows that, like the rest of their kind, had accumulated a store of well-founded knowledge. On which basis, they were relying on the probability that when Matthew had moved on after finishing whatever refreshments he'd brought with him, a reward would await them. At the same time, they were instinctively canny; and until they were sure he wouldn't be doing a u-turn and heading back, they could be depended on to remain where they were before converging on the breadcrumbs and other leftovers they expected to find on the grass. It's also worth pointing out that crows, when it comes to 'who gets what', seldom make concessions to man-made principles such as 'share and share alike'!

* * *

Matthew, as it happened, had no intention of moving on. He was very much at home, exactly where he was, in one of the capital's best known public gardens. But although he stayed put, it wasn't long before his attention was diverted from challenging poetry and a flock of birds to a pair of middle-aged men who, as they strolled past, were absorbed in a conversation of little interest either to himself or, apparently, to the crows. At the same time, he couldn't help noticing that the shorter of the two, whose name turned out to be Bruce, was distinguished by a somewhat craggy upper storey overlaid with a covering of skin ravaged and reddened by the sun. These characteristics struck him more forcibly than they might otherwise have done due to a remarkably short haircut which, being confusable with a scalping, exposed enough bumps to keep a nineteenth century phrenologist occupied for weeks on end.

The latter set of observations, despite their negative bias, introduced a note of levity that effectively altered Matthew's frame of mind. And so, given that the poetry he'd been reading was not only accomplished but taxing, he decided to alter course for a while in order to make some brief notes at the expense of the two men who, by that time, had finally disappeared. To be fair, his intentions were by no means hostile; it was just that his growing collection of character sketches, often enhanced by a spot of satire, was among his several leisure pursuits.

At this point in the story, it's fair to say that Matthew knew himself pretty well; and before he left home that morning, he'd realised there might be a mood swing of one sort or another. He was a restless, uneasy, often indecisive individual; and he frequently made plans open to more than one form of implementation. Which is why, on a day much like so many others, in addition to a book of poetry and couple of smoked salmon sandwiches prepared by his wife, his rucksack contained a clipboard amply supplied with A4 writing paper on which, with the two ageing strangers in mind, he completed an uncomplimentary description whose details are best left unstated.

* * *

For a few minutes, whilst reviewing what he'd written, he was tolerably content, despite the fact that the clatter of passing maintenance trucks was loud, frequent and unwelcome. At the same time, the blue sky overhead provoked a more insubstantial train of thought which was as far removed from his everyday concerns as it was hard to pin down.

By contrast with mere impressions, however, and closer to home, another (this time solitary) figure in his mid-fifties, suddenly appeared out of nowhere. Matthew was immediately struck by his odd appearance and concluded that if his name had been Clarence or something similarly outdated, it would have fitted him like a glove. To explain more precisely what he meant, this rather amusing individual was making his way towards the lake, and was absurdly dressed in a pair of light green shorts which, despite being 'shorts', were incongruously long. Moreover, one other equally striking feature boiled down to the fact that, being notably tall and scrawny, comparisons with a daddy-long-legs immediately sprang to mind. In other words, here was a highly eccentric-looking individual who, in Matthew's estimation, would have made an ideal butt of fun for a Peter Cook and Dudley Moore sketch when 'Beyond the Fringe' was convulsing the nation in the middle of the last century. It was a thought that inspired a self-satisfied, gleeful smile and a fresh set of additions to his notepad.

2

Even so, it was a smile that came and went soon enough in the wake of a quite different matter that presented itself out of the blue and concerned the species of tree under which he was sitting. For most people, no reason for anxiety would have been apparent; yet for Matthew, who had a long-standing interest in the natural world, the problem amounted to whether or not he was at risk from the caterpillars of the 'oak processionary moth' - caterpillars which, if disturbed, are prone to respond by discharging fine hairs that lodge in the skin and cause serious irritation. He'd noticed posters elsewhere in the locality concerning this hazard - and had once observed a mass of threadlike larvae worming their way in total unison along a branch as if they were part of a single sinister organism. At the time, he'd found it disturbing. But on this occasion, as things turned out, everything appeared to be in order... though only until an industrial-size mower (complete with a precariously seated driver at the wheel) blundered into view and started work without delay. Further to which, the accompanying noise was deafening.

At the suggestion of his wife, Brenda, Matthew's plan for the day had been one of quiet relaxation in contrast with the week-long burst of painting and decorating he'd just concluded at home. Unsurprisingly, therefore, he immediately began considering what defensive measures he might take against the mower. But even as he thought about the available options, his concentration was again disrupted - this time by a couple in their thirties who, having rounded the bend to his left, had just come into view. The woman, he observed, was dressed in a mauve frock decorated with sprays of white roses - plus a pink, somewhat loose-fitting blouse. The man, on the other hand, sported an open-necked, Caribbean-style shirt accompanied by a run-of-the-mill pair of khaki chinos.

Not only had Matthew spotted *them*, but they'd also spotted *him*. And in consequence, they glanced at each other and then abruptly altered course. The unintended outcome, inevitably, was that the penny dropped in good time: after all, it didn't take a genius to work out what their plan was as they embarked on a manoeuvre aimed at having a look at what he was doing whilst pretending to take no notice. The fact that he was scribbling notes rather than sketching would obviously have proved disappointing in itself. But given the fact that he was a very private sort of person, he decided to frustrate the couple's scheme with manoeuvres of his own. Consequently, he simply waited until they were looking elsewhere and then turned the clipboard upside down on his knee...

It took him no time at all, of course, to effect so simple a plan and, out of the corner of his eye, to witness the couple's disappointment as they pretended *not* to take a look. And so, as soon as they were out of sight, he rewarded himself with a hearty chuckle before adding a new and lively character sketch to his notes.

3

Time had now moved on. And in keeping with the ups and downs of the real world, although he couldn't quite put his finger on it, Matthew sensed the beginnings of a change in the air. The mower had completed operations and was grunting and chugging as it made off in search of pastures new. No more trucks were tearing by; and no further intrusions appeared to be in the offing - not, at least, until he become conscious, quite suddenly, that the day was unusually still and consequently that the trees were motionless. For a few minutes, he had an odd impression: it felt as if the planet had ceased turning; furthermore, all activity seemed to have dwindled to a point where only a few snatches of birdsong remained in the midst of an otherwise silent void. With the result that, whilst this unexpected hiatus continued, Matthew began packing his bags with the intention of shifting to another, more rewarding spot where he believed there was a better than even chance of peace and quiet. And as for the 'changes in the air' he'd just noticed, he somewhat recklessly disregarded them.

Shortly after moving on, at the tail end of a five-minute walk, he finally reached the lake. With his legs stretched out in front of him, on an empty seat near the water's edge and without unwelcome distractions, he felt at ease. After all, it was a place where he could enjoy nature's peculiar gift of two for the price of one. For most people, such a thought would never have arisen; but for Matthew, the implication was plainly evident in a situation where everything came in pairs. For example, he observed that a yellow flag iris, mirror-imaged in the water, exactly duplicated itself; as did the scarlet copy of a lifebuoy which, as if by magic, was already obligingly afloat in readiness for circumstances less imminent than the explorations of a koi carp to his left as it navigated in and out of the pond weed, lazily flip-flapping its tail as it did so.

4

Notwithstanding what, at root, was a search for perfect tranquillity (and an odd feeling that, after all, he wasn't going to find it), the weather forecast had mentioned late afternoon thunder - although a lone blackbird was still singing when the first, far-off rumbles reached Matthew's ears. This, as he now suspected, was the 'lull that comes before the storm' - a storm which, with luck, might refresh the environment and lift it out of itself. Meanwhile, he faced up to the inevitability of what was coming - and began considering what to do about it.

From the evidence he heard as it grew louder, worsening conditions were getting closer by the minute. However regrettably, the forecast had been accurate; and a regiment of grim, aggressive-looking clouds, although a long way off, suddenly made an appearance. Indeed, the interval between a faint flash and a distant boom told him that the eye of the storm had probably reached the outer suburbs where shoppers, like scurrying ants, were very likely heading for cover - especially those whose umbrellas had been blown inside-out by a wind that was driving the darkening skies in his direction. Meanwhile, standing just a stone's throw away, he spotted the familiar figure of the 'man in green shorts' who was studying a pair of coots whose battle for territory was disturbing the surface of the water.

Abandoning his former hopes of peace and quiet, Matthew was now the only human being among those he could see who was preparing to make a move. By this time, he'd reached a point of no return and was convinced that his intended course of action was the only sensible one. From early childhood, he'd been well versed in the signs: again and again he'd experienced, as at that moment, the sudden drop in temperature and the beginnings of commotion among the trees. Consequently, looking anxiously ahead as he moved off, it was clear that the sun's impending disappearance would be no short-term matter - neither would silence be its hallmark.

5

After a strenuous interval (half walking and half running), with mixed feelings of urgency and relief, Matthew finally caught sight of his destination. He'd been brought forcibly down to earth by circumstances accurately foretold by modern technology and confirmed just in time by sharp eyes and practised ears. 'Better safe than sorry' was the well-worn motto he muttered repeatedly under his breath as he made a beeline for cover.

And not a moment too soon! With only minutes to spare, he took refuge in the spacious interior of a conservatory where he was more than happy to exchange the well tended parkland he'd left behind for what in effect was an all-encompassing jungle. He was lucky: it didn't take long to find another bench; and a feeling of comfort and willing resignation seemed to emerge from the abundant vegetation that surrounded him. The sequel was both unsurprising and perfectly natural: in other words, he resigned himself to a pleasant afternoon under a glass dome where he could listen with impunity to the sound of the wind, the thunder and the falling rain.

All of which enabled him to make the best of conditions foisted on him by circumstances he couldn't alter. Beyond reach of the British weather, he'd now found a ready-made opportunity to go back to his book in an effort to get to grips with those highly accomplished but difficult poems. And this meant, of course, that he'd be usefully occupied until the storm fell silent and it was time to head off home for a cocktail and the first glimpse of a dinner table whose advanced state of readiness was sure to fulfil expectations.

Murder of crows: the collective name for a group of crows.

Daddy-long-legs: the crane fly, Tipula paludosa. A common insect with exceptionally long legs.

Oak processionary moth: one of several members of the family Thaumetopoeidae whose caterpillars behave as described in the text.

Yellow flag iris: Iris pseudacorus. Flowers best in waterside habitats.

THE WINDING PATH OF HUBERT BELLAMY

Frogs and snails
And puppy-dogs' tails,
That's what little boys are made of.

Nursery Rhyme

At the heart of everything, there is a conundrum centred on the question of a being (traditionally referred to as divine and described for convenience as masculine) whose existence or non-existence, in the very particular context cited below, is neither the main nor the only issue. And yet, he, she or it is still the hypothesis without which there could be neither the story that follows nor the rational grounds that in principle supported it.

It was a question of the utmost profundity which had occupied the mind of a young man called Hubert ever since it first arose during his teenage years at a time when questions pop up like bubbles in a glass of fizzy lemonade. And it can best be summarised by introducing it obliquely, as the enigma that it *is*, rather than as a merely philosophical exercise. On Hubert's behalf, therefore, as curious bystanders, let us try to comprehend the nature and direction of his thought.

* * *

Oddly enough, it might be an advantage *not* to begin at the beginning but at the *end* by assuming, for the sake of argument, that a being such as we commonly call God does exist. This may or may not be the case - with equal odds on either side of the fence - but it's nevertheless the presumption without which Hubert's speculations would be reduced to the level of the Higgs boson before it was finally discovered and taken seriously.

Now any external adjudicator, who hasn't guessed already, is entitled to know that Hubert was a religious believer whose theology was orthodox, but basic. And insofar as this is a narrative emerging from one person's highly individual imagination, we need firstly to define God, as usually understood (including by Hubert). Otherwise, the consequent 'conundrum' that foxed him can be neither appreciated nor taken seriously.

For believers and agnostics alike, therefore, God (whether he exists or not) is defined as the one unique being, with neither beginning nor end, who is primordial, infinite and the source of everything other than himself. In other words, in simple language, God is where the buck stops and starts - the alpha and the omega that supervenes at both ends of reality.

And this brings us face to face with Hubert's quandary. Because, if you are the source of *everything* other than yourself, you will have found it impossible from the start to find any material of any description at your disposal on which you could have acted in order to create, manufacture or refashion anything at all. Which would seem, for those of us who are human, to confine God to a solitary heaven, perpetual inertia and a level of boredom greater than the sum total of all the galaxies and black holes in the universe!

And so, after racking his brain throughout the fourth and fifth years of his formal education, these preconditions struck Hubert as imposing a highly counter-intuitive conclusion: namely, that a prime mover without anything to act on must have created Everything out of Nothing - which is the standard theological position and the underlying mystery that had to be grappled with. Beginning with this central puzzle, therefore, Hubert (in between Chemistry, Maths, Latin and French lessons) started off by facing up to it fairly and squarely.

One of the earliest pitfalls that struck him was the possibility that somewhere or other along the line, he was confronting a contradiction. After all, he reflected, if nothing really means nothing, then ex nihilo creation must be an absurd and therefore inoperable proposition. If words really mean what they say, he told himself, neither infinite power nor limitless intelligence can bring about something which is effectively a nonsense - something which, without an escape clause, would tend to confuse creative action with the skill of a conjuror who, by some well concealed means, has pulled a fast one. And in his frequent conversations with the only school-friend he had who was interested, Hubert summed up what seemed like an impasse with the following, frequently repeated mantra. 'Something cannot act on Nothing to produce Something Else', he declared, 'if there is Nothing Else to act on in the first place.'

And on this dizzying pinnacle of an apparent choice between materialism and blind faith, it might be helpful to pause and look back at the early life of that entirely unexceptional amalgam of flesh, blood and conscious mind that was Hubert Bellamy.

* * *

The benefits are as obvious as they are intriguing. We will therefore take a short break from the hard labour of thought in order to gaze backwards at one young man's history - or more precisely, at *part* of it. Hubert had grown up very slowly; and even whilst doing so, he'd realised that 'growing up slowly' was exactly what he was in the middle of. Consequently, during his childhood and teenage years, he marked time in a uniquely ideal environment uninfluenced by the loud-hailers of protest marchers or the conflicting arguments of Speakers' Corner. In other words, he was almost completely unaffected by doctrinaire social presupposition and was governed instead by the characteristics of his particular, in some ways privileged and certainly very unusual background.

Almost daily after school, his interests regressed from parallelograms to birdwatching, from French grammar to model aircraft or, more outlandishly, to the special treetop from which, undetected, he gazed down for hours at the everyday world below. And this meant that, differing from those of his contemporaries whose minds were focussed on first class degrees and brilliant careers, Hubert's head remained firmly in the clouds. Given this level of detachment, it was therefore one of the high points of his fifth year when his only like-minded, academically able schoolfriend greeted his speculations with the following tribute. The name of this obliging fifth-former and confidant was Liam; and his acknowledgement went well beyond flattery.

'I think that's as close as you'll ever get to the truth,' he said.

* * *

Now the truth thus referred to was ex nihilo creation as interpreted by a curious, dilettante Hubert whose insight was this: that when all other avenues were eliminated, only one remained: namely, that with nothing other than himself to act on, it was on *himself* that the divine person acted. And the only aspects of himself on which he *could* act were his own thoughts.

Liam's receptive attitude to this novel theory proved particularly useful when, having made himself as clear as he could, Hubert struggled with the problem of how such an unimaginable event could have been brought about.

'The mystery is probably *not* that the conscious entity we call God can think up universes,' Liam suggested, 'but that he can *reify* them into an independent state of their own... or to put it another way, that he can detach his *thoughts* from *himself*.'

It has to be said that Hubert had never heard of reification. And there was a short silence during which the two friends exchanged undecipherable glances until Liam began to explain that, according to the dictionary, reification was a process whereby something purely hypothetical could become palpable or real. This idea was then discussed for nearly an hour until Hubert's understanding advanced as far as the concept itself allowed if treated as an effective process as distinct from a linguistic mannerism. Inevitably, of course, like a grain of sand in an oyster shell, uncertainty went hand in hand with the emerging chink of light.

'So that makes it pretty clear,' Hubert concluded, 'that when God created the universe, it was out of his own thoughts, and nothing else, that he must have created it.'

'Very likely, as I said earlier,' replied Liam. 'But whether he did or he didn't, we can't possibly know anything more about it unless he tells us.'

What are little boys made of? J. O Halliwell, Nursery Rhymes, 1844.

A LETTER FROM MARIGOLD

I

Close to the common at the top of the hill in Wimbledon village and situated just off the High Street, there is a slightly drab little backwater known as Alperton Way that stands in marked contrast to the refreshing grandeur of Cannizaro Park where the lawns and woodlands slope generously westwards on the far side of the common whose flat, featureless expanse is interrupted only by Rushmere Pond, an avenue of mature trees and a number of straggling, muddy footpaths. It should also be mentioned that when it rains these footpaths play host to many inconvenient puddles which, for lack of visible landmarks within range, reflect nothing but the sky.

Compared with the vast acres of Cannizaro Park, Alperton Way is an obscure and unremarkable location. Not long ago, however, it was there that Ogilvie Mansions, home to about a hundred and fifty flat-dwellers, asserted its particular, if lesser, claim to fame. It did so in the simplest possible fashion by confronting the other, rather shabby properties nearby with a pair of urns brimming with brightly coloured pelargoniums - an audacious summer display which, earlier that year, had supplanted the yellow and orange primulas whose efforts in defiance of winter gloom were beginning to look doubtful. For many years, these urns had stood either side of the ceremonious (if crestfallen) front gates - gates which, at the time of this account, having acquired a fresh lick of paint, contributed an extra boost to the pelargoniums and their assertion of superior status.

Ogilvie Mansions, built early in the twentieth century in a familiar redbrick tradition, owed virtually everything to its Victorian forebears. In its infancy, it had been administered by a charitable trust whose sole mandate was to provide accommodation for poor and needy families at affordable rents. On the other hand, with the passing years, it had been affected by a variety of historical developments, including the almost total gentrification of its hilltop environment. The result was that, in the mid nineteen-seventies, it had passed into private hands and was converted into a limited company whose shareholders comprised those residents and outsiders who could afford to buy the leases.

As time wore on, in response to continuing social change, the flats were transformed into a mixed bag of private leaseholdings alongside short-term lettings offered at market value by Ogilvie Mansions itself. There was also a minority of the original tenants who managed to hang on to their homes at the former, much lower 'controlled' rents to which the law entitled them. Further to which, it must not be forgotten that many of the new owners had purchased their flats solely on a buy-to-let basis. The result was that the so-called 'class of person' enjoying the benefits of pelargoniums and freshly painted gates was somewhat uneven - with the balance just about weighted on the upwardly mobile, aspirational side.

* * *

The several redbrick piles that made up Ogilvie Mansions consisted of five floors apiece, including the ground floor. There were two flats at every level - each group of ten flats being served by a single staircase. There were two or three such staircases in each block - and there were no lifts. On the whole, the top floor was preferable. In addition to having the finest views, these well-placed apartments were affected by the least noise from other occupants. Consequently, despite the fact that reaching the highest level required the greatest effort, it also represented the best deal for those with the requisite stamina to manage the climb.

Although a largely passive observer of her neighbours' activities, central to the present tale was the top-floor owner-occupier of flat 112 - a widow aged seventy-one by the name of Mrs Eloise Williams. Despite her age, she was still sprightly and had little trouble with the stairs apart from an occasional pause to catch her breath. She also had little trouble in finding fault with anyone on the lower floors who stepped out of line. Among her many gripes, for example, was the use of the various landings as parking spaces for private property such as rubbish bags awaiting disposal, unsightly mud-spattered shoes and dripping umbrellas.

Notwithstanding these and similar petty resentments, Mrs Eloise Williams took a very close interest in her neighbours' personal affairs which, to some degree, compensated for their failings. And so it was that, given her frequent presence in the common parts of the building, she was able to listen in to the intriguing noises emerging from behind the closed doors that she passed on an almost daily basis.

'Practice makes perfect': and after many years of habitual snooping, Mrs Williams had mastered the knack of so positioning herself with one hand on the bannisters that she could instantly hoist herself out of view if and when she got wind of a door about to open. And as a result of her long experience, her senses had become very sharp indeed. The result was that musical tastes and cultural affiliations were often deducible in return for a spot of eavesdropping on one or other of the landings. Furthermore, certain general principles became apparent: for example, complete daytime silence indicated an occupant with a regular job; whereas the continuous sound of popular music was a sign either of a loafer on social security or of a student (perhaps from abroad) with sufficiently well-off parents to cover the requisite expenses.

And then, of course, significantly different in kind, there were the party-givers, all of them renters aged twenty-five years old or under. Several of them (following letters from Mrs Williams to the board) had been given notice to quit by their respective landlords on account of the hullabaloo transmitted not only to the stairwell but also, via walls, floors and ceilings, directly to many of the other nearby flats. It was a natural hazard of communal living that had left one overriding principle firmly established in Eloise's mind: namely, that really bad behaviour was almost always associated with lessees or sub-lessees rather than with owner-occupiers.

Last but not least, it must also be mentioned that the occupant of flat 112 was occasionally rewarded with the very particular delight of passing a closed door when domestic conflict was in full swing on the other side of it. Such rare opportunities were not to be missed, despite the danger. But luck always seemed to be on her side; and so far Mrs Eloise Williams, whilst placing herself at genuine risk inches from this or that door, had never yet been caught napping in the middle of a family dispute!

* * *

Now, before detailing the events that substantially altered Mrs Williams' hitherto regular way of life, a broad overview of her circumstances and background will be helpful. She was a naturally resilient character and had adapted fairly quickly to the loss of a husband who, in consequence of heading a successful hardware chain, had left his wife comfortably off. She, for her part, had experienced growing prosperity throughout her married life; and whilst far from being a snob, she had gradually acquired a set of standards governing good behaviour which, other than at family weddings and funerals, had not been characteristic of her childhood.

Notwithstanding this more or less conscious absorption of traditional middle class values, Eloise steered well clear of dressing pretentiously: for example, she had never presented herself in anything like the garb of an East End costermonger's wife self-consciously parading on the platform at Waterloo en route to Ascot; nor had she seized the opportunity when it arose of staggering awkwardly in high heels to the degree ceremony of her best friend's son. Instead, her personal attire was usually bland with just a dash of brighter colour here and there - plus a modest string of pearls on very special occasions when, as at most other times, her knees were concealed by a pleated skirt embellished with an unassuming grey and white check.

As far as appearances were concerned, only one feature suggesting a lack of judgement had ever been observed by her neighbours - and even then only rarely when the first clear signs of summer persuaded her to adorn her hair with a single rose before she made her way across the common carrying in her hand, for the umpteenth time, a copy of a novel by her favourite author, Jane Austen. It was a regular annual response to June that always ended up in the tranquillity of the rose garden which was situated in an obscure and largely unvisited corner of Cannizaro Park.

Rounding off a picture of this well-preserved, childless widow demands just one further set of details centred on the simple but ultimately pivotal fact that the only surviving relative she had was Marigold, her similarly childless sister. Marigold was barely five years older than her sibling; and like Eloise, she was a widow. But she was also a widow of longer standing who had adapted less well to living alone in what was too large a house with a vast, hard-to-manage garden in a leafy suburb of Guildford. More positively, however, it was also a house in a location that held one trump card - namely, a far closer association with open air and sky than was the case in the darker, claustrophobic surroundings of Ogilvie Mansions. And this, of course, was a favourable environmental factor which it shared, somewhat prophetically, with Cannizaro Park.

* * *

Before a game of chess begins, the chess board in its initial neutral state must be assembled with all the pieces in their correct positions. Similarly, with their relevant backgrounds unaltered and in their familiar place, the two main characters in the present story, at the point when unforeseen events began to take shape, found themselves faced with a series of moves which, to begin with, gave no indication of how the game would pan out.

It was in Wimbledon's Alperton Way rather than in Guildford's Imperial Drive that the owner of flat 112 became aware, from a safe distance, of the first unwelcome rumblings. These were connected with the family (father, mother and a young son) who, as sub-lessees, were renting flat 108. Flat 108 was two flights down from Eloise's top-floor residence which, as the leaseholder, she owned outright. She had long been conscious of the noise from the downstairs apartment in question - not only when she passed the front door and paused to listen, but also when relaxing in the supposedly quiet haven of her own lounge where the volume of sound, given the distance between herself and its source, was only a minor nuisance. But Eloise had often told herself that, were she obliged to live directly alongside the raised voices, the loud music and the sound of the child's football bouncing about from room to room, it would be hard to put up with. Consequently, a dark cloud formed at the back of her mind and constantly oppressed her - even when, for once, clear skies prevailed and the silence of Cannizaro Park was golden. It was in the late nineteen-nineties, with summer more or less established, when Eloise discovered that flat 110 was up for sale. Being on the next floor down immediately underneath what had been her home for more than a decade, it was news that provoked instant alarm. Given that suitable buyers cannot be predetermined, it shattered the equanimity she'd enjoyed for many years and became a burden that she carried about with her wherever she went. But despite this, she gritted her teeth. She also changed her behaviour and instead of continuing to spy on her neighbours as she passed their front doors, she began a campaign of eavesdropping outside her own front door whenever one or other of the several estate agents reached the landing below with a new batch of flat-hunters.

During this period of growing anxiety about the future, an envelope unmistakably inscribed in Marigold's hand caused Eloise's letter box to respond with a sharp snap which, in any normal situation, would have raised hopes of a pleasant surprise. The letter was certainly friendly in tone, as she swiftly discovered, but it failed to bring good news. Instead, it conveyed Marigold's considerable discomfort as she rattled about in what she called the very large 'tin can' that was her home - a home which, objectively speaking, was extremely attractive. That, at least, was what Eloise told herself in the light of her own domestic worries. It was clear, of course, that her sister was looking for support; but it seemed she was also hoping to find answers to a dilemma as insoluble as the one affecting her equally troubled sibling.

Whilst considering the unsettling position that both sisters appeared to be in, Eloise's train of thought was interrupted by voices on the landing below which she recognised as those of an estate agent with another group of prospective buyers. She therefore put Marigold's letter to one side, crept along the narrow hallway, quietly opened the front door and listened attentively.

Now it happened to be a day when the couple selling flat 110 were out, thereby causing a hold-up outside the door which in turn enabled Eloise to hear more of the conversation than she might otherwise have done. And it was then that a virtual bombshell exploded in her face when she realised that the visitors about to view the formerly quiet property beneath her feet were none other than the rumbustious occupants of flat 108 who, perhaps wisely, had decided that a mortgage was a better proposition than paying rent. But even worse was to come: for the conversation she overheard whilst the estate agent fumbled with the keys indicated that they had already made an offer (which had been accepted) and were merely indulging an exciting final look at their new home before exchanging contracts in a week or two's time!

* * *

For Eloise, the remainder of that critical day was as bleak as any she could remember; and it revealed to her the full extent of her vulnerability in the face of adverse conditions. She cooked her evening meal with the reserves of energy that still remained rather than as a response to an appetite that barely existed. Both before and after serving and forcing down a mushroom omelette with asparagus and new potatoes, she drank a succession of whiskies and sodas. And then, after swallowing a final glass in lieu of sleeping pills, she went to bed early, shed a couple of tears, and battened down the hatches.

On the following morning, she awoke to bright sunshine and a vociferous blackbird whose cheerful song sounded an encouraging note. But during and after breakfast, Eloise's one and only thought was to escape from the flat, to get as far away from it as possible so as to take stock in some familiar, tranquil environment at a safe distance from everything associated with her troubles.

It happened to be a day that was not only sunny but warm. This enabled her to dress in light clothes, barely remembering to comb her hair and without thinking of the rose which at any other time would have signalled what was, in reality, her first summer trip of the year to Cannizaro Park. Nevertheless, despite her haste and not wishing to leave without something to occupy her, she had enough presence of mind to grab her much-loved copy of 'Northanger Abbey' which she placed in her handbag along with Marigold's letter for use as a bookmark. She then threw in some chocolate digestive biscuits, a packet of cigarettes and a box of matches - after which she made for the front door which she carefully locked behind her before making her way downstairs until she reached flat 108 where she came to an abrupt halt.

The reason why Eloise stopped dead in her tracks was her previous experience of the hubbub behind that door which was now demonstrating once again what she would shortly have to live with. In the first place, there was the noise of moving furniture, of scurrying feet, of objects being dropped on the kitchen tiles - all of which indicated what the future held in store. But in addition, there was another, already familiar sound: namely, that of voices incessantly at cross-purposes, rather like the commotion of rapids pouring with turbulent disregard over a bed of jangling pebbles. While she listened, as in the past, there was no sign of an end to it. And it was finding a means of escape from so dire a threat that confronted Eloise as she fled from Ogilvie Mansions without even noticing the pelargoniums either side of the freshly painted gates.

* * *

As she blundered unsteadily across the common towards the park, splashing her way through several puddles, Eloise presented a forlorn picture. Her eyes were downcast; and her hair grew increasingly dishevelled after the wind, which she failed to notice, blew it this way and that. Her mind was clearly focussed inwardly as she pondered her predicament; and once or twice, she pulled Marigold's letter out of her handbag and then put it back again, without really knowing what had prompted her to do so. Finally, distraught and only barely in charge of her wits, she walked across the road and through the park gates, entirely disregarding the Millennium Fountain and the sound of running water that went with it.

In happier, untroubled days, there were many features in Cannizaro Park that Eloise enjoyed looking at. For example, she often paused alongside the pinnacled aviary, built in the style of a gothic chapel, where the canaries and budgerigars invariably amused her. On this particular day, however, she walked straight past and even ignored the late-flowering magnolias and rhododendrons, neither of which was capable of easing her anxiety. The distant outline of the Surrey hills visible from the lawn fared no better and merely deepened her sense of isolation. She therefore wandered disconsolately on until, guided by habit, she flopped down with a thud on the bench she knew so well in the rose garden where the hedges and crumbling walls sheltered her from the gaze of passing strollers.

It was at this stage in her ramblings, both psychological and geographical, that Eloise tried to pull herself together. The familiar taste of two chocolate biscuits was not wholly redemptive; but at least the gathering gloom gathered more slowly. An attempt at 'Northanger Abbey', of course, failed completely because (as was instantly obvious to her) it could bring no healing influence to bear on a practical dilemma. Instead, she reflected on friendship, on the past, on her sister, on happier days, on childhood aspirations; and having pulled Marigold's letter out of her handbag once more, she read it not only thoroughly but repeatedly.

It was mentioned earlier in this story that Eloise, by and large, was a resilient and practical woman. But until that precise moment on a weathered bench in an obscure corner of Cannizaro Park, she'd had neither the opportunity nor the inclination to scrutinise Marigold's letter in detail. Now, on the other hand, while the sun continued to shine and after two more chocolate biscuits, she realised what had been obvious all along: namely, that both she and her sister needed help. At the same time, of course, she had more than enough common sense to understand that, if a solution is to be found, easily stated problems may still require a great deal of thought. Consequently, she continued mulling things over until, following almost an hour of unbroken meditation, she perceived a faint glimmer of light that seemed to grow steadily stronger. It was a breakthrough that gave grounds for hope; and it commanded her attention more and more closely as she broke several more biscuits in two and demolished each piece slowly, almost with indifference, whilst her mind continued to focus on the central issue.

* * *

The awareness of a problem, acute though it may be, by no means guarantees the existence of a ready-made solution just waiting to be found. But the lack of a solution is inevitable when the problem is not sufficiently well thought through. And it was here that Eloise's rationality triumphed in the wake of Marigold's vague and rather rambling letter. Put simply, she noticed the counterpoint in their shared experience of trouble and swiftly narrowed it down to the fact that Marigold's discomfort was due solely to living alone in an oversized, hard-to-manage house and garden whilst her own somewhat more immediate distress comprised being lumbered with a smaller home threatened by noisy neighbours.

It all boiled down to an equation which Eloise thought must surely cancel out in response to a sufficiently intense effort. And as she pored over the intricacies necessary to achieving that end, she rose from the bench, looked carefully around her, picked a half-open rose in defiance of the regulations - and slipped it behind her ear. She then resumed her seat and, without any further hankering for 'Northanger Abbey', she turned matters over in her mind for a further two hours - at which point the final disappearance of the biscuits by no means dimmed the light into which she began to emerge at what she hoped was the end of the tunnel.

It was a remarkable achievement. And it would be tedious to over-shadow it with a detailed account of the letters and phone calls between the two elderly sisters whom age and adversity had brought into closer contact at a time when kinship suddenly counted for very much more than previously. For Eloise, the solution they agreed on was one that brought relief from an imminent source of anxiety; whereas for Marigold it meant deliverance from the possibility she feared most: namely, gradual decline in uncharted and increasingly choppy waters. Consequently, the sun began to shine more brightly where, until the final decision was reached, darkness and uncertainty had prevailed.

2

Once matters had been agreed in principle, there was good reason for the air of excitement surrounding 137 Imperial Drive when, having placed her flat on the market, Eloise went down for a pre-liminary week's stay in her sister's home on the pleasant outskirts of Guildford. There was still a great deal to discuss, of course; and on the first day, there was an excellent lunch to set the ball rolling - with some good wine to help it on its way. There was no rush, of course: the division of living space was easily resolved, given the existence of two upstairs bedrooms, one with an en suite bathroom, plus ample facilities for visitors on the ground floor. Neither was there any need for monetary concerns to complicate the discussion - for both sisters were sufficiently well provided for.

In broad terms, therefore, it was plain sailing; and consequently, during those early hours of their forthcoming closer association, there was a great deal of light-hearted chatter and jollification. Inevitably, there was also an outpouring of auld lang syne; and above all, in the wake of a rapidly conceived but sensible arrangement, there was much carefree laughter!

It would be naïve, of course, to presume that Eloise and Marigold would duplicate the flawless happy ending of an old-fashioned love story. After all, neither princes, priests nor peasant farmers, not even well-off widows are immune from the march of time and the troubles that go with it. Notwithstanding this, it remains a fact that the clouds which eventually darkened the horizon were sufficiently distant from those first, euphoric beginnings in Imperial Drive as to be well beyond the time frame of the present story.

* * *

It remains true, however, that although unsuspected, unrecognised and long dormant, the seeds of discord were present from the start. Insignificant in summary but highly pertinent in relation to an always-unforeseeable future, there was a characteristic affecting one of the newly formed partners that first reared its head as an apparently generous offer. It was on the third morning of Eloise's preliminary trip to Guildford when she and her sister were chatting during their second walkabout in the garden. As Marigold (unversed in hectares) had just mentioned, the property as a whole was just over an acre; and it was this factor alongside the loss of her husband which had made it particularly difficult to maintain the outdoor areas. Even so, it was a recreational space which was destined to be of central importance not only to Marigold but also (as things turned out) to her sister. And the reason for this, unspoken even to herself, was that as a widow living alone for many years, Eloise had formed a relationship with Cannizaro Park that amounted, more or less, to a romance. And it was Cannizaro Park of which she was reminded as she secretly coveted her sister's neglected back garden.

During the fraught and sometimes muddled moments since deciding to quit Ogilvie Mansions, Eloise had been reminded of a fact she was already aware of: namely, that gardens were something she cared deeply about. Indeed, it was a matter she'd continually dwelt on ever since her arrival in Guildford - perhaps it had even crossed her mind in the train on the way down. However, until this point in time, she'd held back and said nothing whatever about it to Marigold. And for this reason her voice was uncharacteristically tentative and apprehensive when she offered to hire a qualified person at her own expense in order to ensure the upkeep of the considerable horticultural challenge that the property presented. After all, as she pointed out rather awkwardly, she was about to move into someone else's home - and the least she could do was to provide a substantial contribution towards something that so greatly affected both parties. Marigold, of course, was taken aback as well as confused; and although she muttered a few appreciative, rather limp turns of phrase, she was unable to formulate a meaningful response - or to hide her embarrassment.

For a while, the two women maintained a thoughtful, somewhat disconcerted silence - doubtful as to where Eloise's abrupt suggestion (with its appearance of a done deal) had left them. Accordingly, they continued their tour in virtually wordless contemplation of what was, in essence, an exciting new prospect in an already idyllic environment where mutual uncertainty slowly dissipated under the influence of a cloudless sky.

Meanwhile, during the rest of that first week, and mindful of her gradually forming scheme, Eloise continued to cast her eyes about in a garden which, being on a steep slope, comprised three separate terraces at differing levels linked by stone steps. And it was among these that she earmarked certain nooks and crannies tucked away in discrete backwaters where Cannizaro Park (with enough imagination and professional skill) might finally rise again, phoenix-like, for her own and hopefully for her sister's enjoyment.

3

It was on another similarly pleasant morning when the two sisters found themselves strolling in the garden once again. Eloise had spent an uneasy fortnight at home since their previous tours of inspection; and throughout that interval, as the result of much pondering, one particular spot included in the route taken on this later, most recent occasion had remained at the forefront of her mind. Indeed, her thinking, still largely under wraps, had focussed on little else. In other words, without at first realising it, she was now embarking on a speculation whose seeds had been sown during her very first visit.

The site in question was set somewhat apart from the terraced areas, occupying a virtual backwater invisible from the house. It was overlooked on one side by an imposing copper beech in front of which, in a sheltered, unremarkable little quadrangle, ten or twelve rose bushes were struggling to stay alive. Yet surprisingly, these were the bedraggled-looking reminders of a similar, now relinquished, retreat in Wimbledon that confirmed the direction in which Eloise's plans were evolving.

As things stood, it was an area threatened with extinction by advancing weeds less dependent on a regular supply of water than the roses. On the grass verges, dandelions blazed alongside prickly eruptions of cleavers; thistles were majestic, lofty and aggressive whilst encroaching nettle beds were poised to invade the roses that were clearly in want not only of water and nourishment but also of pruning.

Given her frame of mind, none of these challenges dissuaded Eloise from recognising a location so obviously reminiscent of that other, somewhat less neglected rose garden in Cannizaro Park. In the event, it was an affinity that proved the determining factor: and she made a decision then and there that, once a suitable gardener had been found, he would turn this unpromising little spot into a worthy substitute for her former summer refuge, creating at the same time a uniquely attractive addition to Marigold's ailing back garden.

It was during this stage of Eloise's rapidly developing plot that her attitude hardened even more decisively in order, at least partially, to counteract certain troublesome scruples. After all, she told herself by way of mitigation, it was only one among several other substantial schemes that she was offering to finance personally. And particularly in the case of the rose garden, surely the irrefutable evidence of the weeds would override any suspicion of an ulterior motive? She also persuaded herself, in defiance of the same inner voice, that she would not be alone in benefiting from the proposed development - although she knew perfectly well that the underlying objective and the secret purpose it served could never be disclosed to Marigold.

* * *

And there, balanced precariously on a pinhead, she rested her case. But although Eloise found herself within a hair's breadth of believing in the harmless nature of her plans, no amount of special pleading, no carefully constructed provisos and no extra provision of funds could obviate the reality of a pitfall lurking somewhere in the background. It was also a fundamental pitfall - and of a kind that led in due course to the first clouds of disillusion on that unforeseeable, far-distant horizon well beyond the scope of what was, at the beginning, a story with a guaranteed happy ending.

And so, after the many changes and improvements had concluded with a pleasantly bibulous celebration on the patio, what at first was an unsuspected personal defect developed, little more than three years later on, into a fully fledged crisis. It was the result of an all-too-common human failing - a failing to which Eloise, in pursuit of a private ideal, had succumbed without due regard for her sister.

Unfortunately, there is very little more left to say that is actually worth saying. The tragedy of the entire, wholly avoidable affair lay in the fact that it involved such a familiar (and apparently innocuous) pattern of behaviour. And for these two closely linked reasons, without access to a higher authority, it's hard to know how to make a balanced assessment. All that can reasonably be said about it is this: that Eloise, as a general principle, believed she always acted in the best interests of others - but without ever realising the importance of consulting the very people in whose best interests she believed she was acting.

Cleavers: an invasive wild plant, Galium aparine.

Cannizaro Park: early 19th century home of the Duke of Cannizaro.

CAUSE FOR CELEBRATION

In the London Borough of Harrow, less than five minutes' walk from Harrow & Wealdstone station, there was (and had been for at least a fortnight) some small cause for celebration. The position on Planet Earth where this outcome was being felt was in a minute corner of the borough, in a smallish flat situated on the top floor of one of several blocks comprising a much larger estate by the name of Palmerston Place; and it was here, just two weeks previously, that a conclusion was reached to a run of indifference and protraction known in everyday language as *negligence*. To be more precise, action was finally taken in response to approaches from the owner of flat 78 - Mr Lionel Stubbs - whose age and the number of his apartment were separated by a very narrow margin.

Before continuing, it might be a good idea to provide some background information: the central point being that it was only after complaints involving one visit to the company office, two phone calls and two letters delivered by hand that Mr Stubbs' concerns about a smell in the attic above him were finally heeded. Until then, the issue had been left somewhat in the air. The attic, of course, was not part of his flat and was therefore accessible only to the estate workforce; and it took a painfully long time before the odour invading his living space via the plumbing shaft was recognised for what it was. Even then, the acknowledgement only came under cover of carefully written provisos designed to limit the extent of any unforeseen liabilities. This strategy was reinforced by implicitly poo-pooing the seriousness of the original claim in such a way as to be able to deny having done so if and when things went seriously wrong - which they finally did in the form of significant brown stains creeping across the ceiling of Mr Stubbs' bathroom.

* * *

At the heart of such frustrating inertia, easily confusable with apathy, there lay that profound social fault line still common throughout Britain: namely, class - and worse still in the present case, the pretensions of those who lack it. Interestingly, once upon a time, Palmerston Place (a fine example of late Victorian architecture) had been publicly owned; but in response to Margaret Thatcher's 'right to buy' policy, virtually all the flats had been sold to a series of private individuals with the result that the entire enterprise had been a self-governing limited company for at least twenty years. Subsequent to this change, many improvements had been made: flower gardens had been added; saplings, planted early on, had grown into mature trees; and latterly, colourful tubs of scarlet and white dahlias had appeared in various strategic positions. Sadly, however, as time wore on - and particularly after the appointment of the second (and latest) chairman, Mr Silas Martindale - the company acquired a distinct life of its own and the division between its representatives and those they represented grew steadily wider. As a consequence, it was this factor above all others that created the seemingly impenetrable barrier which had caused Lionel Stubbs, after much exertion, to feel that he counted for very little.

Prior to his appointment as chairman, Silas Martindale had had a career in retail, acting as the local store manager for a well-known chain of drapers; and it was the presumptions following from this, along with the gift of the gab, which had secured his election. It was a stroke of luck that gave him particular pleasure - for the position of company chairman not only carried more kudos than that of a store manager, but it also supplemented an occupational pension which, even for an unencumbered widower, had proved painfully insufficient. At the age of 68, therefore, Silas Martindale came gradually to regard himself as a favoured luminary in relation to the other residents amongst whom he lived. And given this underlying reality, it is unsurprising that his flat, number 97, had two bedrooms rather than one and a pleasanter, leafier outlook than that enjoyed by most of his fellow leaseholders.

Notwithstanding his fundamentally haughty attitudes, Mr Silas Martindale had enough native gumption to realise that he needed to exercise a modicum of control over appearances; and by way of subterfuge, he quite often trumpeted his concern for others when his response to their needs, left too long on the back burner, had become conspicuous by its absence. This usually took the form of a barrage of loudly voiced promises which were only finally acted upon under pressure. Sooner or later, however, his sharper side obtruded more plainly; and on no fewer than three occasions, he was overheard telling his secretary that very few people on the estate had any *backbone* - a choice of words implying that particular complaints or demands reflected the wimps who made them.

* * *

The snares of overconfidence can sometimes catch up with even the most accomplished charlatan or snob; and in keeping with this principle, the growing isolation of the company from the mass of residents eventually cut both ways and produced a body of dissent of which the chairman was wholly unaware. Indeed, his Achilles' heel was most marked when he read public admiration into the fawning smiles or waving hands of certain residents - some of whom, behind his back, were among his most uncompromising critics.

And this is where Lionel Stubbs resumes his rightful place in the overall picture. By dint of persistence, the damage to his ceiling, caused by a leaking pipe, was repaired by professional decorators and plumbers at the expense of the company insurers. But although he wrote a judicious thankyou letter to the chairman and downed a glassful of whisky on completion of the works, his liking for Mr Silas Martindale grew no greater. Curiously, he had little knowledge of the gossip elsewhere on the estate; but when the national news bulletins began raising doubts about the behaviour of politicians and bankers, his thoughts, accompanied by the remnants of a smile, strayed automatically towards the chairman of Palmerston Place.

Despite all these considerations, it remained true that Lionel was no fool; and it was certainly *not* the case that he regarded Silas Martindale as dishonest. Nevertheless, as chairman, he was clearly more occupied with his status than he was with the duties that bound him to the people who elected him. Inevitably therefore, over the past few critical weeks, Lionel had suffered much from this deficiency in the chairman's personality, and he continued to resent it.

With the passage of time, of course, these negative attitudes simmered down; and within a fortnight following the refurbishment of his bathroom, having secured his purpose and having finally understood the flawed character at the heart of the delay, he was able to chuckle quietly to himself whenever he was reminded of the damning insight that he'd suddenly gained. And although the company secretary had never repeated what she knew of Silas Martindale's judgemental attitudes, it was Lionel Stubbs' pride in the 'backbone' he never knew he had that repaired, once and for all, the damage to his self-esteem!

OVER THE HILLS AND FAR AWAY

Tom, he was a piper's son,
He learnt to play when he was young,
And all the tune that he could play
Was, 'Over the hills and far away';
Over the hills and a great way off,
The wind shall blow my top-knot off.

Nursery Rhyme

They met only occasionally. And, on this particular afternoon, the fact that Myra and Barry were out for a stroll in Holland Park was no more than typical of an irregular but long-established routine. Unsurprisingly for late October, the wind came in bleak, disorderly gusts. But the threat of drizzle from an overcast sky held off; and now and again, there were half-hearted flashes of light from a fitful sun whose pallor was indicative of darker days ahead.

Both parties to this unremarkable outing were not only in their early seventies but also retired; and both of them were married (although not to each other). Furthermore, to avoid any unnecessary speculation, it's important to understand that the wholly innocuous nature of their connection was well-known and accepted by their respective partners. In other words, everyone was aware that Myra's friendship with Barry arose from the fact that he'd been one of her brother Simon's closest schoolfriends. They also knew that, following the latter's death long before either of them was married, they'd kept the acquaintance going. All in all, therefore, they'd been friends since they were teenagers. And as a result, following Simon's fatal accident, they met once or twice a year at an art gallery or, as on this particular occasion, in one of the London parks.

Given a relationship that spanned half a lifetime, their conversations tended to focus on the past - a past which, beginning with their shared childhood days in Wandsworth, ended with Myra's recent move to Ealing and Barry's longer-term residence in Hampstead. Barry, in the course of his career, had been a Labour MP twice and a maths teacher in between; whereas Myra had progressed through several senior positions in the world of retail management. And so, indifferent to the gloomy weather that afternoon, reminiscence remained (as always) the dominant theme - until a highly improbable disclosure led to a change of tack.

As a coincidence that post-dated their previous meeting, it was something of a surprise. It owed everything to the internet; and what it boiled down to was that each of them, unknown to the other, had been persuaded to attend one of two reunions that were wholly unconnected. In Myra's case, she'd been approached by former work colleagues. In Barry's case, on the other hand, the source was a group of his past students whom he'd neither seen nor heard of for more than twenty years. Inevitably, such news had a marked impact on what, until then, had been a rambling conversation about nothing in particular. With the result that as Myra and Barry carried on towards the Japanese Garden and its ornamental waterfall, the two distinct yet oddly convergent events became the sole focus of their attention.

* * *

Lighting up a cigarette (a practice discouraged at home), Barry took the lead with a summary of his experience. 'It was a mid-week gathering,' he said 'organised by a group of barely recognisable ex-students in a drab, badly lit club down a flight of steps in a side street off Woburn Place.'

'They were all well into their fifties,' he went on with a hint of contempt in his voice that seemed to suggest he held them personally responsible for their date of birth. 'And unfortunately,' he added, 'most of them *looked* it.'

'All the sparkle you associate with young faces had disappeared,' he continued. 'It was like returning from another planet only to find the garden where you played as a boy has gone to seed.'

And on the strength of that gloomy assessment, he took a deep breath, put his hand to his mouth and yawned wearily until, like a deflated balloon, he ran out of the wherewithal to continue.

An awkward silence followed. It was a silence, however, that provided Myra with just about enough time to wonder whether Barry's attitude to his former students might have been be a little hasty. After all, as adults, they'd invited him to their reunion because they presumably thought well of him - added to which they could hardly have foreseen how different they would appear in the eyes of someone whose hindsight they lacked. In any case, she concluded, they couldn't have done much about it even if they'd wanted to!

Meanwhile, in the midst of these considerations, Myra was prompted to glance sideways at Barry who was staring straight ahead with a fixed, expressionless look on his face. And she reflected that if this were the first she'd seen of him for twenty years, she too would be as shocked as he was when confronted by the damage time can do. Myra, however, was a sensitive sort of woman and kept her thoughts to herself. Instead, she broke the silence with a rough sketch of her own comparable, though less taxing reunion at the The Lighterman's Arms not far from Blackfriars Bridge. Moreover, having already noticed a fundamental distinction between the nature of her own experience and Barry's, she conveyed her impressions at some length, hoping they might provide him with a fresh and more positive way of looking at things.

In what (for Barry) sounded like a Sunday sermon in a half-empty country church, Myra laid stress on the fact that, in her own case, the interval between actually working with her former colleagues and the subsequent reunion was only five years. But because this was a mere preliminary to what was coming, she played the incident down by describing it as 'a pleasantly forgettable evening with a group of pretty ordinary people in a city pub.'

She then moved closer to the point of her argument and drew a comparison with Barry's case by referring to the gap of *over twenty years* since he'd last set eyes on 'a bunch of teenagers who were now middle-aged.' In those circumstances, she suggested, the deterioration he'd noticed was inevitable. She then lowered her voice and contrived a quietly persuasive tone in order to deliver her far from convincing conclusion.

'I think that sheds an entirely different light on things,' she said. 'It was all perfectly natural and to be expected... if you think about it.'

But in those last five words lay an element of uncertainty. Myra had made a sincere though naïve attempt to pour oil on troubled waters. Yet she'd accomplished little more than a restatement of the problem without any hint of a solution. And worse still, she'd failed to recognise Barry's principal perception and source of complaint: namely, that his erstwhile protégés had lost all their youthful *sparkle* as well as their youthful *looks*.

* * *

Unknowingly, however, Myra had managed to contribute a number of self-evident truths that briefly prolonged the conversation until, after a sustained effort at playing along with her good intentions, Barry finally ran short of platitudes and resumed his critique of an uncomfortable evening.

'What I particularly noticed,' he said, 'was that they'd all grown up a great deal more than I had. I felt like a fish out of water. And consequently, I couldn't reconcile what I saw and heard with the bright eyes, the bushy tails and the harmless banter which, sad to say, I remembered only vaguely.'

On hearing this, Myra nodded non-committally but pointed out that her own 'blast from the past in a Blackfriars pub', although less dreary, had hardly been more memorable. After which Barry lit another cigarette, commented briefly on the waterfall when it came into view - and carried on regardless.

'One of them,' he remarked, 'very much a Jack the Lad back in his college days, was clearly embarrassed when I cracked the sort of joke he would have cracked himself when the sun was still shining.'

In response to which, Myra looked Barry straight in the face and did as much as she reasonably could to cheer him up - though rather less, she feared, than was needed in order to persuade him to pull himself together.

'Those were the days, I'm afraid,' she murmured 'when the sweet wine of youth was something we took for granted at a time when the grass was a great deal greener than it is now.'

Barry took no notice of this. 'Frankly,' he replied 'I was so bored that I thought they'd notice it. And after making the best of a bad job for nearly two hours, I politely shook hands with all of them, smiled, disappeared up the steps, and made a beeline for the Russell Square underground!'

'Well, I can't say I blame you,' answered Myra rather helplessly.

Over the hills and far away: from 'Tom, Tom, The Piper's Son'. A nursery rhyme, one of many variants: c1795 - 1908.

The red sweet wine of youth: Rupert Brooke, 'The Dead', 1914.

THE HOSEPIPE BAN

A few years ago when there was a blazingly hot summer that led to drought conditions and a hosepipe ban throughout East Anglia, great concern was felt by the management and staff of the Riverside Botanical Gardens about the survival of numerous trees and shrubs which in some cases were more than a century old. And their anxiety was felt even more strongly when they considered those rarer, vulnerable species that were more dependent than most on a plentiful supply of water.

Among the residents of the surrounding area, Mr Royston Bland was not the only fully paid-up 'Friend of the Riverside Botanical Gardens' who, during a visit at the time of this crisis, noticed that certain plant varieties were beginning to droop. Even some of the sturdiest and most resilient-looking trees were showing symptoms of stress - a fact clearly evident from the way in which their leaves had become flaccid and pendulous - with the result that they swayed limply to and fro in the breeze.

But Royston, who was a great fan of the Riverside Gardens, didn't allow these warning signs to spoil his afternoon - although, as he emerged from an area of pleasant woodland shade, he was some-what disconcerted to find that a number of silver birches, whose leaves had turned yellow, were already more or less dead in consequence of their shallow root systems. Equally alarming, whether due to abnormal weather conditions or to longer-lasting climate change, there were further indications of malaise in the cultivated garden areas. For example, every one of the sky-blue flower heads of a stately agapanthus seemed to have withered over-night; and virtually all the blooms of a swamp rose had dropped off prematurely, leaving behind nothing but crumpled, lifeless leaves that looked more like wads of screwed-up paper than the former engines of photosynthesis.

As he altered course in search of refreshments and made his way towards a small cafeteria on the far side of a lawn whose colour had faded so far from green that it looked more like stubble, it struck Royston that whatever needed doing in the face of an obvious emergency showed few signs of actually being done. And after mulling things over, he began to ask himself why no one seemed to have considered the potential implicit in the enormous lake that was one of the Gardens' principal attractions. Given that this was a lake uniquely equipped with a system of pipes and stopcocks by means of which it was periodically topped up from the nearby river, he wondered why water from such an abundant source was not being made available and then redistributed with the aid of pumps to the various key locations in the greatest need.

* * *

Two or three days later, with the use of hosepipes prohibited and no end to the hot, dry spell in prospect, Royston was reminded of these concerns whilst, with the help of a watering can, he ensured the continued welfare of his runner beans - reflecting at the same time that compliance with local regulations made the upkeep of his allotment a bit too much of a good thing. And he was still daydreaming along these lines when a neighbouring plot-holder put in an unexpected appearance, bringing with her a nonchalant, yet resourceful show of resignation to the demands of the moment.

A more or less cheerful, run-of-the-mill exchange of generalisations ensued - after which, following a glance at the state of each other's surviving crops, both parties launched into a random flurry of moans and groans about the inconvenience and hard work the heatwave was causing. And so it went on until, with further variations on the dominant theme in increasingly short supply,

Royston seized the opportunity to point out how the threat posed by the weather was creating mayhem in the Riverside Botanical Gardens just a mile down the road.

* * *

Julia Ford-Wilson was a pleasant woman in her late fifties. By contrast to the tall, willowy figure of Royston, she was on the portly side; and her ample topping of fair hair was tied back rather jauntily with a ribbon. She also wore a dog-eared pair of trousers whose seat was covered by the tails of a brightly coloured, floral smock which not only proclaimed the light-hearted, jolly personality of its owner, but also deflected attention from the fact that Julia Ford-Wilson was rather broad in the beam.

In terms of social standing and education, both Julia and Royston were on a relatively equal footing - although Julia, with her easy-going, extrovert personality, kept far more in touch with local events than the somewhat retiring plot-holder standing next to her. They were at one, however, in that like Royston, Julia was a 'Friend of the Riverside Botanical Gardens' - but a friend who, *unlike* Royston, always read the Friends' magazine from cover to cover and assiduously absorbed its contents. In addition to this, she was also on personal terms with some of the Riverside staff; and these factors, taken together, helped her to engage immediately with Royston's remarks about the lake and its problem-solving potential.

It was therefore with a meaningful glint in her eye and a cryptic smile on her lips that she was able to reveal the circumstances under which Royston's entirely feasible solution to the water shortage had been considered and rejected by the top brass at the Riverside Botanical Gardens. And given that both she and Royston were mature adults who scorned what they saw as the never-ending succession of fads imposed by trend-setting officials with nothing better to do, there was an outburst of contemptuous laughter when Julia, somewhat mockingly, made a clean breast of what she knew.

And like so many apparently perplexing questions, the explanation in the present case proved disarmingly simple. For as Julia was at pains to make clear, it all boiled down to something which, over time, had repeatedly spawned ridicule in the press: namely, the anomalies associated with *Health & Safety* legislation and the ludicrous ways in which its terms were often implemented - to which plain statement of fact she added that the worst offenders were those local authorities who were keen to appear forward-looking but equally keen to steer clear of trouble. And despite the ambiguity, Royston was almost as amused as he was incredulous when Julia finally disclosed that it was the perceived risk of infection and a consequent fear of litigation that compelled the directors of the Gardens to oppose the introduction of untreated water despite the desperate need.

There was just one more crucial consideration that popped up before the above lively exchange among the cabbages and cucumbers eventually gave way to watering cans and wet feet. It was an observation to which Julia was wholeheartedly sympathetic when Royston remarked that, without a single warning notice anywhere in sight along the banks of the river, countless canoeists and anglers were allowed to pursue their leisure activities on or beside it without any concerns about the water quality. And he added, with a certain amount of wry sarcasm, that this could mean only one thing: namely, that water, presumed free from contamination *before* entering the Gardens, was transformed, by means unknown, into a grave risk afterwards.

'I couldn't agree more,' replied Julia. 'You obviously didn't read last week's East Anglian Gazette. The editor made exactly the same point!'

Agapanthus: also known as the African Lily.

Swamp Rose: Rosa palustris. Favours marshy habitats.

WHEN THE PENNY DROPS

I

Dominic Fitzgerald was of ample proportions, very tall as well as plump - and consequently rather overbearing in appearance. He was forthright in manner, had just turned fifty-two; and, once upon a time, had been regarded as very good-looking indeed. During those earlier years, he'd naturally been the object of much female interest which he encouraged up to a point just short of the self-indulgence now considered routine; and through this decidedly dubious strategy, his education at a church school had (just about) preserved his innocence until he married his first wife who provided passing pleasure without the encumbrance of any consequent issue.

Melanie died at a relatively early age; and following her death, his second acquisition, Anna, being a quiet character approaching fifty at the time of their wedding, provided reassuring continuity to an easy-going domestic life in which both parties ended up in bed each night reading barely distinguishable novels and magazines. Anna also derived satisfaction from her new surname, Fitzgerald, which she considered a marked improvement on her own (less resonant) maiden name of Simpkins. It was a revealing sentiment, of course, that she naturally kept to herself.

Despite the advancing years, Dominic Fitzgerald remained energetic and almost as voluble as he was when, at thirty, he'd set out to obfuscate the fact that his twenties were behind him. And now, at just over fifty, he could still persuade friends that he was a bright spark whose mature looks were not yet due for the scrap heap. He also remained adept at giving an impression of genuine concern for other people; and even his less intimate acquaintances were convinced that he was on their side and had their wellbeing at heart. On this basis, therefore, he frequently elicited confidential information without supplying any of his own.

2

Samuel Crosby and Dominic Fitzgerald lived in Holland Park, and in the same fashionable block of flats whose name, Lakeland Mansions, appeared on a brass plate beside the main gates. Furthermore, they were both regular users of the Holland Park underground; and it was to chance encounters at this location that their relationship was normally confined. Their conversations - a combination of politeness, the weather and other repetitive themes - were, as far as Samuel was concerned, something of a strain. He was a shyer individual than Dominic and many years his senior; and consequently, he rather dreaded the routine barrage of questions about where he was going and what he was up to - enquiries which he felt had a patronising, non-reciprocal air reminiscent of an adult talking to a child.

It was on the eastbound platform, on a particularly fine Tuesday morning when Samuel, by no means as dumb as he felt sure he looked, was overcome by the feeling that his pale face and dry skin were insufficiently offset by a blue Marks & Spencer sweater together with a pair of nondescript grey trousers. He would not have entertained such misgivings, of course, had it not been for the presence of Dominic who was dressed in a formal suit. But despite being uncomfortable with this and with the attendant, one-way series of questions, he also felt the warmth of what he took to be Dominic's approving manner. In short, somewhat ambivalently, he felt appreciated - and was duly flattered. Indeed, it was an ambivalence that became a constant feature of their ongoing relationship.

3

Friday the fifth of June that year, given a disappointingly reluctant summer, was part of a sunny bonus during the wet sequel to a spring drought; and it marked a day when Dominic and Samuel had again bumped into each other on the eastbound platform at Holland Park. The conversation, which began lightheartedly, followed the usual line; but Samuel, who had recently noticed that the white paint was peeling from one of the uprights supporting the gates at Lakeland Mansions, rather awkwardly remarked how very unusual it was to encounter negligence on the part of the estate's management team. Surprisingly little, however, was said in reply; and following an embarrassing series of hastily cobbled-together provisos, Samuel boarded the next train to Oxford Street with some relief, leaving behind Dominic, dressed in his somewhat loud pin-striped suit, who declared he was waiting for a work colleague to join him en route to a conference in the City.

* * *

From that point onwards, broadly speaking, there was a period during which nothing of significance occurred. And by the time the annual Lakeland Mansions Newsletter arrived on the first of August, Samuel and Dominic hadn't run into each other since their last, slightly tense meeting in the Holland Park underground. For Samuel in particular, life had been drably routine in the interim; but when he arrived home that very same evening - namely, on the first of August - he suddenly noticed that the formerly neglected front gates had been treated to a brand-new coat of white paint.

At Lakeland Mansions, of course, as with every other institution throughout the country, there were often contentious issues to be ironed out; and so, anticipating a spot of scandal as soon as he discovered the Newsletter on the hall floor, Samuel sat down on the sofa with a cup of coffee and eagerly began reading in the hope of discovering whether any important issues had been resolved or whether, alternatively, one party or another had suffered a well-deserved setback.

To begin with, however, the overall content proved disappointingly bland. But just as he was preparing to pour a second cup of coffee, Samuel spotted the words 'main gates' in a short paragraph headed 'Newsflash' on the last page. And the penny suddenly (and rather shockingly) dropped when he read that, in response to 'a recent complaint', the tried and tested firm of Bartholomew Wentworth & Sons had postponed pressing business elsewhere in order to repair the damage inflicted by the previous hard winter on the main gates at Lakeland Mansions. This was followed by a statement to the effect that the work would be carried out in time for the distribution of the Newsletter.

But although, at first, he couldn't quite put his finger on it, the tone of this announcement didn't seem quite right. Moreover, the order in which the information appeared struck Samuel as rather odd. It was an uncertainty, however, that lasted only until he realised that the somewhat confused presentation betrayed a challenge. And for Samuel, it was a challenge that amounted, rather alarmingly, to a thinly disguised rebuke (directed at himself) of which the writer and the writer's sources were plainly aware.

THE LONELY LIFE
OF MISS CYNTHIA GLOSSOP

I

The red mason bee, Osmia rufa, is one of Britain's *two hundred or more species of bees that disdain colonies in favour of an independent life - from which arises their collective title of *solitary* bees. During her brief month-long existence, the female keeps busy by providing for the future offspring she will never see; and she does this by clearing out tunnels not only in sandy banks or hollow stems, but also in a variety of man-made structures such as nail holes where she leaves a deposit of pollen and nectar along with an egg. She then blocks off the cell thus formed with mud, taking a whole day to do it before repeating the exercise up to twenty times during her all-too-short life span. Finally, after fourteen weeks and the demise of their mother, the larvae emerge but remain cocooned in their cells throughout the winter that lies ahead. Other than this, there is very little else worth mentioning about a solitary mason bee whose short experience of Planet Earth took millions of years to evolve.

I was suddenly reminded of Osmia rufa one day on arriving home at my flat in Lansdown Park House which was situated in a non-descript enclave on the borders of built-up, stockbroker-belt Esher and the wilder, rolling countryside of Surrey. On reaching the flat, I discovered that the neighbour with whom I shared the first floor landing was in the midst of isolating her premises from the outside world by applying a strip of insulation tape all the way round the inside of the door frame. She was a new tenant, and it was early days in our acquaintance; but I ventured the familiarity of calling her Cynthia, having been introduced to her as such by the flat's owner and former occupant who had recently moved away. So far, for no particular reason, our encounters had been few, far between and always short; and having ventured a light-hearted aside about draughts which she answered by referring to cooking smells from the other flats, I acknowledged her evident desire for physical and social seclusion by disappearing indoors as gracefully as I could.

2

Before proceeding further with a somewhat curious and enigmatic story, it would no doubt be helpful to give form and substance to a person with a name like Cynthia Glossop in whose wan smile and brief greeting I had discerned a note of melancholy from the moment of our introduction. Her age lay at some indeterminable point between thirty-two and thirty-eight. She was pale, extremely thin, and her features were long and drawn. What must once have been dark hair had faded prematurely, and hovered like a disorderly puff of smoke around her head. Furthermore on this particular day, alone in the stairwell and looking like a vagrant, she was dressed in battered jeans and a crumpled black sweater - a combination that seldom varied except by the addition of a brownish mackintosh whenever required by the weather. Any passing stranger would have deemed her innocuous, in all probability dull and, going by appearances (which can be deceptive), in every respect unremarkable.

Looked at from all of the very few vantage points available, a description of Cynthia Glossop's way of life is a hard task because of the degree to which she lived within the bounds of a sealed capsule which, although on a short lease, she altered in ways which spectacularly betrayed a character that remained indefinable. A series of incidents, however, alongside inadvertently disclosed practices and attitudes, gradually created a picture that I found intriguing - despite the sometimes tenuous links between isolated fragments of information.

* * *

The first and most striking manifestation of something new in the air was noticed by many residents because of its adverse effect: namely, the fact that the windows in the common parts were being repeatedly thrown open - even when the frost was sparkling on the lawn or the snow falling. Consequently, a chill invaded the entire stairwell and made its unwelcome presence known in the form of an icy blast streaming in under the doors of the various apartments. People were naturally puzzled and annoyed; but it took several months to work out that it was the newcomer in flat 8 who was continually opening and *reopening* the windows. This made it all too apparent that, for Cynthia Glossop, fresh air had a strong affinity with insulation tape and hygiene - a fact she reinforced by ventilating her own kitchen and bathroom in a similar way. At the same time, unfortunately, the persistence of a measure designed to disperse those cooking smells at large in the common parts seemed to indicate that the insulation tape was performing badly - unless, of course, it was a case of missionary zeal in furtherance of a private obsession with cleanliness.

It was shortly after these revelations that I spotted a parcel outside number 8 from which I learned that my neighbour's surname was *Glossop* - the inelegance of which amused me in relation to the Kensington-and-Chelsea note sounded by *Cynthia*. Even more surprising was the fact that the package remained untouched day after day - although its owner was clearly at home. Indeed, so great was her apparent indifference to this link with the world in general that it lay in the same spot for just under a fortnight - although the person to whom it was addressed was repeatedly forced to step over it.

Notwithstanding the similarity of her existence to that of a part-time anchorite, Cynthia Glossop was not averse to matter-of-fact conversations with the plumber and various other contractors making alterations to her kitchen and bathroom in pursuit of a tidier, cleaner lifestyle - a lifestyle to which the attribute 'sparse' should be added. This latter feature was easily deduced, given the minute bags of domestic waste occasionally carried down to the communal dustbin; indeed, it was anybody's guess how she managed to avoid the welter of twenty-first century packaging as implied by the meagre size of her rubbish bags. And it was also a remarkable fact concerning number 8 Lansdown Park House that, although the washing machine was sometimes just about audible after the statutory 11pm embargo on noise, there was never the faintest smell of cooking from the newly refurbished kitchen to compete with the scents of Wright's Coal Tar Soap and Dettol escaping from the bathroom when the front door was ajar.

3

We need to remind ourselves once again that the improvements Cynthia introduced after moving into her flat were carried out in accommodation on a short lease - and at her own expense. Alterations to the kitchen and bathroom were substantial changes aimed at cleanliness and order - although these factors were subordinate to the need to personalise an interior world sealed off from the universe beyond. No measures, of course, were more indicative of the underlying pattern than the exposure, sanding and high-gloss varnishing of the original parquet floors - on top of which, the landlord's canary-yellow wallpaper, modestly embellished with stars, was over-painted in unadorned matt white. Taken all together, these measures pointedly underlined and complemented the somewhat pharmaceutical odours of soap and disinfectant that seeped out on to the landing and stairwell where, once the works were complete, Cynthia put on her shoes every morning and took them off again at night before re-entering the flat.

Consequent upon all of this, and given the great care taken with the details of her apartment, readers may well be surprised by the apparently irrational uses to which the space was put. The accommodation, other than kitchen and bathroom, comprised a small bedroom, a large bedroom and a brightly lit, even larger lounge - and yet the small bedroom was used as a utility room, the sparsely furnished lounge wasn't used at all, and the large bedroom functioned as Cynthia's somewhat monastic bedsit where she spent many silent hours immersed in impenetrable mystery behind a door closed against the cold air from the bathroom and kitchen windows. As a recipe for living, these were elaborate yet weird arrangements for a tenant who, on top of everything else, had received no visitors whatever after more than a year in residence. In fact, to all outward appearances, she was every bit as solitary as a solitary bee.

4

For an interested observer of what was a puzzling but thankfully quiet neighbour, there were times when it was easy to assume that Cynthia Glossop had regular employment of some sort. After carefully locking her door, and carrying a threadbare holdall, she sauntered off morning after morning to join the queue at the nearby bus stop in Blaise Road, reaching home again in the early evening. Her return was signalled, at ground floor level, by the hollow thud of the double doors; and shortly thereafter, repeatedly reacting to the fact that closed human habitations do not smell as sweet as Sherwood Forest at daybreak, she continued to throw open the windows of the common parts - whatever the weather conditions outside and without regard to the concerns of other residents. She then crept into her own flat, closing the door gently behind her - after which the only regular means of knowing whether she was at home or not was to consult the windows to see if any lights were on; but even that wasn't a wholly reliable test, for the occasional sound of cupboard doors inside an unlit flat suggested that she sometimes spent hour after hour in virtual darkness.

* * *

One evening, not long after she arrived home, my bell rang; and I was surprised to find that the caller was Cynthia. She was anxious to know whether any strangers had been spotted that day, since there were signs of what looked like a break-in. I had seen no one, but was asked to take a look in the small bedroom where the door of a wardrobe, allegedly left closed that morning, was slightly ajar. Upon enquiry, I was informed there was no other evidence of interference or of forced entry. In consequence, although I steered well clear of saying so, it was overwhelmingly obvious that no one at all had entered the flat and that Cynthia herself had left the door open. It was an incidental circumstance that provided me with a glimpse of an unexpectedly disordered mishmash of clothing, towels and assorted junk hidden in the entrails of a plainly undisturbed flat. And that was the end of the matter: Cynthia had clearly got hold of the wrong end of the stick - and nothing more was ever said about it.

5

Despite her periodically regular comings and goings, there were other times when it seemed doubtful whether Cynthia really had a job at all. Now and again, for periods of a week or more, she stayed shut away at home in almost complete silence, never emerging - and sometimes remaining in apparently complete darkness with no lights on until late evening. At these times and at most others, no sound of a radio or TV was ever heard; and no phone calls were received. Only the occasional, faraway rumble of a washing machine or the faint thud of a footstep suggested a living presence immersed in the quiet gloom of flat 8.

As to reasons and explanations, no one ever found out what extraordinary ordinariness or peculiarity occupied these long, sometimes short periods of suspended animation; and there was perhaps some cause to wonder whether at such times, confined to her box like Schrödinger's cat, she might be both dead and alive at one and the same time until some unseen hand raised the lid and transformed her state into that of a living person. At least this would explain how she resumed the appearance of an ordinary working woman at about half past nine on each of the many such mornings after.

* * *

There is one final revelation that I *can* make, and feel I *ought* to make, in order to do justice to the tenant of number 8 Lansdown Park House. I believe I owe it to her to point out that she was not entirely unlike the rest of us: in other words that she was, after all, as human as many people are when their eccentricities are disclosed.

As to the revelation itself, it comprises a minor event following the redecorations which marked the point in time after which she always put her shoes on and took them off on the shared landing outside my flat. One morning, having locked the door before leaving for what may or may not have been gainful employment, Cynthia was bending down attempting to tie her laces which had got into a hopeless tangle. An unforeseen knot then developed; and everyone knows how infuriating this can be - in or out of a hurry; and it turned out that Cynthia was in a hurry. Consequently, after some heavy breathing, she suspended her characteristically withdrawn manner and loudly cursed the shoelaces. This might have been quite unremarkable of course; but it came as a great surprise when her complaint was qualified by an audible and extremely reprehensible expletive beginning with f. And I see no reason to apologise for finding it a cause for silent laughter as I witnessed the incident unobserved from behind the spyhole in my own front door!

*Two hundred or more species: this figure and other data are either taken from 'Bugs Britannica', by Peter Marren and Richard Mabey, Chatto & Windus 2010; or from 'Butterflies and Other Insects of Britain', Reader's Digest Nature Lover's Library, 1984.

MAKING IT CLEAR TO BOSWELL

Having set out from the village of Pixham where we live, it took us barely five minutes before we reached the cemetery in Reigate Road; and according to the timetable we had in mind, another five or ten minutes would bring us to Dorking's main shopping street at the southern end of which a righthand fork would lead us back into open country on our way to Coldharbour. Coldharbour, a village four or five miles further on, lies on the southern flank of Leith Hill which, at an altitude of just under a thousand feet, is one of the highest points in the south of England. Unsurprisingly, therefore, the panoramic views from the summit make the uphill slog to get there well worth the effort.

Whilst still abreast of the cemetery at the beginning of what was a six or seven mile walk, we were overlooked from the north by Box Hill, an impressive beauty spot much favoured by day-trippers from throughout Surrey and Sussex as well as from the southern fringes of London. But despite its compelling grandeur, Boswell showed very little interest when I indicated a cloud-shadow gliding serenely across its western slopes where the high ground falls sharply away towards Westhumble and the Mole Valley.

* * *

Unfortunately, there was a solid reason for his indifference - for although our walk had only just begun, we were already approaching the borderline between an earnest discussion and a heated argument. To detail the precise issue that divided us would be detrimental to the progress of this narrative. But it's worth mentioning that the rôle of ethics in the public arena was at the heart of it.

* * *

Also worth mentioning is the fact that Boswell and I were (and still are) old school pals. Added to which, readers might like to bear in mind another detail to the effect that Boswell, no spring chicken by the time of this story, retained a crop of dark hair which, untarnished by time and groomed with conspicuous care, looked far too youthful compared with the wrinkles and crow's feet that reflected his age more accurately. It was a combination which, speaking entirely for myself, I've always found rather amusing - but which, out of due consideration, I've never tried to exploit.

* * *

After crossing the hazardous junction with Deepdene Avenue and London Road, and having progressed some distance along the High Street under continuous bombardment from Boswell's strongly held views, to say that I was getting fed up with it would be a mild expression of the truth - whereas in Boswell's case, the same assessment would have been a gross understatement. I should add that Boswell is a man of strong opinions who doesn't always think things through. Consequently, he often gets into a muddle - at which point, with an angry glint in his eyes and a very red face to go with it, I sometimes find it hard (even in retrospect) to stop myself laughing.

Eventually, once I'd managed to get a word in edgeways, I made it clear to Boswell that I had no problem whatever with admitting to *my* limitations but that I *did* have a problem with the fact that he seldom admitted to having any of his own. At which point, with the f-word and a stationary bus only a few metres away, and noticing we were next door to the White Horse pub, we agreed it would be a good idea not only to take a deep breath but also to pop inside for refreshments!

Encouraged rather than otherwise by a series of strong drinks, Boswell continued to argue the toss on a particularly sensitive side-issue in a way which, to *my* mind, made no allowance for everyday human failings. By this time, like him, I too was under the influence; but although I had a just-about-relevant advantage up my sleeve, I was still acutely embarrassed when I revealed that on several recent occasions, close to the Pixham village green, I'd personally seen him in animated conversation with a young woman called Elizabeth Banks who was less than respectfully known in some quarters as Busy Lizzie.

I was overwhelmingly confounded, of course, by my lack of tact and self-control - as was Boswell by his sudden and unexpected embarrassment. And so, in consequence of the awkwardness, an extended and rather tense silence ensued accompanied by two pairs of downcast eyes and the absurdly ineffectual sounds of alcohol repeatedly sipped and swallowed - with an occasional cough thrown in for good measure.

* * *

Boswell was not alone in feeling an urgent need to save face. And as a result, I was more than happy to avoid further tension by disowning my implications regarding Lizzy Banks. After all, it was precisely by this rather underhand expedient that I'd sought to resolve a political issue easy enough to defend through reasoned argument. But far more importantly, thank Heaven, I was still sufficiently compos mentis to curb even the slightest suggestion in my tone of voice to the effect that, despite an open-minded willingness to eat my words, I'd certainly *not* resorted to the brand of cover-up characteristic of the losing candidate in a general election!

A PARAGON OF RECTITUDE

I

Mr Francis Maitland radiated dignity - an impression that arose, in a variety of ways, both from his personal character and from the status that accompanied his position in life: namely, that of a barrister. Bob had known him as a friend since their school days together when his (Francis') behaviour was less constrained than it was as an adult. He remembered, for example, those deafening outbursts of laughter - a feature once immortalised en route from one classroom to another at a point in the daily routine when silence was mandatory. It was also the moment when Frankie just happened to brush shoulders with Mr William Ashcroft, the then headmaster and paragon of rectitude, who warned him off in a highly accusative tone initiated by the words 'That was *deplorable*, Maitland' and followed by a lengthy drumming home of the school rules!

It was an incident that Bob never forgot. And much later on, more than fifty years down the line, a similarly noisy response could be coaxed from the lips of Francis Maitland whenever he was reminded of it.

* * *

Bob was not at all clear why these recollections had popped up precisely when they did. After all, he was relaxing on a bench in the Royal Botanic Gardens. It was little more than a week since Midsummer's Day - and therefore inevitable that the grass had begun to fade as the sun bore down unremittingly from a succession of cloudless skies. On the other hand, this was a regular seasonal hazard - a hazard significantly tempered by the flutings of a thrush. Furthermore, a half-hearted wind stirred the treetops; insects of all varieties were about their business; and all in all, the presence of Frankie at the back of Bob's mind remained something of a mystery.

Not far in front of where he was sitting, an enormous cedar had created a patch of shade where one of its lower branches descended at a modest angle; and then, about a metre above the ground, it flattened out - thus providing a seat for several visiting school children from among a larger group whose botanical interests were conspicuously inapparent. At the same time, some of the bolder members of what amounted to a very large class had hauled themselves up along the same branch to the higher limit where it joined forces with the trunk. And there, perched somewhat awkwardly, their triumphant arm-waving was making no impression whatever on their classmates at ground level who, like a pack of hounds in pursuit of an equal number of foxes, were chasing each other, at breakneck speed, in and out of the rhododendrons.

All of this evoked personal memories very much in tune with what Bob was seeing; and as he gazed with mild interest at the comings and goings just a few metres distant, he was propelled back to those carefree, tree-climbing days of his own. And he could still picture himself, high up in the canopy of a copper beach close to the blue of a sun-soaked and uncomplicated heaven which, then as now, delighted the reckless teenager he undoubtedly was so many years ago. For which reason, and for many others like it associated with the passage of time, it was a pleasure to absorb some of the juvenile energy on the loose nearby. And thus at ease, in a state of casual self-examination, he repeated out loud the question he'd asked himself only a few minutes before.

'Why on earth,' he mumbled 'am I harking back to my old friend Frankie in a place like this with nothing I can think of to explain it?'

2

The children, led by their teacher, moved on after twenty minutes or so, leaving behind them an emptiness with which Bob was not entirely at ease. It affected him like a wave that, having swept inland and rattled the pebbles on the beach, crashes with a muffled roar and then slips back out to sea, leaving little evidence that it ever existed. All the same, he fought off what felt like the beginnings of a downward spiral; and so, despite the absence of anything like a good reason, he spontaneously pressed the rewind button, stopping short at a point in time when he and Frankie were both in mid-career: Frankie in his comfortable West End chambers whilst he himself had charge of a group of history students in a newly established London university.

It was also a time when being in mid-career meant that youthful pursuits were by no means dead in the water - at least not as far as Bob was concerned. And unfortunately, in his case, it led to a spot of bother with a young woman who, as it happened, was expecting to gain more from his attentions than he was prepared to give. The result was that the connection broke up rather rancorously at his front door where, after about an hour alone together, he said goodbye for the first and last time. The break-up, as he vividly recalled, was therefore far from amicable; and being a born worrier, he instantly felt at risk from possible repercussions - the result being that he was burdened with anxiety as soon as he slammed the door shut.

By the following morning, his concern had grown sufficiently to persuade him that it would be best to prepare for the worst by taking the bull by the horns. And he immediately thought of Frankie. With the passage of time, however, he could no longer remember whether he'd phoned him in advance or turned up unannounced at his chambers early the same afternoon. Either way, he was granted an immediate audience. And despite the uncertainty about how the appointment had been arranged, he could still clearly recall that Frankie was dressed in a carefully tailored off-white suit - which told him, of course, that it must have been summer. And that set him thinking.

'Perhaps it was something as flimsy as the weather,' he said to himself 'that reminded me, in similarly bright conditions today, of my old friend Frankie.'

And once again, as clear as a bell, the headmaster's voice rang in his ears with the unforgettable words...

'That was *deplorable*, Maitland!'

* * *

There's no telling why human beings remember some things rather than others of equal or greater importance. For which reason, recollection failed Bob once again after so considerable a lapse of time. He realised, of course, that he must have acquainted Frankie with most of the details of the unfortunate incident that so concerned him. Nevertheless, all he could remember as he relaxed in the sunlit environment of a twenty-first century public garden was that, after absorbing all relevant factors and having risen slowly to his feet, Frankie assumed a somewhat po-faced expression as he put the million-dollar question which, in a nutshell, lay at the heart of Bob's dilemma. And it was a question he phrased in the following, strikingly down-to-earth language.

'Did intimacy occur?' asked Frankie at a leisurely pace that oozed with the professional dignity he was attempting to present as plain, matter-of-fact English.

And happily, since intimacy had *not* taken place, and since no unpleasant sequel had ever developed, Bob looked back with unalloyed amusement at the memory of Frankie's solemn expression - and with renewed relief at his assurance that there was nothing to worry about.

3

Now that the headstrong days of youth were over and the sweat had been wiped retrospectively from an anxious brow, Bob felt glad... glad to be alone, out of doors, on a sublime summer afternoon. The sky was still cloudless; and all the sounds were cheerful - including tourists on a guided walkabout, the cries of the schoolkids confronting him less than and hour previously, and the magpies chattering away like machine-gun fire in the treetops. And then, of course, there was that most mesmerising sound of all: namely, the rustling of foliage on a hot day in conjunction with a leisurely breeze.

And so, although within sight of the wrong end of a lifetime, Bob took pleasure in contemplating once again Frankie's never-to-be-forgotten, strictly to-the-point question. It was vitally important, of course, that nothing had actually happened. But there was more to it than that: and when he looked honestly at the past, he concluded that even if he could turn the clock back, even if he could be certain there would be no repercussions, he genuinely wouldn't *want*, much less *consent*, to seize the opportunity he'd declined at the time. 'Far better,' thought Bob 'to leave such matters to the birds and the bees that live out their lives in this marvellous spot that I've enjoyed so often and so much.'

THE BALCONY ON THE THIRD FLOOR

Thanks to the human heart by which we live,
Thanks to its tenderness, its joys, and fears,
To me the meanest flower that blows can give
Thoughts that do often lie too deep for tears.

William Wordsworth

I

It's now getting on for the end of May; and this morning I find myself at home, comfortably seated on the balcony of my third floor flat. Luckily, after a drab start, the sun has finally appeared and is dispensing a gentle warmth whose effect, as I've so frequently noticed, is to soften the noise of traffic in the street below.

Despite the small size of this space, I'm surrounded by self-seeded saplings of buddleia and sycamore which, potted on at intervals for several years, are now taller than I am. Pinks in profusion, just a few days short of bursting their buds, are beginning to reveal their colour. The geraniums are fighting back after the March pruning and will soon rival the Chelsea Flower Show with a display of crimson and pillar-box red.

There are also signs of life from further afield. For example, I can hear the tinkle of birdsong in the woods on the other side of the road - a sound, modified by distance, that puts me in mind of loose coins in a pocket whose owner is rummaging for change. To my right, children's voices from the infants school augment and con-fuse the many other sounds reaching me from every point of the compass. No doubt it's break time and the playground is awash with juvenile banter.

As far as I can see, at least from where I'm sitting, all the signs are convincingly positive. Unadulterated contentment has taken hold of me. I have neither need nor desire for change. I am in thrall to the mood of the moment and to the conditions that have brought it about.

* * *

Just above my head, the campanulas are already well advanced. Along the full length of the containing wall, flourishing in planters aligned with the top edge, their unique shade of blue affects me profoundly. It evokes impressions of another world - a world that lies somewhere between heaven (as commonly understood) and the myths of Shangri-La. This is an association I've often felt before, in particular after sunset when each bloom seems to glow with a light that comes from within. I've also noticed (and today is no exception) that the bumble bees react to campanulas as favourably as I do - although they linger inside each bell-like structure so briefly that I can hardly believe it's worth their while.

The generic name for bumble bees is 'bombus' which, until an hour ago when I looked it up, I'd always assumed was the Latin root of the English word 'bomb' in recognition of the manner in which members of this genus lurch like missiles from one bloom to another. It was an idea further reinforced by the common metaphorical use of 'beeline' to describe a decisive form of motion - usually with a defined destination (target) at the end of it. And much to my surprise, I eventually discovered that 'bombus', whose true Latin meaning is a booming or buzzing noise, is indeed the reason why bumble bees and an explosive weapon of war share the same link with classical antiquity.

Historical questions aside, I'm more than happy to have the company of these industrious insects as they busy themselves hereabouts without any regard for the perfume of just two prematurely opened pinks. I'm also delighted that, although I'm situated about 12 metres above ground level, the curiously named 'tree of heaven' towers at least another 12 metres into the sky. This species, originally from China, is in full flower; and its white panicles, suspended from delicate stems and looking like upside-down lupins, are releasing their scent in response to the heat of the sun.

* * *

Immersed in doing nothing, I have abandoned the book I was reading, partly because it was at odds with the 'spirit of place' and partly because, although it wasn't exactly a bore, it was just too much effort. And this is certainly not a day for anything resembling *effort* - at least not for me; it is, rather, a day for quiet contemplation of a world turning, apparently untroubled, on its axis - a world, more-over, that for anyone who cares to look closely, provides exceptional reasons for wonderment. In fact, from what I can see of it, Planet Earth is more complex than a galaxy - and it's also the only known spot in the universe where life has gained a foothold.

Unsurprisingly, for these and many other comparable reasons, I'm perfectly happy to remain alone, here in a place where frantic office workers on a pedestrian crossing cannot knock me down as they brush past obliquely rather than at right angles to the kerb. With the following result: that they collide with and endanger other, more orderly members of the public - leading in some cases to an exchange of abuse. On the other hand, in this strictly private environment of my own, I can safely rely on the non-human life-forms that share it with me. After all, they hardly ever demand sudden, evasive action; and long experience assures me that each carries on with the business of living without disturbing the tranquillity of this unique location.

2

I ought to make it clear that, when I mention 'non-human life-forms', it's not just the bees that I'm talking about. This balcony supports a surprisingly wide range of inhabitants which, without the benefit of flight, have arrived and taken up residence by means entirely unknown. Setting aside spiders, woodlice and centipedes, for example, consider the snails. I've no idea how they got here. But what I do know is that they can't be got rid of - and that however many of them I take downstairs to the garden, there's an equal rate of reproduction behind the flower pots that serves only to maintain the status quo. It's possible, of course, that being the 'common garden snail' is no bar to fecundity. But perhaps a simpler and more likely explanation is this: that since I stopped feeding the birds, I've noticed no visiting predators such as thrushes whose preferred means of survival is smashing snail shells into pieces before making a meal of the contents.

There's more to snails, of course, than a bunch of trailblazing opportunists nibbling away at the leaves of my geraniums. And I have particular reasons for saying so. I remember, for example, those nostalgic summer holidays in Catalonia where, whenever it rained, hordes of snails emerged from hiding in order to scavenge the roadside fennel - a habit well known to local villagers who used to go out in force, filling their baskets and plastic bags with wild nature's cost-free source of a square meal. It was also well understood that fennel-fed snails added their own special flavour to the various local recipes of which they were the main ingredient. And, just to be clear, these were not the *Roman* snails served in expensive French restaurants; they were, instead, exactly the same species which is surprisingly well represented *here*, within a few feet of where I'm sitting.

It may be obvious already, but I'm bound to admit to having a soft spot for those molluscs condescendingly known as 'the common garden snail.' I like the rich brown and black markings on their shells, their solidity, their surprising weight and their exotic, almost antediluvian appearance as they pop up, for example, in the everyday setting of an allotment. For which reason, I'm equally bound to hang my head in shame when I acknowledge that, in Catalonia, I also found them delicious ('common' or 'garden' though they may have been) when served in their shells with chunks of pork belly and a hot, savoury sauce.

These are memories for which I feel an even greater affection when I think of the mountainside restaurant, somewhere near the French border in the Pyrenees, where I first encountered snails (cargols) piled high in a rough stoneware bowl. It wasn't just the novelty of eating snails for the first time. It was also the *atmosphere* - an atmosphere enhanced by the light-hearted holiday chit-chat of the diners, the flames of an open fire, the wine, the friendly waiters and the continuous plash of a waterfall just beyond the verandah.

And there was something else, too - something which, although extraneous to the central culinary event, added a unique dimension to what might otherwise have been a pleasant, but less memorable experience. It caught my imagination to such a degree that it remains an even more enduring recollection than the only item on the menu I can still remember: namely, the 'cargols.' And, as I strolled uphill from the car park to the restaurant, that special 'something' presented itself, as if by magic, in the sky immediately overhead.

3

The two friends accompanying me were Bruno (a long-standing

friend) and his wife Clare with whom I was staying at their country-style holiday home in Vilabertran. Vilabertran is a small village situated about an hour's drive from the restaurant. And to my particular satisfaction, the house - although equipped with basic modern conveniences - was nearly a century old and built entirely in the local style. In other words, it was *not* a suburban-looking expatriate bungalow with a fish and chip shop to go with it. And consequently, during breakfast in the kitchen, I felt just as far removed from the likes of Southend-on-Sea as I did around the corner on the steps of a mediaeval Catalan church.

Compared to what some might regard as my distinctly whimsical view of reality, my hosts were much more down to earth. They probably thought of me as someone with his head in the clouds whilst their own feet remained firmly on the ground. For which reasons they were less likely than I was to consider the enigma and implicit mystery attaching to the things that most people take for granted.

As it happened, on that memorable evening, by the time we left the car, the sun had already set; and once our eyes had adapted to the dark, as we gazed up at the night sky, the Milky Way appeared brighter, sharper in outline and more majestic than any of us had ever seen it before. With the result that, to begin with, a stunned silence prevailed, interrupted only by a few, almost wordless exclamations.

Unsurprisingly on the one hand, but also unusually, the conversation veered towards religion. I say 'unusually' because this was a subject that rarely featured in our exchanges. Nevertheless, on this occasion, I remember the quiet, almost reverential tone in which Bruno (knowing I was a believer) explained that among his problems with the idea of a supernatural being was the 'incredible vastness' of the universe. It was something he found hard to grapple with - *particularly* hard, if I understood him rightly, when it came to imagining a god who was 'big enough' to account for the immense scale of what was plainly visible above our heads.

By sheer chance on that occasion, I was in no mood for a heavy-going, controversial discussion on an evening when I was wearing a tourist's rather than a theologian's hat. It was my first visit to Catalonia; I was in love with the landscape, with the warm mountain pool where I'd swum the day before - and with the prospect of the local cuisine in a restaurant whose praises had been rapturously sung during the long drive to reach our destination. Consequently, I suppressed my conviction that a universe which existed *now*, but hadn't always done so, deserved some sort of explanation notwithstanding its vast size - a vastness which, in our differing ways, continued to affect us as we completed the uphill slog.

4

Returning to the here and now on my West London balcony, it can truly be said that among the advantages of a day like today is the absence of appointments, a dearth of unwanted phone calls and a relaxed attitude to domestic chores. That, at least, is how things stand at the present moment. It's a condition that brings with it a degree of mental lebensraum - an open space that I've been enjoying for several hours whilst loosely connected fragments of the past have crossed my mind in a pleasantly unsettling manner.

It would not be unreasonable, of course, to say that it's been an odd assortment, some might say a rather *tangled* assortment, of recollections, impressions and hankerings - a blend that includes a top-class restaurant in a mediterranean setting alongside a spectacular, if challenging view of the heavens. Nor would it be unreasonable to add that, since then, I have never experienced so particular an evening. And even now, nearly thirty years down the line, the dish of snails and the panoramic view of the night sky remain as clear a collection of images as they were at the time.

* * *

And what conclusions, I ask myself, are to be drawn from all this? In answer, however, I'm inclined to hold back; and on second thoughts, I wonder whether *conclusions* are in any sense a desirable proposition. Instead, I feel as I did when Bruno, in the darkness of the Catalan night, first raised his profoundly fundamental question. And consequently, rooted once again in the present among the familiar sights and sounds of a home-grown environment, I prefer to avoid structured thinking altogether in favour of quiet, retrospective contemplation - contemplation, that is, of a series of specific events overshadowed (and yet illuminated) by the Milky Way.

Although less spectacular in their impact, it's also worth mentioning that I've gained a similarly clear view of the Milky Way on only three occasions since that early encounter. The first was during a drive across the high ground above Las Vegas; the second, accompanied by the distant sound of breakers, was on a sandy beach in Bali; and the third, whilst the horizon still bore traces of the sunset, was on the deck of a passenger vessel chugging its way from Mumbai to Goa.

5

Whether in the past or present, of course, events such as these can be unforgettable yet indefinable experiences that somehow evade analysis. A colour in the corner of one's eye, the far-off sound of a goods train embedded in landscape or the rocking of a ship at sea -

all of these can serve to fix not only a memory but also the sensation that accompanied it.

Which brings me back to the present moment - to more or less precisely where I started, here, at home in well-heeled, leafy West London. And I'm left with just one definitive fact in mind which I admit amounts to the *conclusions* I said wouldn't reach. And it boils down to this: that whenever the crepuscular glow after sunset ignites the blue of the campanulas on my third floor balcony, I'm struck by the same sense of wonderment I once felt on the slopes of that mountain in Catalonia. For me at least, it's not an uncommon experience. But at the same time, it never fails to suggest that much remains out of reach, and always will do, beneath the surface of the things we take for granted.

Introductory verse: William Wordsworth: Ode. Intimations of Immortality, 1807.

Campanula: Canterbury bell. Name derived from the late Latin diminutive of 'campana' - a bell.

Tree of heaven, Ailanthus altissima. Brought to the Chelsea Physic Garden from China in 1751 and now widespread. See 'Flora Britannica', R. Mabey. Publisher Sinclair-Stevenson.

The common garden snail, Helix aspersa. Widespread throughout Western Europe and the Mediterranean.

A VERY PARTICULAR PLACE

And Frensh she spak ful faire and fetisly,
After the scole of Stratford atte Bowe,
For Frensh of Paris was to hir unknowe...

Geoffrey Chaucer

I

Today is the last day of October. I am alone, at ease on a bench in an ornamental garden whose legendary name, if I mentioned it, would obscure the splendid particularities all around me, exchanging them instead for an avalanche of visual clichés concerning a place whose special merits I am eager to endorse.

It is for no trivial reason that I've just removed my sweater. Although the year, on the verge of its demise, is at a turning point, an unusual level of warmth and light continues to fill the air. And with thoughts of summer still uppermost, this provides a positive, if unorthodox prelude to tomorrow's brush with November - a month which, at least for now, seems indifferent to its long-established associations with hoar frost, snow showers and the scent of bonfires smouldering on allotments.

2

A ladybird, revelling in these benign conditions, has just touched down on my scribble pad... but has instantly flown off again, leaving me without enough time to count its unusually large number of spots. Less attractively, a horsefly has also settled in exactly the same position at the top of the page but (given my abrupt intervention), it has fled to pastures new with even greater readiness than the ladybird. Looking back, however, given that it managed so skilfully to evade the sticky end I had in mind when I attempted to swat it, I'm genuinely delighted rather than otherwise that now, having erased all recollection of the past, it could well be at peace, sunning itself on a toadstool.

Not only ladybirds and horseflies, but insects in general seem to be doing well in response to current weather conditions. For example, a larger-than-life butterfly with a hint of iridescent colour on its wings has just crossed my field of vision in great haste and, apparently, in pursuit of a very particular, if inscrutable purpose. Its identity, for me at least, is something of a puzzle; and I'm beginning to wonder whether or not I might have stumbled across a once common, now seriously endangered species - namely, a purple emperor.

And yet I rather doubt it: instead, it seems that I've emerged this very moment, in the nick of time, from a prolonged daydream. And now that I have my wits fully about me, I realise that what I *thought* I'd seen was not a butterfly at all but the shadow of a leaf scudding across the lawn in front of me at a speed identical with that of the same leaf's rate of descent from an overhanging branch.

3

I have now shifted my attention further afield to the middle distance where shimmering, angular, late-season light and dreamy shadows combine to create a mysterious landscape where doubts arise as to whether or not those inconclusive shapes that linger, murmur and move on again are genuine flesh and blood or perhaps much stranger, mirage-like presences from another reality. After all, where is the evidence that rules out a collision of worlds in which visitants of uncertain origin are somehow in the same league as those ring-necked parakeets which, down through the generations, have made their way here from the temples of Trivandrum for no other purpose than to settle on a branch not far above my head in an English garden?

*   *   *

But am I perhaps getting too embroiled? When I bury my face in my hands and block out the kaleidoscopic images at the back of my head, a composite picture of what I've been looking at lingers, albeit briefly, on my retinas. Objects fade, then brighten and assume an altered state where imagination steals a march on solid facts. Here presences shift and gesture as in a shadow play - only to be blown off course, suddenly, without warning, by the mew of a seagull declaring that winter is just around the corner on a day when there isn't the slightest evidence to confirm it.

And yet, given this apparent interaction of worlds, I wonder if I'm still dreaming even though I know I'm not asleep. There can be no doubt, for example, that in order to outsmart an enormous oak whose shadow continues to pursue me, I've just moved the bench I'm sitting on for a third time. And even now, at this very moment, if so minded, I could virtually *touch* that woman strolling past in front of me. Indeed, she's so close that her footsteps among the brittle leftovers of a maple tree sound as clear as a child munching crisps in the next seat on a train.

But although the shadows twist and lengthen, the sun still shines. This is no time to weaken... nor is there any excuse for cold feet. Now, at last, I am fully awake and fully alive - as indeed I have been all along. I shall therefore take stock as a prelude to taking action.

4

The afternoon has certainly grown cooler: which is why my sweater has resumed its primary function of keeping me warm. And so, for at least another hour, I shall make the best of Shanks's pony. Until the park gates close, I shall explore shady paths; I shall examine spiders' webs sparkling with this morning's dew; and I shall admire the late autumn flowers still glowing in the light of the sun as it makes its way west towards Fishguard and Cardigan before crossing the sea to New York.

I shall keep smiling, too. It doesn't take a degree in astronomy to remember that, in the morning, the same sun will pop up again - this time over the Thames on the opposite side of town, to the *east* among the skyscrapers of Canary Wharf. Nor does it take a genius to understand that it's been doing so as regularly as clockwork every day since long before Canary Wharf was even dreamt of. And with that thought in mind, I'm prompted to look back even further: and it's sobering to consider how the same unchanging sun brightened up the world in exactly the same way, in more or less exactly the same spot, when a well-chronicled mediaeval nun, on the quayside at Stratford, was making a hash of speaking French to an assortment of traders from Calais.

Opening verse: Geoffrey Chaucer's Canterbury Tales: Prologue, the Prioress.

DOCTOR McDERMOTT'S DIAGNOSIS

Despite the modest sting reserved for the tail end of this story, Mr Ronald Price-Fairweather had a lot to be thankful for. His relationship with his wife was a happy one; at forty-four years of age, he had two strapping sons on the brink of Cambridge University; and, as an established graphic artist, his considerable financial success had placed him well beyond the reach of domestic criticism.

Good fortune, however, brought with it a corresponding set of claims on the plentiful resources which much hard work and many unsocial hours had generated. Among his first priorities, of course, was the maintenance of a happy and varied family life. On the other hand, care had to be taken with regard to his sons who, being used from infancy to considerable luxury, were expecting their easy circumstances to continue undiminished as undergraduates - something Mr Ronald Price-Fairweather had wisely prepared for by building up an offshore account of which, until the money was actually needed, no mention had ever been made within the walls of the family's Cadogan Square flat.

As a merely intellectual proposition, of course, everyone understood that the wherewithal to sustain an extravagant lifestyle could only be procured through hard work - although the two youngest Price-Fairweathers never really appreciated the consequent strains imposed on the family breadwinner. For example, there were the frequent meetings with demanding clients who changed their minds every five minutes and then blamed Ronald for fulfilling their original briefs with unquestioning precision. Nor, on their way to bed, did those thoughtless young men ever stop to think that when the source of their well-being was still riveted to his AppleMac at gone midnight, it was probably because he'd had to revise his latest commission in time for a presentation early the next day.

And then, of course, on top of business pressures, there were family-specific concerns which naturally grew weightier as time passed. To illustrate this aspect of Ronald's life, consider the inevitable, if innocent needs of little boys, big boys, teenagers and incipient adults who required the presence of their hard-pressed father at the infants school's nativity play or on the football pitch at Harrow for the last match of the year (every year). And latterly, of course, there was the small matter of membership fees owed by Harry and Christopher Price-Fairweather to several glitzy nightclubs in the vicinity of Sloane Square where they were building up a colourful reputation before their first term at Jesus and St John's College Cambridge respectively.

* * *

Now, Ronald Price-Fairweather could not rely on his relatively young age of forty-four to act as the sole means of maintaining good health; and as time wore on, imperceptibly, step by step, he'd begun to feel the effects associated with premature middle age. There were reasons in addition to the passage of the years to account for this: his clients had never made an effort to improve their modus operandi; and as the nation's culture became more lax, so did his clients' briefings become more pressing and less precise. The result was inevitable; and the outcome of these relentless changes was a gradual increase in all-round stress, a lot more clandestine alcohol and a somewhat shorter supply of domestic give-and-take! In other words, as his stamina began to weaken, he became less able than in the past to use his time efficiently - notwithstanding the marginal relief when his two sons, with barely a year between them, moved on to Cambridge at the beginning of their first term.

Ronald's wife Valerie was by no means unaware that something was wrong as the tremors outlined above increasingly focussed her attention. And when her husband's stresses and strains eventually seemed to threaten a serious breakdown, she persuaded him (without much trouble) to book a fortnight's holiday in a top-class hotel on the French Riviera where she expected to benefit from the experience as much as he did.

* * *

By the time this stage in the story was reached in the autumn of Ronald's forty-fourth year, there was no longer a problem about leaving Harry and Christopher alone at home, given that they were already living in Cambridge. And so, with the prospect of warm sunshine and Mediterranean beaches before them, Ronald and Valerie made a devil-may-care online booking in less than twenty four hours after deciding to take the plunge - whereupon, jointly and severally, they started to anticipate the forthcoming break with the enthusiasm of virtual newly-weds. The result was this: that without delay shortly after arriving at their hotel in Biarritz, they began as they meant to go on with a slap-up, three-course dinner served on their private veranda. They then had a good night's sleep; and the following morning, after champagne and savoury snacks at the bar, husband and wife strode forth to enjoy themselves with a vengeance, stopping off for a light seafood luncheon at the Café de la Mer with its enticing picture-postcard views of the sea.

Throughout their fortnight away, there was never a dull moment - nor was there much in the way of rest. Nightclubs and restaurants benefited from their patronage; there was a refreshing dip in the sea every morning before breakfast; there were excursions inland to historic chateaux and romantic villages... and then, of course, there was the shopping, not to mention the casinos and a stroll arm in arm along the promenade after dark where the soft lapping of the waves evoked heart-warming memories of their early years together.

There was really no end to it. And yet, of necessity, the end *did* come - even if it was only to enable the breadwinner to *continue* winning the considerable amount of bread needed to keep everyone happy. And so, to cut a long story short, no one will be surprised to learn that, after the return flight home, the grey clouds and showers encountered at Heathrow proved something of a shock. Not only that: for Ronald in particular, it amounted to an abrupt and distressing anticlimax.

* * *

Much has been said and much has been written about the various forms of indulgence that lead on to a miscellany of regrettable mornings after; and when dawn broke to the sound of rain outside the couple's bedroom window in Cadogan Square, a downhearted Ronald Price-Fairweather realised that he wasn't anything like as well in body, mind and spirit as he'd anticipated after take-off on the outward flight. He tried to pull himself together; but at the end of two days of diarrhoea, depression and fatigue, he made an appointment to see his doctor at the latter's private Harley Street practice in London's West End.

There was an exchange of pleasantries before the consultation proper began; and the verdict that followed must surely be a lesson of one sort or another for those who look at life with a view to understanding it. Furthermore, even if the name of Dr Andrew McDermott isn't specially familiar, it's important to know that, although he had a natural interest in his bill, he nevertheless examined Ronald minutely and listened with close attention to the description of his symptoms. In the end, his reassuring diagnosis was not without its lighter side, although the patient found it less amusing than he did embarrassing.

'I've seen this sort of thing before,' said the doctor with a confidential smile. 'In fact, there's absolutely nothing wrong with you. The technical term for what you've got is 'exhaustion.' And I strongly recommend another, much quieter holiday with considerably more rest!'

WITH HINDSIGHT

At an exhibition of paintings, she glimpsed
an extraordinarily beautiful young person
who was her junior by an immense margin. And
she wished that passing stranger, although
uncognizant of her admiration, a happy life
and abundant issue in the years to come.

Michael Hill

Whilst browsing Tate Modern's 2015 exhibition entitled 'The World Goes Pop', Audrey found that her attention wasn't focussed exclusively on the featured images and themes dating from the nineteen sixties and seventies; instead, and by contrast, she experienced an almost equal fascination with the contemporary dress sense and hairstyles of the visitors - particularly those of the younger generation some of whom, going by appearances, were little more than fifteen years old at the time of her visit. This indicated, of course, that they were born round about the year 2000 - a fact in painful contrast to her own arrival on Planet Earth long before the new millennium.

Audrey was not an unqualified supporter of the belief that time and progress necessarily go hand in hand. She was more than willing to admit, nonetheless, that the passage of the years had put an end, particularly for men and boys, to what must once have been the country's dowdiest period. From her own infant school days in post-war Britain, she remembered the dreadful, pudding-basin haircuts worn by scruffy louts. And then there were the grey shorts, the scabby knees and the long socks with elastic bands to hold them up. And there were the girls, too, with pleated skirts, second generation woollies - and a pair of pigtails secured with ribbon! As to bright colours, in the case of boys, that was for sissies; and you could forget the smell of a decent bar of soap which implied a pampered individual of either gender from the posh part of town near the bowling green!

These images and others like them flashed past Audrey but didn't linger for long as she divided her time at the Tate that afternoon between the pictures and the young people of anything up to twenty five years old who were showing a genuine interest in an exhibition of Pop Art that occupied ten salons. Streetwise elegance was wide-spread; living copies of illustrations from fashion magazines looked amazingly spontaneous; bold colour schemes crossed the boundaries of sex; and bodily postures were confidently casual or agreeably assertive.

For Audrey, it was a very enlightening experience; and she had only one seriously negative admission to add which boiled down to the fact that, although a decisively senior citizen, she was certainly quite well, if unassumingly, presented. All the same, the sheer freshness and poise of the younger visitors, plus the prospect of a virtual life-time still ahead of them, left her feeling rather as oil must feel when obliged to float on water as a separate layer, distinctly different in kind and therefore subject to nature's very uncompromising version of apartheid.

This was a disturbing line of thought. But Audrey was a realist and, to a lesser degree, an optimist. And these factors helped her to adopt an easier frame of mind when she remembered something a now long-deceased friend (and old flame) had said to her many years ago. He was describing his recollections of a holiday at a beach resort in Devon which was some way off from the nearest town and a favoured haunt of hippies.

Other than beads and bangles, Audrey could no longer remember much if anything about hippy culture. But that friend of hers was someone she'd known since their time together at college. He'd always been extremely easy-going and non-judgemental. Nevertheless he displayed what was for him an uncharacteristic departure when, with an ambiguous smile on his face, he'd referred to one noisy bunch of hippies he'd seen cavorting among the breakers as 'long-haired gits.' He was, of course, speaking ironically; and in the context of that conversation, there was a sympathetic undertone in his voice that matched the twinkle in his eye. It was simply his way of characterising a group that saw itself (and was seen by others) as a distinct tribe somewhat less well adapted to work than to play.

That afternoon at Tate Modern, as Audrey looked back, it amused her to recall that her friend (whose name was Denzil) had been something of a layabout himself; and his liking for the sun, together with a mindset opposed to regimentation, had inclined him to ignore barriers and divisions and to disregard status. He possessed an outlook that had its advantages as far as Audrey was concerned as she reminisced among the energetic, sometimes irreverent works of art. And she reflected that he'd developed a way of looking at things that enabled him to perceive a plain if commonplace truth when he remarked that, when the so-called 'long-haired gits' emerged completely naked from the water, they looked and were… 'exactly like the rest of us!'

Although so many years had come and gone since that conversation, Denzil's laissez-faire assessment sprang back to life and provided a stabilising influence which had survived his death - for Audrey, the death of a much-loved friend whom she could still picture in her mind's eye with a cigar hanging out of his mouth and a glass of red wine in his hand. However, it was the enduring memory of what he'd said, re-emerging from the past, that persuaded her to shed the mood of self-pity. It prompted her to search for a silver lining; and so it was that although she was aware of envying those young people whilst simultaneously admiring them as they chattered about the paintings, she resolutely performed an about-turn and suppressed what was essentially the fear of being worsted, of being on the wrong side of an impassable barrier, namely that of age.

The result was a modest level of enlightenment. Within the unseen confines of an active mind, she adopted an alternative attitude and wished them all well. This enabled her to share with them, and with one particular young man, what 'The World Goes Pop' undoubtedly had to offer. It was a colourful and vibrant exhibition with something for everyone; and she suddenly felt a renewed enthusiasm on that warm yet unexceptional afternoon when the third millennium, still in its infancy, confronted head-on the 'cloud of unknowing' that was the necessary future both of herself and all those young people around her.

The Cloud of Unknowing: title of an English work of mystical prose; anon, 14th c.

FUNDAMENTALLY AT ODDS

The enormous scale of the universe is no sort of measure of man's importance or his lack of it. Furthermore, the demise of the geocentric model has not yet challenged our probable uniqueness whilst, for similar reasons, the mere possibility of other beings elsewhere cannot materially undermine our current claim to fame.

It has also been pointed out that if our universe were not as vast and as ancient as it is, it could never have developed those special features that make life possible. And so, whether we are alone or not, the stunning immensity of the All remains not only a precondition but also a sustainer of our existence.

I

This story, however indirectly, owes a great deal to Clive Ormiston's extremely popular book entitled 'The Revolution in Physics' which was first published in 2017, by which time Ormiston had already established an international reputation as a theoretical physicist. It was also a book which, in addition to its broader public impact, had made a deep impression on an elderly, retired librarian by the name of Patrick Fairclough who was persuaded to recommend it to his old schoolfriend Ashley for reasons which were only partly concerned with the fluent, everyday manner in which the author summarised the complexity of the cosmos as then understood.

The way Patrick saw things, although Ormiston's book described an almost incomprehensible witch's brew of subatomic particles and forces, it was still genuinely compatible (though not identical) with his own picture of what the world was like. The point being, in the present context, that it lent itself (or so Patrick thought) to a notion of reality about which he'd differed from Ashley for something like fifty years.

Likewise retired, though much more recently than Patrick, Ashley Clitheroe had been a solicitor throughout his working life; and together with his old friend, he'd often discussed what the universe really boiled down to. And yet, no genuine progress had ever been made due to a fundamental difference of view concerned with whether or not a supreme being could be postulated as the cause of 'everything' - a belief favoured by Patrick but not by Ashley. And interestingly, despite the length of time the discussion had been going on, neither party was clearly aware of what the other thought about his opposite number's stance. Indeed, when taxed about what his position really was, Ashley had once spoken rather abruptly in defence of what he saw as his independence of mind. 'Position?' he asked with a self-deprecating, somewhat mischievous smile on his face. 'I *have* no position!'

To be quite clear, Patrick's beliefs were *religious* beliefs; and in a way, it was rather odd that he interpreted Ormiston's book as being more compatible with his own convictions than with the scientific world's consistently belligerent materialism. This was especially so in the light of the last chapter, number five, which attempted to define the nature of man's place in a universe which, as presented in the earlier sections, Patrick took as evidence for his own view that, at its heart, all reality is fundamentally 'strange' - a condition that, for him, was made more rather than less evident by the latest conclusions of physics.

But as far as that *final* chapter was concerned, he stood to one side and dissented from Ormiston's clearly negative drift because it struck him as philosophically rather than scientifically founded. It was a world view to which Patrick felt the writer was entitled as a personal opinion; but he also considered that, as a certainty, it was in conflict with the material set out in the preceding four chapters which left such questions open.

Notwithstanding these reservations, Patrick was still inclined to recommend Ormiston's illuminating summary to Ashley whose views amounted simply to saying that the nature of the world had been broadly diagnosed already by the likes of Charles Darwin, Albert Einstein, Niels Bohr, Ludwig Boltzmann and a few other, mostly twentieth century megastars of whose writings he was only vaguely aware and to which he had given relatively little consideration. After all, in Patrick's judgement, Ashley had spent a lifetime of legal arguments and tight-lipped conformity diluted by little more than discursive, convivial evenings dining out with colleagues who were happy to dispense with their professional straightjackets when given the chance of a share in Ashley's predominantly mandarin sense of humour. By contrast, as Patrick saw it, Ormiston's succinct little volume amounted to a wake-up call that might well challenge Ashley's laissez-faire, disengaged philosophy with the counter-intuitive menace of quantum uncertainty, wave-particle duality and the meltdown of virtually everything commonly thought of as solid from the Koh-i-noor diamond to steel girders and pyramids!

Patrick was also vaguely aware of something else which he was determined to confront despite his suspicion that the attempt would fail - the suspicion being that his friend's beliefs (and by implication his own) were dependent on psychologically predetermined factors. He also realised that in Ashley's case these factors would always favour the continuance of life as he knew it, unaffected by the intrusion of speculative concerns bringing with them the possibility of habit-changing demands. In other words, he was almost certain to persist in taking things at their established face value; and having carried such long-standing convictions into his seventies, he was unlikely to abandon his comfort zone - as was also the case for

Patrick who nevertheless congratulated himself on having given these fundamental questions much more thought than his friend.

2

In London's National Gallery there is a large and rather august portrait, painted by Sir Thomas Lawrence in 1789, which depicts the wife of George III, Queen Charlotte, seated by a window in Windsor Castle beyond which, to the left of the figure, there is a dark and louring landscape showing the chapel of Eton College just visible in the distance. This stands in contrast to the serene appearance of the sitter who is clad in a delicate blue gown. She is also conspicuous for a vast halo of white hair, elegantly styled; and during his frequent visits to the gallery, this latter factor used to remind Patrick of Ashley whose age, if not his gender, was on a par with that of Queen Charlotte as she appeared in 1789.

Although irreverent, this evocation in no way implied anything effete about Ashley Clitheroe. It was purely a matter of the hair, its colour and widespread distribution that forced the comparison in Patrick's vaguely perverse mind. Once perceived, unfortunately, there emerged another suggestive link in that the aloofness of the royal person was reminiscent of Ashley's rather lofty self-assessment which was never far below the surface. And because the Queen's abundant coiffure was the result of careful attention whilst Ashley's somewhat thinner topping was correspondingly extensive due only to the action of the wind, the similarity was forever a source of amusement.

3

Now in the wake of Patrick's encounter with 'The Revolution in Physics', his first meeting with Ashley Clitheroe took place in the autumn of 2018 in Ashley's two-bedroom apartment on the second floor of a tall, redbrick villa. To tell the truth, the flat was on the small side; but this was more than compensated for by its situation in the Vale of Health whose village-like collection of Victorian dwellings was enclosed on all sides by North London's delightfully rustic environment of Hampstead Heath.

On that particular day, the seasonal colours of autumn were over-shadowed by a melancholy sky rather reminiscent of the backdrop in Sir Thomas Lawrence's painting. However, once inside Ashley's apartment and having dispensed with his hat and coat, Patrick soon found himself comfortably seated on the nondescript leather sofa which his host had bought with the lump sum that came with his retirement from Cunningham & Radcliffe, Solicitors. Thereafter, any remnants of the gloom bearing down on the Heath were soon dispersed by mutual enquiries about health and further dissipated by a glass of red wine which turned out to be the first among rather fewer than Patrick would have liked.

Nearly a year had elapsed since their last get-together. And so, unsurprisingly, Patrick couldn't help noticing that his friend of many winters was looking slightly older. If anything, his hair, though still just as white, was somewhat thinner - and it also looked less professorial than he remembered it, given that the wind had had no chance that day to take matters into its own hands. All the same, the health of both parties was clearly unimpaired; and each was glad to see the other. Subliminally, too, the continued well-being of one gentleman bolstered the high hopes of longevity in the other.

But there was always an underlying element of divergence! Patrick's appetite for politics was unequal to that of Ashley whose reasonable interest in parliamentary debate competed with a sportsmanlike fascination with the way in which the participants played their cards. To him, it was almost like watching a game of chess where the strategy adopted by the winner was the principal source of interest - and often the main point of any discussion about it.

For Patrick, on the other hand, any interest in political affairs was more exclusively focussed on those issues which, for one reason or another, he considered important in relation to himself or to the moral well-being of the world in general. Accordingly, comfortably seated with a glass of wine in his hand, it was this divergence of interest that prompted him to steer the conversation away from Ashley's emphasis on the latest examples of one-upmanship in the House of Commons. Consequently, with that end in view, he took a step sideways, perhaps a little prematurely, and raised the question of the Middle East conflict which by that time had cast such deep shadows far and wide.

Ashley was perfectly willing to follow Patrick's cue because the gravity of the situation in Iraq and Syria was a plain matter of fact. This story, of course, is not about 'wars and rumours of wars.' Nevertheless, during the long conversation that followed concerning that very topic, Patrick seized the opportunity to refer once again to something which (as he well knew) had never been close to Ashley's heart; and this 'something' was religion. And his point was this: that whether or not 'religion' was of any interest to Tom, Dick or Harry, the fact remained that the war in the Middle East had a substantial religious bias.

And with that rather inadequately prepared introduction implying a host of plain or possibly obscure facts buzzing around like a swarm of bees in the intellectual air, he began a far-too-abrupt summary of Ormiston's book; and then, with an easily spotted breakdown in the logic, he cited, as a cause for wonderment, the wild improbability of the globe, *any* globe, rotating on its axis in the emptiness of space - all of which, in his opinion, was made so very much more mysterious by Ormiston's outline of the latest physics. But ill-prepared though his argument was, his hope remained this: that he (Ashley) would be persuaded to look again at the most important unanswered question of all, given that the strangeness of *everything* was so extreme that it called *all* positions, fixed or otherwise, into question.

But unfortunately, in the emotional urgency of what he was getting at, Patrick had made the fundamental mistake of failing to pinpoint the counter-intuitive nature of what modern science itself tells us about everyday perception. And by so doing, he'd also failed to mention that his account of reality is now universally accepted as a well-nigh incredible and yet well demonstrated truth.

And it was in the proposition that today's *scientific* truth can appear as outlandish as what the internationally known scientist, Richard Dawkins, has labelled the 'god delusion' that Patrick had sought to revive the lifelong discussion between himself and his friend.

4

In this vein, the conversation maundered on without much evidence of any shifting of positions until the exchange of ideas began to slow down to a pace which persuaded Patrick that it was time to leave. Matters therefore remained unresolved and unaltered, as they always had done. And so, after Ashley had rather pointedly enquired whether Patrick had any further commitments that afternoon, the two old friends shook hands, smiled benignly and bade farewell. In all probability, it would be a matter of many months before they met again - or so Patrick surmised when his friend's front door closed quietly behind him rather sooner than was comfortable.

In the aftermath of the ennui implied by the manner of parting company, Patrick wandered off at a loose end. It was still barely two o'clock when he strolled downhill towards the underground. And as he paused outside the Cornerstone Gallery to admire the paintings in the window, he was reminded of something Ashley had said nearly twenty years previously in the course of a conversation similar to the one which had just concluded. And it made him realise, finally, that the reason why his friend never had and never would alter his stance was that it concerned something in which he felt not the slightest interest. After all, he reflected, had Ashley not given his own game away when he posed the most extraordinary question ever raised all those years ago? Looking back, it had probably been as much defensive as rhetorical. And he remembered it clearly. 'If God exists,' Ashley had asked with telling composure, 'why should I worship him?'

And to Patrick, of course, this was not only a burning issue, but also a question to which the answer seemed so obvious that he'd never been prompted to formulate it!

Wars and rumours of wars: St Matthew 24, 6.

Richard Dawkins: a renowned biologist and prolific writer - almost equally famous as a critic of religious belief.

MR JEREMY BRADSHAW
MEMBER OF PARLIAMENT FOR THORNTON HEATH

I

At the precise point where the London and Surrey borders meet, Richmond Cemetery has a considerable number of attractions in addition to the quiet: it is flanked on one side by dense secondary woodland owned by the National Trust... and the remaining boundaries are occupied by so many shrubs and other, taller garden species that the impression given is convincingly rural. The entire area, moreover, is on a steep slope, green and, but for the large acreage, strikingly reminiscent of a traditional country churchyard. Soothed by the stillness, one also notices that the headstones in this, the older section to the west, tilt with casual indifference to good order; and, on a fine day like today, they evoke that longed-for contentment of which the inscriptions so readily remind us. Of equal significance, too, the late-lamented are not only at ease, but also tight lipped... thus providing a welcome contrast with the garrulous world outside as it fights its way by bus, train or Shanks's pony to join the crowds on the riverside promenade.

What better place for a pleasant afternoon, I ask myself. Encouraged by the flamboyant butterflies basking on tombstones heated by the sun, I can actually hear myself think. Overflying aircraft drone on towards Heathrow Airport. The distant voices of children supplement the occasional twitter of birds interrupting their siesta. So all in all, it really is a perfect day to be alone - mulling over this, that and the other and wondering what on earth has brought to mind the person of Mr Jeremy Bradshaw whom I've known on and off since our formative years at an excellent school for boys not far from where I'm sitting.

* * *

Funnily enough, I've only known Jeremy Bradshaw intermittently. Indeed, in the most positive of senses, I've always thought of him simply as *Bradshaw* because of the way in which that manner of speaking succinctly encapsulates both the character of the person and the cultural norm of many schools in the nineteen fifties. In a curious way, even the faintest visual recollection of the aspiring fourth-former and the sound of the word 'Bradshaw' belong to each other. Furthermore, there's a weird significance in the fact that Bradshaw shares his surname with that of the nineteenth century author of railway travel guides - the unlikely coincidence being that my earliest memory of the elder Bradshaw's lesser known twentieth century namesake involves the two or three summer holiday reports that he wrote for the school magazine - all of them partly or wholly reliant on trains.

Bradshaw's scintillating coverage of a visit to Italy, including a description of Vesuvius seen from Naples, was like a space odyssey to the ears of someone like myself who had never strayed further afield than the beach at Southsea. Neither was his account in any way tarnished by the accompanying rumours of a guided tour of Pompeii, including the well-known Roman brothel with its mural illustrations of precisely what was on offer. More exhilarating still, of course, was the following year's report on a trip to Nigeria and the much trumpeted 'Bradshaw Interview' with a tribal chieftain.

Seated here in sunny comfort, I remember all these things so clearly... and yet, at the same time, they seem strangely distant from the physical reality of a person whose sights were clearly set on a future far and away beyond my own childish world of sticklebacks and tree-climbing. In short, I perceived even then, as an inexperienced teenager, that Bradshaw saw himself as a future man of affairs - an objective that he initiated at the age of twenty-two when he set sail on a voyage of discovery to Machu Picchu as the roving correspondent for a national newspaper.

2

Bradshaw's first excursion among the headlines lasted less than a year. His employers felt that his insights lacked sparkle and, fatally, that his literary style was not only long-winded but also somewhat imprecise when it came to information. Consequently, he was given two months' notice and, in deference to his youth, generous compensation along with a good reference. Jeremy, somewhat at a loss, then went back to the drawing board and studied banking at a college of further education where, after two rather dull years, he obtained a certificate printed in two colours plus gold on paper that an unkind critic once described as more impressive than the qualification.

This return to a world reminiscent of school had put the brakes on Bradshaw's rise to fame and fortune; it had also put a strain on his nerves. Consequently, once it was over, he took a holiday in Jamaica at his parents' expense. And he did so in the company of a former classmate by the name of Maurice Chamberlain who had recently completed a degree course in English Literature at Cardiff University. By sheer coincidence, it happened that Maurice was also a friend of *mine* - which remains the case today. And it's therefore to *Maurice* that I owe much of my information about Bradshaw's exploits during and after the trip to Jamaica where both parties revelled in the excesses of youth without regard to the risks. And however briefly, they also cast aside every consideration of that pervasive bugbear, commonly known as 'the future.'

The subsequent two years in the sphere of banking reinforced Bradshaw's desire for a degree of advancement and status that showed no signs of materialising. Inevitably therefore, life in the City began to pall - and the compensations provided by seedy Soho nightclubs together with the influence of alcohol failed to persuade him that he was anything other than bored. He therefore resigned from the Threadneedle Street branch of Lloyds after getting wind of the fact that he was among those singled out for staff cuts - after which he obtained temporary employment in a coffee bar, taking care not to tell his parents.

It was neither the first nor the last time that chance came to the rescue. And it was by chance alone in this unlikely environment that he once again ran into his former holiday chum, Maurice Chamberlain. In consequence, their friendship (which had lapsed) was enthusiastically re-established - thereby providing a stroke of luck that no one could have foreseen and which, equally improbably, had a pivotal influence on the future of both parties.

3

From the outset, Maurice made a clean breast of the fact that he too had grown tired of his first job as a teacher; and now, within eighteen months of completing teacher training, he'd already made his mark in pastures new. Unlike Bradshaw, however, Maurice was more of an idealist and, as the son of an Anglican vicar, he still hankered after an occupation with a social purpose at its heart. Consequently, following a heated debate in his local Islington newspaper, he'd decided (rather precipitately) to apply for Conservative Party membership at the time of its campaign in support of a well-known North London arts theatre which the Labour Party had criticised for indifference to left-wing issues.

The coincidence of bumping into Bradshaw again in a high street coffee bar had a surprisingly immediate effect on the lives of both young men; and encouraged by a shared liking for the Islington scene alongside the fact that Bradshaw was already a Conservative Party member, they decided to join forces. Without even pausing to think, Bradshaw then snapped up a convenient vacancy at the party's local office where Maurice already worked in the publicity section. After which, for Jeremy, all recollection of cappuccino coffee became a thing of the past.

The local headquarters proved a congenial environment in which both parties felt that their contributions were making a differ-ence. In this they were correct; and as a result they were extremely well liked - a factor which consolidated their commitment. And it had one more, extremely important consequence: it fuelled their ambition. And after the local election just under a year later, both Maurice and Jeremy woke up the morning after a very late night in the knowledge that they were the youngest of the newly confirmed borough councillors.

Early political success proved the making of Bradshaw in particular. He now had a booming, confidence-inspiring, middle-class voice and an expanding waistline which, once established, communicated status and dependability along with a reassuring presence. It was a combination that soon attracted the attention of influential party officials whose chief spokesman persuaded their up-and-coming standard-bearer to set his sights higher than the town hall and to put himself forward as a parliamentary candidate as soon as a seat could be found.

Bradshaw accepted this invitation with considerable pride; and two and a half years later, after an arduous campaign, he was elected as the Conservative member for Thornton Heath by a large majority. It was a success to which his friend Maurice's heartfelt congratula-tions added material satisfaction; and it was to Bradshaw's credit that Maurice was not omitted from a celebratory dinner at the Reform Club in Pall Mall. Also present, in addition to party officials, was a pleasant, talkative woman whose age was comparable with Bradshaw's. No one quite knew who she was, however; and her relationship to Bradshaw was left unexplained in the course of a dinner during which the new member for Thornton Heath made ample use of a microphone.

These events, of course, marked a turning point: Mr Jeremy Bradshaw MP, like many others, had found his feet in a milieu of which he'd hardly dared to dream during his formative years - years during which escapades such as those in Jamaica had been out of keeping with the presumed dignities of a future House of Commons which had turned a blind eye in the past to many an indiscretion whilst remaining, in certain quarters, rife with prejudice.

Jeremy, whose eyes and ears had been sharpened by experience, had now joined an institution far more exposed to scrutiny than mere members of the Reform Club; and as someone with much greater economic independence than before his election, he decided to enhance his public image by getting married to none other than his mysterious companion at the Reform Club dinner - a widow, formerly Mrs Copperfield (née Baldwin), but now the mature and effusive Mrs Edwina Bradshaw.

Buoyed up by his success, the new member for Thornton Heath took like a duck to water when it came to parliamentary life which, being a platform on which to puff out his chest, he much preferred to the local Islington council where he'd found the triviality and petty bickering something of a dead end. These were reservations, however, that were never made public because Bradshaw had long ago perfected the art of positive communication, of blowing this way and that with the wind (as long as his diverse suppliants were dealt with in isolation so that the elasticity of his position wasn't unduly obvious). In the event of any slip-up joyfully reported in the press, of course, Bradshaw was able to smile convincingly and to prevaricate in ways far removed from the stern principles of his former headmaster, Mr Brian Barraclough-Wilson, who was still alive and wondering what the devil the world was coming to.

4

At the end of the day, this is not a story about politics as such - not even those politics that specifically concerned the only-too-human Mr Jeremy Bradshaw. As it happens, his exploits in the public arena lasted the life of only one parliament - after which the conservatives were resoundingly defeated. And sadly, although his status was underpinned by membership of many committees and associations, the memory of his grandiose outpourings from the back benches, his plummy voice and his carefully considered espousal of good causes didn't long survive the fall of that parliament.

If Parliament didn't remember Bradshaw, it was no surprise that Bradshaw himself remembered it as the one and only place on Planet Earth where he'd truly been able to spread his wings and fly. And so, although thereafter he was obliged to earn his living by less exalted means, his need for some sort of platform on which to speak his mind found expression in the addition to his portfolio of even more boardrooms and committees than he'd been able to acquire whilst in office.

But the ultimate hardship for Jeremy Bradshaw was this: that although his name, by dint of determined effort, was associated with so many institutions and organisations, virtually none of them could make up for his former place in the House of Commons. Notwithstanding which, as the clock ticked on, those among his colleagues who were able to distinguish the wood from the trees continued to regard Bradshaw with the understanding and affection for which he'd always fought so hard. And that, when all was said and done, proved an infinitely more significant conclusion than the fall of a government - whether it was to the right or to the left... or somewhere in the middle of the political spectrum.

THE JOURNEY HOME

I was making my way home from a visit to the doctor and was contemplating the remedial action I'd had explained to me in the aftermath of a collision between my left shin and the handle on a chest-of-drawers. This had occurred in the middle of the previous night when the bedroom was in complete darkness. With the result that, by morning, my leg had responded with a lump nearly as big and almost as red as a beetroot.

It was May 4 and a disappointingly drab day for the time of year - a fact that made a small but tangible contribution to the depression caused by the injury to my leg. On the other hand, given that for the same medical reason I'd become a little unsteady on my feet, the half empty bus made navigation somewhat easier; and just as I alighted at the stop closest to home, the sun improved matters even more by emerging, albeit furtively, from behind a cloud.

Once on the pavement of the Lower Otterbrook Road where I live, I immediately noticed a raised planter built into the boundary of number 365. And I also noticed that the wallflowers growing there, already in full bloom, were making the best of it. And so, given they were within spitting distance, I walked across, leaned over them and inhaled the evocative scent.

Now ever since my childhood days, I've loved wallflowers - not only because of their association with bumble bees and the secluded little park I enjoyed so much as a boy but also, at least as I look back, on account of their old-fashioned perfume which seems to preserve the memory of incidents and places that time has swept away. With this result: that as I prepared to move on, I experienced a benign influence that tempered the prevailing mood of foreboding brought about by a fear of old age and declining health - fears, moreover, that were already closer to accomplished facts than I cared to admit.

* * *

To reach my flat, I needed to make it to the far side of the road by means of a nearby pedestrian crossing; and having reached what was no more than an interim staging-post, my attention was again diverted - this time by a prominent lilac (also in full bloom like the wallflowers). Conspicuously untended, it formed part of a natural division between the pavement and the forecourt of a small, red-brick church; and for the second time within minutes, long forgotten associations made themselves felt.

In this particular instance, my reflections, provoked as before by Mother Nature, took a very different, distinctly fanciful turn. And not for the first time during the course of a long life, the scent of the lilac struck me as inexplicably related to the mauve colour of the flower-heads in a manner reminiscent of time to space - both of which, in accordance with current thinking (but without considering how), I took as interchangeable aspects of one and the same thing. In other words, the perfume was coloured mauve and the colour mauve was scented.

This bizarre, dreamlike idea, of course, was only made possible by a thoroughly imperfect understanding of 'general relativity.' No doubt it was also made possible by gazing, through rose-coloured spectacles, at my early teens when it first arose in conjunction with another, related fantasy in which the scent of lilac had acquired a mysterious association with Heaven - a *childlike* Heaven of whose reality it nevertheless seemed a convincing and reassuring manifestation. And so, as I looked back over my shoulder at those early years, I distinctly recalled wondering whether, when the time came, I'd encounter the scent of lilac when I arrived at the pearly gates!

* * *

After an unnerving overnight accident and an emergency visit to the doctor, all these recollections, like a passing shower, came and went in just a few minutes. Despite which, there on the pavement, for what was only a brief interval, the doldrums seemed distinctly further off than they had done under the influence of the wallflowers alone. In a more relaxed frame of mind, I therefore returned to my flat where a glass of milk and the doctor's medication headed the list of priorities before I ended up half asleep on the sofa.

But sadly, as soon as I resurfaced, the short-lived outbreak of euphoria gradually diminished. The overall experience, once I'd had a chance to consider it from the beginning, felt rather like a toothache that returns with a vengeance after the palliative effect of aspirin wears off - or so it seemed at the time as I mulled things over. Consequently, I reverted to the doldrums and a period of thoroughly unproductive self-pity that focussed on the march of time, its effects on my health and, of course, on the inconveniences of an injured leg.

Not without an element of desperation, I inevitably tried to offset so unwelcome a reversal with the help of a few carefully spaced out glasses of wine - a slow process that occupied much of the run-up to the evening meal. Unfortunately, it was an evening meal that suffered from being a supermarket 'ready' - and therefore virtually tasteless due the nationwide clampdown on salt, sugar and more or less everything else capable of enhancing flavour. After which, I sought to bury my sorrows in the television; but apart from an interesting documentary on Turkey, the programmes were even less inspiring than the ups and downs of the weather, the swelling on my left leg and a kofta curry that bore no resemblance whatsoever to its oriental paradigm.

In the end, as a last resort, with all alternative means having proved ineffective, I decided to deal with the problem in the only way I could think of: namely, by going to bed. My fundamental hope was this: that deep sleep and a long period of rest would put a stop to the downward spiral. Those who know me well, of course, will not be surprised to hear that, despite the adverse conditions, I adopted a note of levity when I called to mind the slogan so often bandied about by politicians at election time. And eventually, with the words 'a better and brighter tomorrow' on the tip of my tongue, I managed to get some sleep.

A RATHER ODD SORT OF DAY

Headstones at angles swelter in the heat;
a fallen angel crumbles at my feet.
Magnolias limply petalled lightly fume
the yews' primordial dalliance with gloom.
Time for one lazy hour has slackened pace;
and music out of tune seems out of place.

Michael Hill

'Has anything interesting happened today,' I ask myself, 'other than the plain fact of unbroken sunshine in a clear blue sky?' Which, looked at more closely, seems somewhat too vague a line of enquiry to take seriously. But it follows, of course, that since I haven't been asleep all the time, certain things, apart from the state of the weather, must have happened. And some of these may well enable me to answer this question in plausibly meaningful terms.

I mustn't forget, of course, that the key word is 'interesting' - and in that regard, I'm not wholly convinced. At the same time, having nothing better to do at the present moment than to raise trivial questions, I may as well cast my mind back over the day's events - ending up, in all likelihood, with a set of equally trivial conclusions - or perhaps not.

So here goes. In the first place, I've delivered a repeat prescription form to my doctor at the local health centre. For the umpteenth time since the weekend, I've also done the shopping and carried it home in a reusable plastic bag. Before boarding the bus, of course, I visited the library to see if anyone had borrowed my latest book - they hadn't. I then went to the bank to extract cash from the ATM. And finally, safely back at home after what had been a strenuous early-morning sortie, I made up for my exertions by wolfing two delicious tarts courtesy of the local supermarket whose patisserie section is a regular source of temptation.

I am however, a firm believer in the inevitability of snags; and taking an impromptu look at life's love affair with inconsistency (today excepted), there's no escaping from the fact that, at many British supermarkets, several of the items on the daily shopping list are likely to be out of stock. But this morning, as I've already hinted, the problem didn't arise - thus enabling me to mention the day's events alongside an exceptional *non*-event!

Which brings me to a watershed - because, after the tarts, I then restocked the same plastic bag with a cheese and tomato sandwich, a thermos flask of iced water and a newspaper. Following which, I made my way to where I'm sitting now: on a shady bench in the tranquil surroundings of St Peter's churchyard which, as I continue casting my mind back, is still the same oasis of sunshine and bird-song that it was when I arrived round about lunchtime. It's there-fore fair to say that I'm much more relaxed than I was when I got here. And rather appropriately, in between a series of naps taken precisely when I felt like it, I've also devoured several pages of world news and local chit-chat - although I was distracted now and again by clear evidence that there are fewer butterflies about this year than in the recent past.

* * *

Unsurprisingly, in weather like this in a place like this, the feel-ing that all is well has intensified since I arrived - qualified only by the fear that it might be different tomorrow morning when a bundle of letters lands on the hall floor. For the time being, though, my frustrations have worn off; there are no further obligations in the pipeline; and, rather like holidaymakers leaning against rusty railings as they stare at the sea, the headstones around me are tilting at amusing angles. With this result: that looking back over my shoulder at all the happenings that have occurred within only a few short hours since I got up this morning, I seriously question whether, in the face of so flawless an environment, there are any more lessons left to learn or reflections worth indulging.

On the other hand, I'd rather not abandon my original purpose. I've asked the question and, positive or negative, I ought to find an answer. It could be argued, for example, that up to three circumstances stand out sufficiently well to arouse interest: namely, the brilliance of the sun, the awareness of passing events and the decreasing number of butterflies in the South of England. Today, all of these points, supported by observable reality, seem to have a wider relevance that I find striking. So on the basis of a reasonably positive outcome to my question, I now feel free to add just one more element to the list: namely, that the only impediment to taking another nap is a growing urge to saunter quietly along the banks of the Thames, only a stone's throw away, where the regular flow of the current embodies so succinctly all those minor events which, for most people, constitute a lifetime.

Magnolias limply petalled: Magnolia stellata, whose petals are as described, is also perfumed.

EARTH AND FIRE

I

Rick had a particular interest in handmade studio ceramics - an interest which, broadly speaking, he confined to vessels and, most importantly, to vessels capable of serving a useful purpose consistent with their form.

Accordingly, over time, he accumulated a significant collection of objects answering to this description - although he never risked using them for the functional ends implied by their shape or size. The reason for this was simple enough to grasp given that, although cost was a factor, his interest was almost entirely aesthetic. And it was this emphasis that precluded practical use as a matter of course. In other words, he was an art collector (within the bounds set by personal preference) rather than a dealer in household goods sold (and bought) with an exclusively workaday purpose in mind. Which didn't mean that his collection was entirely bereft of examples which, although marketed for use, he deemed too fine as 'objets d'art' to be subjected to the rigours of a kitchen.

* * *

During the many years it took to put his collection together, Rick also developed a theoretical platform consonant with the criteria he instinctively applied when deciding on any new purchase. Various principles were involved; and high on the list was a rejection of those ceramic artists whose creative work was fundamentally impractical insofar as it *did* not, *could* not and *wasn't intended* to perform a function. For Rick, this amounted to a basic distinction that applied even when, coincidentally, such artworks were hollow enough and sufficiently waterproof to act as containers.

In such circumstances, he argued, the only link between functional and non-functional items amounted to the clay they were made of.

In the latter case, it also meant that the maker, instead of throwing vessels, was operating more like a sculptor. Rick, incidentally, was by no means lacking in common sense, and was sufficiently clear-minded to realise there was nothing wrong with being a *sculptor*. But he was equally well aware that being a sculptor was significantly different from being a *potter*.

2

However briefly, this sums up the thinking that governed Rick's attitude; and it explains precisely why he collected the sort of pots he so lovingly displayed but never used. Purely sculptural work clearly didn't interest him; and on that basis, he consistently excluded it from his collection. It was a view that held good whether or not any such item was figurative, abstract or, in his own words, reminiscent of a 'found object' discovered on a building site and revamped for the benefit of those gullible enough to fall for it!

To be fair, he'd chosen a perfectly legitimate, consistently argued set of principles; but like most such expressions of personal opinion, Rick was unable to demonstrate that his own way of looking at things was superior to any other way. And indeed, by resorting to 'odious comparisons' instead of simply stating a preference, he un-necessarily complicated his position. Consequently, he stuck to his guns without asking himself if there were really any guns worth sticking to; and thus encumbered, the best resolution he could think of was twofold: in the first place, in relation to a straight-forward, functional *vessel*, he maintained that the only issue boiled down to whether or not it was attractive. This was a rather obvi-ous stand on which he conceded that individual opinions differed. In the second place, although compelled to agree that the world was full of sculptural forms of the highest aesthetic order, he also saw it as the area of contemporary art most open to the ideological abandonment of beauty in pursuit of grass-roots relevance - an ideal he considered least well understood by those who actually *lived* at the grass-roots level!

3

Inevitably, the result of Rick's 'either-or' way of thinking was a rigid set of distinctions vulnerable to a charge of inconsistency. And now and again, the consequence of this reality was a red face. Further down the line, he also found that whenever he needed to establish a firm starting-point for discussion, the only plausible argument he could find was his much-vaunted attack on building sites. It was a strategy that worked well - up to a point. And in the absence of an alternative, it was a serviceable defence that provided him (more or less) with the vindication he needed. Moreover, considering that he needed it rather often, it proved a standard escape route (if sufficiently well argued) from the perennial conflict between hard facts, personal taste and ill-advised dogmatism.

* * *

When all's said and done, Rick had an excellent collection of pots - a self-evident point in little need of questionable value judgements. Consequently, in conversation with friends or visitors, a simple proclamation of his central interest would have been sufficient. At the same time, to be effective, he would have needed to take one further, crucially important step towards enlightenment. For the very good reason that no such private manifesto can ever *compel* a third party to share the likes or dislikes of another person. On the other hand, a clear picture of where the boundaries lie can often lead to a better understanding without forcing hot-headed rivals into an identikit convergence.

But human nature is notoriously obstinate; and yet, one last resort holds good in the case of anyone who remains indifferent to Rick's ceramics when all approaches have failed. 'To know all is to forgive all' is a wise and much quoted proverb. And when things get tricky, it can still pour oil on the troubled waters that follow a heated argument.

Odious comparisons: various forms, Shakespeare and Lydgate, mid 15th century.

'To know all… etc': proverb mid 20th century. See Oxford Dictionary of Quotations for historical comparisons.

THE SIGNIFICANCE OF OLIVER JUPP

I

The Angel Islington in North London includes the point alongside Vincent Terrace where the Regents Canal, commencing at Duncan Street, continues its westbound course through a tunnel which, almost immediately, passes beneath the main Upper Street shopping area. It then runs parallel with Chapel Market which, in addition to more than two hundred stalls, once featured a long-established and much favoured eel and pie restaurant that, very unfortunately, has now closed.

Across the road in Camden Passage, only a stone's throw away from Duncan Street and in startling contrast to the hustle and bustle of its near neighbour, lies a second, quite different market whose array of antique shops, art dealers and jewellers attracts tourists from across the globe who, in the context of this story, can be summarised either as casual sightseers or committed bargain hunters.

Before going on, of course, it's important to emphasise that for many years Islington has amounted to more than a pair of highly distinctive markets and a subterranean, largely invisible canal. Indeed, these attractions are only part of a much bigger picture. And whilst many people will not even be aware of the lively street scene, almost everyone will know that among the area's principal claims to fame is the number of resident politicians - many of them traditionally left-leaning and widely rumoured to enjoy a glass of champagne whilst plotting the overthrow of the nation's historic institutions! On top of this, the fringe theatre is well represented; Sadler's Wells is just down the road; and at the top end of Upper Street lies Highbury Fields - one of London's most admired green spaces surrounded by elegant and beautifully preserved period properties.

At the time of this story, however, whilst tradition states that every cloud has a silver lining, Islington (in common with the wider world) had a dark side; and just past the antiques market, one of several examples of this could be found by taking the righthand fork into Essex Road where conditions became more and more down at heel the further one went. Nevertheless, there is no reason to conclude that it was an area bereft of interest - given that Westborough Terrace, close to the main thoroughfare, was a backwater where the once fashionable properties had been subdivided into maisonettes such as the ground floor dwelling occupied by Oliver Jupp and his somewhat ancient cat whose name was Clara. Noisier and less slavishly attached to humans, there was also Rosy - a blue and white budgerigar whose absurdly featherless rump went some way towards justifying an otherwise inappropriate name.

Broadly speaking, at least for now, this completes all the essential background information. And so, embedded in an environment involving famous names and virtual nonentities - plus vibrant local colour alongside examples of serious deprivation - the scene is set for an intimate tale focussing on a much maligned resident of Westborough Terrace known, on formal occasions, as Mr Oliver James Jupp.

2

Over the years, of course, times have inevitably changed; and, as a result, the character of Islington has altered. In particular, the Westborough Terrace of today has resumed its original standing since Oliver's tenure ended with his confinement to a nursing home almost two decades ago. Local land values have increased significantly; and consequently, the three-storey houses which were formerly bare brick now sport façades cheerfully overpainted in white or cream. Furthermore, the telltale signs displayed in many ground floor windows (including an occasional potted orchid or cyclamen) are such as to clinch the widespread evidence of gentrification.

But thankfully, although only a handful of survivors closely acquainted with Oliver Jupp are still alive, their number remains sufficient not only to exchange anecdotes but also to preserve the story of an old man who deserved better than routine dismissal by a selection of neighbours who, in the same breath, laughed at his jokes (and then repeated them to others as if they were their own rather than his). For despite the fact that, both before and after his wife's death, he was typecast as 'the local window cleaner with a comic streak', his reputation amounted to precisely that and nothing more. And whilst his appearance on the pavement aroused smiles before he'd even uttered a word, the very same smiles dissolved into downcast, preoccupied stares as soon as he and his ladder turned the corner into Clevedon Mews and disappeared.

* * *

Oliver (Ollie) was shorter than average, stocky and rather thin on top. Similarly built but with a more abundant supply of hair was his wife who, when she died at sixty four, left him childless and alone. In a way, of course, their physical similarities gave the couple the appearance of being well suited. On the other hand, among the virtual strangers Ollie encountered every day, many found it hard to imagine what (if anything) they could possibly have seen in each other.

But despite this, it was apparent, that when the attraction (whatever it consisted of) was brought to its tragic end, the surviving spouse was left drained of his former high spirits and ready wit. And so it was that, for three or four years after Nora's funeral, her bereaved husband dragged himself around the familiar streets of Islington, sheltering behind a façade of light-heartedness that fooled no one. It was also noticeable that his repertoire of witticisms had become constrained and repetitious, drawing heavily on the outpourings of happier days.

Following Nora's demise, the next bombshell that came Ollie's way occurred when he arrived home one evening and discovered Rosy, his blue and white budgerigar, lying dead at the bottom of the cage. What made matters worse was that the poor old thing was flat on its back with each leg, surmounted by a bunch of claws pointing defiantly upwards. It was rather like a moment of madness in a Disney cartoon. Ollie, of course, saw no grounds for amusement. And although the source of his lamentation was barely eight inches long, it doubled overnight the feeling of loneliness which had borne down on him ever since the death of his wife. It was a misfortune guaranteed to exacerbate his sense of isolation; and apart from the feline company of Clara, it left him with only two genuine friends - friends who, between them, acted as a vital life-support system.

One such friend (and the most important one) was his neighbour Andrea, a Good Samaritan as well as a widow who lived in the house opposite Ollie's; the other, from the borders of Highbury, was Mike whose history was largely unknown - although his windows had benefited for many years from Oliver's professional skills. Mercifully, both of these acquaintances persisted in knocking on his door at regular intervals - something that was particularly consoling in winter when the dark evenings preyed all the more on the old man's loneliness.

* * *

Nearly a year passed before another far more serious crisis marked a turning point in Oliver's life. It was discovered by Andrea who, on seeing his front room light shining one evening on her way home from the shops, rang the door bell on impulse. Receiving no answer after several tries, she darted back across the road and grabbed a spare set of keys from the kitchen sideboard where they were wisely kept as a precaution. She then returned and rang the bell once again without success; after which she let herself into the hall where she ventured several cheerful halloos ending with a precautionary joke as a means of softening the impact of her intrusion. She then repeated the name 'Ollie' several times. But apart from the sound of her own voice, there was no break in the silence.

The 'front room', known more usually today as the 'lounge', turned out to be empty - although the electric heater was glowing brightly if forlornly in the fireplace. The toilet was in darkness - as was the bedroom. But there was a shockingly different picture in the kitchen where Ollie was discovered lying semi-conscious on the floor, muttering incoherently. There was no visible sign of an injury; no bloodstains appeared on his clothes; and there were no bruises to compete with the familiar birthmark under the left side of his chin.

Now Andrea was a quick thinker; and whilst not certain of her suspicions, she had a shrewd idea of what was amiss and immediately called an ambulance from Oliver's telephone - a telephone, it has to be said, which was not (even then) among the world's most up-to-date models; and it had certainly never seen the inside of the now long-forgotten Design Centre in the Haymarket. That was plain enough - but at least it worked.

The outcome was equally providential; and the required help arrived in record time. With similar promptitude, having sized the situation up, the medical team acted swiftly; whereafter the surviv-ing, grey-blanketed pile that was still a functioning Oliver Jupp was carried off, accompanied by much clamour, to the nearest hospital.

In many ways, with his front door sufficiently wide open to reveal a single light bulb dangling from the hall ceiling, and in the presence of Andrea and an assortment of neighbours sporting 'Mrs Mop' pinafores and knotted headscarves, it was a very British-looking incident. Had it not been for the bleakness of the circumstance (and that of the weather), it might have been a clip from an Ealing Comedy - an impression underlined by the fact that the Hampstead District Hospital was situated improbably close to the Angel Islington in a location disconcertingly distant from that implied by its name.

* * *

Eventually, after the neighbours had exhausted their wise words or negative suppositions about lifestyle and diet, things quietened down in Westborough Terrace; and having contacted the hospital a few hours later, Andrea phoned Mike to tell him that Ollie had had a stroke and was paralysed on his righthand side with no movement either in his arms or in his legs. Worse still, she pointed out that although he had a good chance of survival, he was unlikely ever to walk again. Naturally, both she and Mike were taken aback by the immediacy and obduracy of these firmly stated conclusions.

After all possible means of alleviation were attempted, the medical opinion so unreservedly and so promptly dispensed proved stubbornly accurate. Oliver's stay in hospital was lengthy; it was punctuated by well-meaning visits (mainly from Andrea and Mike). But neither their honest-to-goodness fussing nor the carnations and bunches of grapes arranged on the plastic worktop to the patient's left could overcome the fact that the future was as bleak as it looked.

It was a sombre prospect; and consequently, there's little benefit in overloading this story with the ancillary detail leading to the inevitable outcome; for when all was said and done by officials and friends alike, Ollie was obliged to dispose of his flat in order to finance the expenses of a nursing home known as The Oaks. And inevitably, the cost proved so great that, even including the cash received from the sale, the local authority was obliged to pay for his upkeep when, all too soon, the patient's personal resources were reduced to the bare minimum which, under the law, he was entitled to keep.

3

The Oaks derived its name (but not its use of the plural) from the single representative of that species surviving on the lawn by the main entrance of an old people's residential home that had been a vicarage until the vicar, faced with a dwindling congregation, was moved by his bishop into a much more compact residence nearby. His former dwelling was then put on the market; after which, as a prospective nursing home, it gained a certain kudos from a wooden plaque on which 'The Oaks' was inscribed in bold, gilded lettering.

Inevitably, of course, the attendant alterations associated with the change of use were far from brilliantly handled. And consequently, the remnants of nineteenth century grandeur were ruthlessly obscured by tawdry, makeshift structures which ultimately housed the likes of Oliver Jupp in a cheerless environment where life's basic needs and very few of its pleasures were just about catered for.

To make matters worse, not only was the vicarage no longer a vicarage, but it was also situated in a part of Hackney, East London, whose drabness at the time in question was undeniable. And still more concerning was the fact that once *inside* The Oaks, the drab-ness of Hackney was reinforced by conditions where the letter but not the spirit of the law was applied to the needs of the elderly.

Like Mike and Andrea whenever they paid a visit, anyone else had only to look closely at the situation in the day room which had once been the scene of spirited parish councils. Instead of that, what invariably met their eyes was a group of old people of mixed sex seated in a semi-circle around a flickering TV screen that none of them was watching. This was partly because most of them spent half the day asleep, and partly because the sound was inaudible. Further to which, irrespective of whether or not the programmes might have been of interest, no one was ever given a choice. And this describes very accurately the repetitious prospect confronting Oliver himself as he ate breakfast each morning - liberated for the time being from the matchbox-cum-bedroom he shared with a gruff and taciturn stranger.

To keep matters in proportion, it's true to say that whenever Mike or Andrea went to see him at The Oaks, there was a perceptible improvement in Ollie's demeanour. The righthand side of his body was permanently paralysed; but once he woke up to who they were, a somewhat lopsided grin usually crept across his face accompanied by a cheerful 'Hello, dear.' And this was a form of greeting that gradually developed into standard fare for everybody and anybody - irrespective of relationship or gender.

Over a period of about two years, almost always preceded by the same verbal formula, Ollie's encounters with his friends gradually acquired a fixed and faraway quality such that all signs of animation dwindled to nothing as soon as those who came to see him, who-ever they were, began leaving the room. For example, well-wishers observed that even before they reached the exit, his chin had resumed precisely the same spot it occupied on his chest when they arrived, conveying the impression of someone whose mind was focussed inwardly on a world of his own.

4

In his heyday, Ollie's interest in other people and especially in other people's affairs was a defining characteristic. Westborough Terrace was within easy reach of Camden Passage; and the Chapel Market in particular provided an ample supply of stallholders with whom, between cleaning dirty windows, much lively (often bawdy) conversation proved that unguarded gossip was the spice of life for someone who seldom paid much attention to the niceties of conventional behaviour.

Both before and after his wife's death, the market's ins and outs - its hustle and bustle - lay at the heart of Oliver Jupp's universe. And what the faithful few who came to see him at The Oaks couldn't possibly be expected to realise was that when his chin rested on his chest and his eyes seemingly stared into the abyss, he was in fact back on his rounds consumed by the hurly-burly of lewd banter, raucous laughter and the commotion of breadwinners and layabouts alike - all of them hunting for bargains.

It's even more important to remember that, in those once happy, now irrecoverable bygone days, Oliver had developed a particular attachment to the owner of a flower stall who rented a pitch just short of the junction with Baron Street. The woman in question, buxom to put it mildly, travelled all the way from Bethnal Green to earn her living in Islington. Furthermore, she was usually accompanied by her two thoroughly dissolute sons, Zac and Benjy, who formed a sympathetic relationship with the length of Oliver's tongue which, at times, could be as long and as loose as theirs. And naturally, the fact that *their* tongues were just as loose as *his* likewise recommended *them* to Ollie.

Now the stallholder herself, whose East End origins went hand in hand with a rather generous self-assessment, was persuaded by Oliver's familiarity to extend to him the privilege of calling her Topsy - an intimacy otherwise restricted to the family. She had not, in fact, made any specific invitation to this effect; but Oliver, having overheard the name on the lips of her sons (and having taken the liberty) was given carte blanche as a reward for his overtures which, it must be emphasised, were entirely innocent of any dark designs. A tacit agreement was therefore established in which Topsy deigned to be amused by Oliver's quips, whilst Oliver (the proud intimate of a Chapel Market stallholder) made ample and loud-mouthed use of Topsy's, Zac's and Benjy's names which he repeated with an absurd degree of pretence and swagger.

* * *

On one of his regular visits to The Oaks (this time on his own), having successfully raised Ollie's chin from his chest, and having also provoked the by then traditional lopsided smile, Mike was presented with a particularly intimate glimpse of the invalid's preoccupations which were focussed that morning, as they almost always were, on Chapel Market.

He was aware, of course, that a significant slice of Ollie's past had been centred on that bustling venue about which he'd always spoken a great deal more than he had about his own business or the latest goings-on in Parliament. Accordingly, Mike was less confounded than he might have been when Ollie, in his befuddlement and without any introduction, broached a subject which he evidently assumed would be understood without any background detail. And in so doing, of course, he made it clear that it was precisely on recollections of market life that his thoughts had been focussed when Mike's presence led him to voice an aspiration closer to his heart than any other: namely, the restoration of links with those vividly remembered personalities from the past whose flower stall flourished only a mile or two away in Chapel Market.

The outcome was as follows. With an abruptness that was almost alarming, Oliver launched into a rapidly spoken, somewhat garbled campaign littered with allusions and disconnected asides that far exceeded Mike's sparse knowledge of a group of stallholders he'd never met. But although he spoke haphazardly, and despite the constant reiteration, he successfully concentrated Mike's attention on the central issue and on the part he was asking him to play.

Eventually, in the aftermath of much verbal toing-and-froing, his purpose became clear. Without describing their differing person-alities or his precise relationship with them, he persuaded Mike to carry a disarmingly simple message: namely, to pass on his regards in person to Topsy, Zac and Benjy whose names, once uttered, seemed to acquire a special energy of their own. No doubt they were wondering what had happened to him, he suggested; would Mike please fill them in? And let them know where he'd got to? He recalled them so clearly, he said; and he repeated their names again and again in token of his close attachment. 'Topsy, Zac and Benjy; Topsy, Zac and Benjy,' he mumbled. 'Tell them how much I'd love to see them all again'…

But sadly, even for an old friend like Mike, once this tirade was over, the questionable air of Hackney proved something of a relief as soon as his feet were back on the paving stones in an area that provided little by way of an antidote.

5

On his way home, having recovered from the assault on his nerves, Mike felt less daunted than at first by what seemed like a straight-forward task. He'd never met the individuals concerned, but vaguely recalled a formidable woman in a flamboyant apron loudly pontificating whilst a local mum with a buggy, hoping for a special price, fondled a bunch of daffodils. And so, under an obligation fortified by his long association with Ollie, he set out early the following morning to find that corner of the universe where flowers and friendship, recollection and regret had become, in the imagi-nation of an old man, the one and only light at the end of a tunnel very much longer than the Regents Canal's underground odyssey between Vincent Terrace and the Caledonian Road.

Shortly after reaching Chapel Market, Mike successfully tracked down Topsy and the boys who, in the absence of customers, were huddled in conversation when he drew abreast of the stall which presented a colourful contrast to the damp grey morning. Topsy's voice was as brassy as he remembered it; and, in the intervening years since that fragmentary recollection had first lodged in his brain, 'the boys' had clearly crossed the boundary that divides fresh-looking teenagers from pub crawlers in their mid to late twenties.

Mike braced himself and took a deep breath in readiness for the task ahead. Unfortunately, however, the consequence of preparing himself rather too precisely was that he failed to handle his mission with the casual ease of manner he'd planned. All three stallholders looked bewildered and perhaps a little put out when his somewhat uncertain voice interrupted their conversation with a nervous 'excuse me.' All four parties to the encounter were instantly embarrassed and, for a few moments, the awkwardness bore down heavily. It was the sort of situation that Mike was not best equipped to grapple with. And unsurprisingly, in his effort to explain who he was, he was presented with much more of an impasse than expected.

At first, being a friend of Oliver Jupp didn't seem to cut much ice.

'Who the hell's Oliver Jupp?', Zac demanded.

'Oh, that's the window cleaner,' replied Topsy in a tone of voice that betrayed neither curiosity nor much in the way of concern.

Benjy, venturing a lighter touch that fell flat, then chipped in with a form of words altogether at variance with the conciliatory outcome he'd intended.

'I 'spose you mean the old boy with the ladder?' he said. 'We haven't seen all that much of him recently round about these parts.'

'He could talk the hind leg off a donkey... don't you remember?' added Zac in an attempt at easing tension that dissolved into a yawn.

Even after Mike, to the best of his ability, had outlined the purpose of his visit, the apathy evident on all sides was impossible to ignore. After all, he was a quiet sort of individual at heart; but at the same time, he was no fool; and consequently, realising he was facing a brick wall, he prepared to slip away with his tail between his legs.

All the same, it was a rather *public* sort of stalemate. And realising how things might look, Topsy (mindful of her reputation) altered her approach and changed her tune. It has to be said that, for Mike, the change of tune offered a glimmer of hope. Nevertheless, it was a volte face that failed to obscure the insincerity of her allusion to visiting The Oaks 'in due course', as she put it, before adding 'when I can find the time.' And worse still, in the midst of this all-too-obvious evasion, Zac sounded an even more ambiguous note when he wondered whether Ollie would appreciate a bunch of tulips 'when we're over that way.' On top of which, whilst he and his mother continued beating about the bush, deaf-eared Benjy was serving a customer and fingering the change before grudgingly handing it over.

6

As often as not, there are good reasons for steering clear of profundities when confronting irreconcilable forces. People are who they are; they form attitudes and perceive what is essentially the same world in quite different ways. There are some, of course, who manufacture a picture of the cosmos in which their personal inclinations are suspiciously close to their theories. With Topsy and her family, however, this was not exactly the problem. They just happened to live in a box-file of their own in which a mere window-cleaner and gossip like Ollie was distinguished only by the significance that eluded him. And consequently, although Zac's reference to tulips and Topsy's mention of a trip to Hackney were not outright lies at the time, they still failed to materialise. Indeed, Ollie never saw *any* of his old friends again. Instead, in the day room at The Oaks, just over a year later in front of a flickering screen, he died in his sleep as unaware of Topsy, Zac and Benjy as he had been of the TV soap opera that neither he nor anyone else around him had been watching.

7

With Andrea's cheese and tomato sandwiches and a selection of freshly baked cakes served in her own home as a final tribute, one might reasonably suppose that the somewhat crowded sequel to Oliver's funeral service would mark the end of a depressing story. But not quite.

To begin with, it's worth remembering that Andrea's flat was immediately opposite Ollie's former residence; and this alone was bound to stimulate a wide range of anecdotes subtly improved by spurious recollections. But, as a proviso, it has to be added that most such contributions (true or false) were brief snapshots rather than detailed histories, given that the majority of those present had been little more than acquaintances. Indeed, a significant proportion of the mourners knew Andrea better than they'd known Ollie. With the result that the number of guests was surprisingly large (as was the supply of alcohol) - all of which, taken together, facilitated much gossip about the character and interests of the deceased whose significance seemed greater in the aftermath of his death than during the seventy six years of his life.

8

When everything was over, and long after the front door had closed on the last departing guest, there was an unexpectedly brighter side that left two genuinely heart-warming consequences arising from the story so far told. In the first place, immediately after Ollie's stroke, Andrea had carried his understandably bewildered cat across the road into her own home where, after a few days of feline diffidence, it settled down and was excessively pampered until, rather less scrawny than when it arrived, it died about two years after her former owner's funeral.

Secondly, seemingly out on a limb after the loss of his old friend, there was Mike whose previously casual acquaintance with Andrea had firmed up in consequence of the fact that their trips to see Ollie at the nursing home had often been a joint venture. And so, once The Oaks became a thing of the past, there was a vacuum that led Mike to knock on Andrea's door with no special purpose in mind on a day when he just happened to be passing. He was made very welcome, of course; and in response to an open invitation, he continued to drop round for a chat several times a month.

It was a development which, for both of them, kept something alive that might otherwise have dwindled to the status of a black and white photograph in a family album. Instead, in a mysterious sort of way, it credited the memory of Oliver James Jupp with a permanence oddly in harmony with the 'tea for two' that Andrea invariably provided.

Mike, for his part, returned the compliment on these occasions by a variety of means. For example, while Clara remained alive, his visits unfailingly included a range of delicacies whose approval by a fastidious cat was established fairly early on. And for Andrea, he seldom forgot to bring a bunch of flowers - flowers, moreover, which highlighted the fact that Zac's tulips had never travelled the easily negotiable distance between Chapel Market and The Oaks where, beyond all question, they would have made a very great deal of difference indeed.

FLIGHT OF FANCY

How desolate will seem each tree
unknown by sight or sound through me
when I, observer, having gone,
dissolve the world I gazed upon
and, from its solids as I flee,
quit unobserved reality.

Michael Hill

I

According to the breakfast-time news bulletin, official records confirmed that, although it was only halfway through June, weather conditions thus far were better, brighter and more promising than they'd been since the twentieth century gave ground to the twenty first. And for an inconspicuous forty-year-old man making the best of it in Battersea Park, this meant that his enjoyment of another sunny afternoon had become a largely routine experience. In other words, like a repeat performance of the previous few days, the sun was obligingly warm without overdoing things. On top of which, among the surrounding trees, the sibilance of wind and foliage had unruffled his feathers yet again. The same thing had happened the day before; and to cap it all, weird and wonderful thoughts kept popping up out of the blue without a consistent pattern. After all, it was a day as perfect as anyone could wish for. And as far as Calum was concerned, this was a state of affairs that he hoped would continue until the forecasters said otherwise. Meanwhile, very little else seemed to matter.

Ever since he'd arrived in the park, a succession of minor events had come and gone all around him - virtually without a break: for example, an inquisitive robin, eager for crumbs, had just emerged from the undergrowth with species-specific bravado; he also noticed that a hover fly, instead of carrying on hovering, had settled on a wild flower that looked like an undersize dandelion. Slightly more startling, a fungus crawling with maggots had also caught his eye; and out of sight behind a privet hedge, an overheated conversation had been in full swing for ten or more minutes - although, despite his efforts, he couldn't quite catch the gist.

In fact, as he thought more about it, it seemed amazing how much was actually happening so close to the relatively small space he occupied. Minutes earlier, a pair of swans had flown overhead en route to the Boating Lake; an infant in distress had begun howling for no apparent reason; and only seconds later, a stray cricket ball had landed with a thump just in front of him. Indeed, his natural curiosity, combined with long experience, persuaded him that numberless minute events - events so small he could neither see nor hear most of them - were occurring on every manhole-sized patch of ground within range. Yet for Calum, despite their insignificance, they enlarged and enlivened a tranquillity that strengthened his composure and gave rise to daydreams that seemingly popped up of their own accord.

2

In thrall to the influence of the immediate environment, yet inclined to doze as the afternoon wore on, Calum was sitting by himself on a bench, finishing off a lunch that consisted of two croissants and a selection of pastries from his local baker. On the negative side, the influence of a cloudless sky was such that he'd so far made no additions to his diary for which he was equipped with an A4 notepad plus a red and a black felt-tip pen. His laptop (to which the handwritten material would be added later) had been left at home for security reasons. And as things stood, this was just as well, given that no progress was being made - a fact that brought a certain uneasiness to bear on Calum's otherwise relaxed mood.

Whilst, at one level, the stream of consciousness rambled steadily on, the appeal of fresh sights and sounds gained the upper hand until his attention wandered off to anywhere that sprang to mind such as Carlisle, Truro, Holyhead or Lowestoft - places he'd never actually visited. In due course, he began to feel like a bird flying through the air ten or twelve metres above the ground; and during these flights of fancy, as he sank even deeper into reverie, he encountered a wide cross-section of his fellow countrymen gathered in family groups around carefully laid tables on neatly mown lawns in the middle of their Sunday lunch.

At first, like the writer of Alice in Wonderland, Calum gave full rein to his imagination; and from time to time while the illusions lasted, he was persuaded to pause in order to take a closer look at this or that intimate scene. And interestingly, whenever he did so, he could almost hear the tinkle of the wine glasses and the light-hearted banter. The metallic plink of cutlery had an odd way of sounding disorderly yet cheerful; and the periodic outbursts of laughter conveyed an impression that all was well with the world as the temperature of the Arkwright's crazy paving rose steadily whilst, in another county, the Johnson's family pet lay asleep in the shade of a mountain ash. For Calum at any rate, these distinctive sights and sounds, in their several ways, had a life of their own - a life enriched by the chimes of an imaginary ice cream van he encountered in Warrington and an ambulance ploughing through the back streets of Gosport. Both of which, later rather than sooner, served as timely wake-up calls at the back of his mind.

3

Whilst he was still dreaming and dozing in roughly equal proportions, another jolt to Calum's complacency occurred when he
noticed that an elderly couple had appeared not far off to his left
and seemed about to intrude on his comfort zone. Raising his hand
to his mouth, he at once manufactured a strategic yawn after which,
as an indication that he was in no mood for company, he stretched
his arm lazily along the back of the bench he was sitting on. It did
the trick - and both parties altered course without realising they
were being manipulated. However, almost as if by design and just
a minute or two later, an ominous cloud drifted overhead and
obscured the sun - the result of which was an instant, seemingly
unnatural gloom that only faded away after a tedious and disquieting
interval.

Despite being both trifling and relatively short-lived in nature,
the combined effect of these interruptions was enough to remind
Calum that the tangible, incontestably *real* world was still present
all around him in the form of Battersea Park. It also reminded him
that he'd failed to make a start on the task he'd earlier set himself.
Feeling something of a failure, he therefore lifted his backpack
off the grass and dumped it down on the bench. After which, he
unzipped one of the pockets, selected the black felt-tip pen rather
than the red one and began twiddling it between his fingers.

* * *

For Calum, keeping a regular diary was associated with a decidedly
longer-term purpose. Known only to a few intimate friends, it was
therefore much more than a collection of jottings undertaken for
lack of anything better to do. On the contrary, it arose from the
underlying fact that he was a little known painter with a minor

reputation who nevertheless planned to mark his departure from life on earth with a record of his existence that went well beyond the commonplace. The diary, in other words, would end up as a book - a book which, if and when it was printed, was to be a combination of biographical incident, carefully chosen images of Calum's own making and a selection of his private thoughts.

That at least was the plan: and it confirmed that the diary was primarily a reservoir of source material - the build-up of which was the only true motive behind the entries he made almost daily. On the other hand, the entries themselves were never considered in advance but were allowed to occur at random. Structurally speaking, therefore, Calum's diary amounted to an unbridled flow of information comprising both minor and major elements accompanied by the widest possible range of factual observations and impressionistic reflections.

4

Fully awake at last, and egged on by a fear that he might be losing his touch, Calum took the A4 notepad out of his bag and removed the cap from his felt-tip. To begin with, he was at a loss for words because although he had a motive, he lacked the necessary energy on that particularly soporific day. Nevertheless, in order to regain his confidence, he decided to summarise everything he'd seen, heard and above all *imagined* since he'd arrived in the park. After which, he continued to convince himself that although writer's block was waiting in the wings, he would eventually fight it off! And in order to do so, with a resolute flourish, he began putting pen to paper.

Calum was a staunch believer in two, fundamentally distinct types of reality which, at their simplest, boiled down to 'material facts as observed' and 'fictitious experiences as imagined.' In relation to that specific day, the first type, in the heart of London, had consisted of an audacious robin, an errant cricket ball and a heated argument. On the other hand, scattered throughout the country, the second version had amounted to a daydream involving cosy family gatherings in typically British gardens. Between them, of course, as Calum fully realised, there was no connection... apart from the shared timing imposed by the workings of his mind. In addition, all the circumstances, whether real or fictitious, were insignificant beyond their immediate spheres of influence; and the only common denominator that linked them was consciousness (namely, his own) which, unburdened by forward planning, had drawn them together.

Just to be clear, this was not the first time that Calum's thoughts had explored areas regarded by many as beyond reach. Despite which, he'd allowed himself to stray yet again into uncharted waters that left him struggling at the boundaries of knowledge - boundaries, it has to be said, that he shared with everybody else stranded on the same side of the grave as himself. And therefore, to put it plainly, clarifying his ideas and finding the right words to express them was a perennial headache.

In a show of defiance, however, he continued scribbling; and gradually, his efforts developed into a series of speculations about 'events' - events that are here today and gone tomorrow... incidents that endure by reason of having happened in the first place. He then questioned where this line of thought was leading; after which, in pursuit of an answer, he paused and concentrated on where the mystery ultimately lay. He knew, of course, that petty squabbles as well as historic battles arise and then dissolve in submission to the arrow of time. But inevitably, this highlighted the fact that 'time' and everything connected with it was an area of unresolved scientific debate. 'When all's said and done, what the hell *is* time,' he wrote in an ill-disguised effort to obscure his lack of a solution. It was a mere ten-word response to a centuries-old conundrum. Nevertheless, he considered it worth scrawling in the margin of his manuscript before underlining it with three impetuous strokes of his felt-tip pen.

What the hell time is (in the absence of an agreed definition) was a seemingly rhetorical question without much scope for original ideas. The result being that Calum opted for the only honest answer he could think of; and he quietly congratulated himself as soon as the words 'nobody's got a clue' appeared on the page. At least this was a fact - if nothing else. Despite which, he supplemented this train of thought, somewhat tentatively, with another question.

'And what about the people who tell us that time doesn't really *exist* at all,' he asked.

This left him with little else to say (and perhaps concerned for his future readers), he paused briefly before returning to his conviction that, whatever their link with time, historical and imaginary events are on a par 'simply by reason of having happened in the first place.'

* * *

With this mishmash of speculation weighing him down - yet still under the benevolent influence of sunshine and shadow - Calum was almost persuaded to call it a day. It was no longer a question of writer's block; instead, it was the sheer impossibility of accessing any further layers of understanding. He nevertheless continued writing in the forlorn hope that the 'famous last words' destined for the end of his book would suddenly materialise unprompted. Inevitably, of course, he was disappointed. And in the end, he bowed to necessity by resigning himself to the fact that, for the present, all further efforts would be a waste of time.

There was then a brief struggle, after which he opted to 'look on the bright side' by laughing at his own frustration. He was entitled to take it easy, he decided; and nothing else of importance was going to emerge until the sun had yielded to the night as a condition of rising, full of new potential, at dawn on the following day. He then held back for just a few moments longer before finally recognising that something of genuine significance had emerged *already* in the form of his written notes on the day's events.... events real and unreal which, according to Calum's way of thinking, could *never* be deleted from history. In the long run, it was all part of the universe as a whole and its vast armoury of mysterious principles and structures.

'And that, if nothing else,' he calmly wrote, 'is a conclusion well worth reaching.'

Unobserved reality: a reference to the 'Copenhagen Interpretation' of the quantum world developed in the mid-1920s by Niels Bohr and Werner Heisenberg.

Dandelion, Taraxacum officinale: there are many other wild flowers of similar appearance but of comparatively diminutive size.

Mountain ash tree: alternatively known as the 'rowan tree', Sorbus aucuparia.

JAMIE

Gather ye rosebuds while ye may,
Old Time is still a-flying:
And this same flower that smiles to-day,
Tomorrow will be dying.

Robert Herrick

I

Whilst listening to the BBC news, I was not at all surprised to hear that the temperature had reached a high of 27 degrees Celsius. During the same bulletin I also learned that, according to official records, it was the hottest April day since the nineteen forties. And for me at least, although it was still spring, 19 April 2018 felt more like May or June than a month usually associated with showers and brief glimpses of the sun.

From dawn till dusk, there was brilliant wall-to-wall sunshine. It was therefore an ideal moment, long awaited, for a shady deck-chair in Regents Park; and it was also a perfect opportunity to observe how, since the heavy snow of only a few weeks previously, the world of nature had burst into flower whilst, in response to the same root cause, the world of human beings had moved on from overcoats, turned-up collars and scarves to a blizzard of floppy white hats and outsize shorts which, in the latter case, were the sole province of middle-aged men. It was also noticeable how the female visitors had similarly cast aside all thought of winter clothing in favour of much flimsier garments which, in a few cases, offered rather scant coverage; and this, for seasoned people-watchers like me, provided a spectacle on a par with that of the men's shorts. All of which conjured up a picture of eager rummaging among those wardrobes where, more often than not, the smell of moth-balls still lingered.

Under the sonorous influence of city blackbirds alongside the satis-factions of a critical eye and the scent of freshly mown grass, I was gradually lulled into a state of contentment and carefree reflection. The shadows of the trees were reminiscent of enormous ink stains spreading unevenly, as if the lawns were made of wet blotting paper. In the distance, the white façades of the Nash terraces projected a dazzling image of well-being. And a butterfly of the commonest kind, powered by its pale, ivory-coloured wings, audaciously confirmed that spring was well advanced.

Close at hand, in the shade of a neighbouring tree, there was a family group comprising six or seven individuals. Seated on the grass and enjoying what must have been their first picnic of the year, they were a centre of lighthearted chatter that seemed softer than it might otherwise have been but for the effect of the sun's heat on the density of the air.

The group's youngest and smallest member went by the name of Jamie. And it was as plain as plain could be that Jamie was a recent arrival whose age made his crumpled white sun hat a more com-pelling necessity than was the case for the similarly clad grown-ups responding more to custom than to pressing need. Be that as it may, however, and with due allowance for the older men with bald heads, the child struck me as a quintessential and none-too-steady toddler whose tendency to toddle greatly added to his charm. For a few minutes, therefore, he commanded my attention and, in the longer run, he provoked a surprisingly challenging thought experiment.

Applied to a human being at such an early stage in life, the 'innocence of children' is a truism rather than a cliché or an error of judge-ment. And that, perhaps, lay at the heart of my interest. At every step, this was a child on the brink of stumbling; his awkward movements were reminiscent of a badly handled puppet; and predictably, as an infant, he was wholly oblivious to the dangers of walking on two limbs rather than four. Yet despite his limited awareness, before being grabbed by his father, it was plain that every bit of the five or six metres he covered was as deeply interesting as it was profoundly new. And as a person conscious that the world, for those with open eyes, is never short of interest, I recognised in the child a faculty which, in the case of adults, is all-too-frequently snuffed out by the 'familiarity that breeds contempt'.

2

These considerations certainly marked the beginnings of a line of thought which led on into the murkier waters that soon confronted me. But it was no love affair with the devil that induced me to reflect how Caligula, Pol Pot and Genghis Khan had all been innocent children during the early years of their existence. By contrast, here was a simple case of a recognised if negative aspect of human nature which was tempered on that exceptional day by perfect weather conditions in a more or less perfect environment. And consequently, being off guard, my mind rambled on without discomfort or any felt need to alter course. This was despite my clear understanding that sunny days could never guarantee immunity from a downturn - not even in the case of that picture of innocence I was looking at only a few metres from where I was sitting. 'Here today and gone tomorrow,' I whispered to myself.

Impacted by the high temperature and the overwhelming tranquillity of my surroundings, I inevitably drifted off at a tangent and gave free rein to my imagination. And the first thing that bubbled up at the back of my mind was the image of a fifteen or sixteen-year-old boy, at the end of the school day, scribbling two hundred lines during prefect's detention - a circumstance I construed as a punishment for sniggering at the Latin master whose glasses, initially propped up on his forehead, had slipped and struck the bridge of his nose whilst reciting a passage from Ovid.

After a pause, I casually pressed the fast-forward button and moved on from the third to the fifth form where, by then somewhat more calculating and certainly more sure of himself than previously, I glimpsed the same, now taller boy arguing with the history teacher who asked him to leave the room when his use of language on a current affairs issue overstepped the mark.

Having thought it over, however, I passed this incident off as a minor misdemeanour that amused his friends and was soon forgotten. After all, I told myself, it was a common enough tendency among the young, as they found their feet, to challenge the older generation by blaming them for most of the world's ills.

At the same time, there was something about this line of thought that had the makings of a dead end. And after another tap on the fast-forward button, for the third time and at the end of his sixth form year, I caught up with the same, conspicuously taller schoolboy. By now, of course, he was nineteen years old. And, as a fly on the wall, I was lucky enough to arrive at the exact moment when he disconcerted all his teachers (and shocked some of them) by receiving a letter from Durham University confirming his acceptance as an undergraduate. And it was there, with a certain amount of triumphalism directed at anyone who cared to hear it, that he later launched into a three-year course in mathematics and computer science.

Durham University - or rather his achievement in managing to get there - transformed Jamie overnight from a cocky teenager into a young adult who exemplified the latter description by spending endless hours with friends in the local pub, even more hours in bed with his girlfriend and, following an increasingly characteristic pattern, just enough time spent on his studies to earn him a second class honours degree at the end of his course. 'So far, so good' you might say, for a fictitious character whose addiction to 'living it up' was balanced by the realisation that he needed a brilliant job and a decent income in order to finance his grandiose aspirations!

3

By the age of thirty-six, this young man whose youthful looks were beginning to fade, had been married, had got bored with it (as had his wife) and was now divorced - luckily without any children to complicate what was, in the event, a fairly smooth process. On the other hand, in terms of his career, he was getting into a rut - something he vaguely realised despite lacking sufficient drive to fight back. This was a gradual and relatively recent development which had crept up quietly behind him: in other words, well ahead of schedule, he was beginning to run out of steam.

Despite what amounted to the first signs of a downturn, Jamie nevertheless plodded on. He declared war on his declining self-confidence and, at least for the time being, he retained his reputation as an efficient operative in the service of the same financial institution where he'd spent most of his working life. And up to a point, he was still well liked by those of his colleagues with whom, after hours, he spent much time with a beer glass in his hand - something which reminded him, with growing frequency, of his student days in Cambridge.

Distinctly less edifying in my judgement was the fact that, rather late in the day for a person past his prime, he became entangled with a never-ending succession of girlfriends; and it was this factor added to the drink that lubricated the after-hours chit-chat with work associates until, subjected to more of the same over a period of years, most of them grew tired of his increasingly repetitive sexual adventures and drifted away... And so life went on until he was nearly fifty... by which time he had only three friends left who genuinely liked him and consistently spoke up in his favour.

4

The downward spiral was gradual but steady. As the candle burned lower and his sixth decade drew closer, his contemporaries noticed that he was ageing more and more rapidly whilst his response to the demands of his job grew slower and less effective. Significantly, too, almost everyone stopped calling him 'Jamie.' Somehow, the diminutive form sounded inappropriate; and the consequence was that 'Jim' became the norm - thereby inadvertently recognising that the smooth skin and rosy cheeks of the infant, noticed so long ago by a stranger in Regents Park, were gone forever. And most sadly of all, apart from his three remaining friends, he was increasingly looked down upon and regarded as a drag by the survivors among his longer-term associates who, by then, were more interested in their pension funds than they were in a former companion who once cracked amusing jokes and told dirty stories in the Fox and Hounds... And to cap it all, the three friends who continued to support him finally woke up to the fact that they'd been tarred with exactly the same brush themselves.

Gather ye rosebuds while ye may. From a poem by Robert Herrick: 'To the Virgins, to Make Much of Time', 1648.

Here to-day and gone to-morrow. From J. Calvin's 'Life and Conversion of a Christian man', 1549. See Oxford Dictionary of English Proverbs.

UNTIL THE CLOUDS GATHER

To Maureen, even the falling leaves left a positive impression: florid as newly minted coins, they tapped dryly on the hard foliage of a holly bush whose berries sparkled in the November light. It was a day when the sun transformed whatever it touched. Among the grass blades, for example, the overnight hoar frost had dissolved into a scatter of uncut diamonds that flipped from colour to colour as she strolled serenely on. Even the shadows glimmered; and reality, however impermanent, seemed to have achieved perfection.

From 'Peacock Blue', page 241.

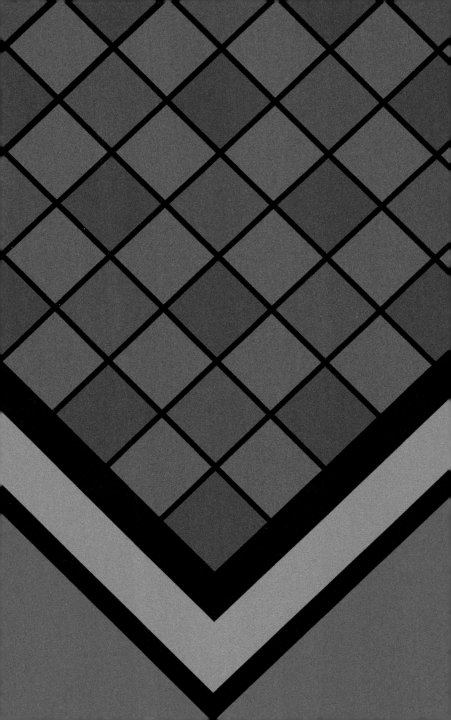

PETERSCOMBE SANDS

High tidal barriers of vagrant stones
shelter, above the clustered shingle
and slanting sand,
a medley of bungalows
from the cold hand
of the water's rising pressure on the land.

Seaview and Broadshore are well defended.

Michael Hill

As if airlifted either from a thirties London suburb or from the fringes of John Betjeman's much maligned Slough, there is, among many similar dwellings in Peterscombe Sands, a mock-tudor-cum-ribbon-development-style house that is somewhat grander than its neighbours. Its bold frontage confounds passers-by with the name 'Sunnysyde Up' which is burnt, with rustic pretension, into the varnished cross section of a log screwed to its front door. In addition, on closer inspection, it is clearly evident from the neatly draped curtains and spotless window panes that all its other details are likewise intended to make an impression.

In the same leafy avenue, equally well maintained but less remarkable and closer to the beach, stands a freshly painted bungalow whose white pebble-dash walls bear the cast-iron image of a schooner accompanied by the words 'Ship Ahoy.' However, anyone out for a stroll will notice that although the proud owners are competing for admiration like everyone else, their front garden is less well endowed with shrubs than the mock-tudor rival a few yards further inland.

* * *

Thus far, we have the merest snapshot of a virtually self-contained world as it *seems* to be, and actually *is*, in summer. It is also a world well and truly under wraps when winter winds cut across the channel from France and hurl twenty-foot walls of water against a natural barrier that holds back the sea from a low-lying environment perpetually at risk but for its stony defences.

There are some, during these months of suspended animation, who doubt whether retiring to Peterscombe Sands was a wise move. Others, however, are content with slippers and afternoon tea in a comfortable armchair - or resigned to a snooze by an 'electric' coal fire whose reflections on the rug remind them of the hard slog before the war when the flames (as well as the smouldering ashes) were real. Nevertheless, for most people, whatever their differing attitudes, winter is seen as something simply to be endured until it comes to an end.

By contrast, on bright summer days, the well kept lawns of Westmead View, Staplecroft and the like are exuberant with pink hydrangeas or lupins; and sprawling in the shade of a tamarisk, an overheated spaniel with its tongue hanging out is a common enough sign of a happy home and winters long forgotten. Moreover, at times like this, in the one and only village high street, there is much bustle and gossip; and the shops, with additional customers from the outlying farms, are always busy.

Trivial by comparison with the early morning news, but important to locals intimately acquainted with each other's business, a chance encounter en route from the butcher's to the newsagent can lead to much exchange of information. With the result that the impending visit of relatives is likely to compete significantly with unwelcome rumblings from abroad. In consequence, when it comes to describing the many hours of hoovering and the minutely planned lunch awaiting the visitors, there is little opportunity left for world affairs.

* * *

And so it seems that, all in all, despite its fair share of human misery and disappointment, there is something about Peterscombe Sands on a fine summer's day that is special - although there's no shortage of carbon copies in other, more or less similar locations. It's true, of course, that we're likely to laugh at a bungalow by the name of Ancona in an English seaside village - although we may look more favourably at Chestnut Cottage whose sole occupant is nearly as old as the thatch on its roof. What we need, perhaps, is a broader vision - and a greater willingness to probe beneath the surface.

But there's one rather particular thing that ought not to excite ridicule; nor should it greatly surprise us. I refer to the plain and simple fact that at the EU referendum in 2016, the constituency of Peterscombe Sands (by a comfortable margin) rejected the 'Remain' option. Furthermore, quite out of the blue during opening hours on the day the result was confirmed, there was an unaccountable increase in attendance at the village pub 'The Francis Drake.' On top of which, there was a virtually continuous queue at the nearby fish and chip shop.

It was all very perplexing. Indeed, it was such a remarkable phenomenon that it gained a mention in the local newspaper. But despite much wild speculation, neither the pub landlord, the proprietor of the fish and chip shop, nor the editor of the Southern Courier could find a convincing explanation.

Come, friendly bombs, and fall on Slough! From John Betjeman's poem, 'Slough', 1937.

RETREAT FROM NO-MAN'S-LAND

According to the date on his morning newspaper, it was the middle of March - a fact highlighted on page 3 by a short article alleging that spring was on the early side that year. But although he saw very few grounds for the writer's optimism, he'd nevertheless ventured into Kensington Gardens where, unsurprisingly, he found conditions (especially the temperature) less springlike than those he'd read about only a few minutes ago on the bus between Hammersmith and the park.

Having braved the cold, Lawrence headed off from Alexandra Gate along West Carriage Drive in the direction of the Serpentine Gallery. And on top of his uneasiness about the weather, further concerns began to present themselves at the back of his mind that made him feel even more like a fish out of water. For example, only yards in front of him, he noticed a young man (not a day older than eighteen) exercising his Jack Russell which, despite being constrained by a lead, had succeeded in cocking its leg against the railings. Consequently, in deference to necessity, the young man came to a standstill; and as he overtook him, Lawrence noticed that in addition to unnaturally pale skin, he was staring straight ahead like a zombie and showed no interest at all in his dog's bodily needs. He was also somewhat unsuitably dressed in a formal black suit. And as a result, given his present commitments combined with the low temperature, both his appearance and demeanour seemed at odds with the ordinary world from which he appeared to have cut loose.

Marked by a similar level of incongruity, Lawrence then remembered that only a few moments ago, just before he'd spotted that strangely anonymous young man, he'd also been aware of a butterfly, prematurely out and about, flitting across the road where it was blown off-course by a passing vehicle. After which, it zigzagged unsteadily towards the rhododendrons where it was absorbed so completely by the dense, gloomy foliage that, practically speaking, it might just as well never have existed.

* * *

Ever since he'd got off the bus that morning, impressions like these had been building up… alerting his mind, step by step, to possibilities that may not have been as absurd as they appeared. For instance, despite the petals falling as harmlessly as snowflakes from a wild cherry tree, he was overcome by a feeling that the world, under pressure from another dimension, was no longer fully present in the round. Instead, it seemed to be drifting away into no-man's-land; and once he'd passed the gallery and reached the bridge dividing Long Water from the Serpentine, he could tell from the impressions emerging all around him that a transformation of reality, so plainly recent, was still gathering pace.

As a result, to his discomfort, he noticed that familiar landmarks appeared less solid than in the past. Furthermore, the visible world seemed to be shrinking significantly so that, obscured by an inner-city haze, no hint whatever of the London he knew and loved was observable beyond Park Lane. On top of this, as if to confirm the prevailing trend, the cold air cut across his face like a knife, bringing with it a sense of foreboding.

Surviving nature, however, remained aggressive and intolerant of intrusion: a coot pursued a rival… half-flying, half-sprinting like a crazy athlete across the surface of the waves. And as the sky darkened still more and the first raindrops began falling, he felt out of his depth in a rapidly disintegrating and unstable environment.

* * *

Helpless as a ship becalmed on open water, Lawrence consequently began to think about emergency action. He decided it was time to pull himself together; and so, although the weather showed no signs of improvement, he prepared to alter course. With sudden conviction, he unfurled his sails in readiness for a favourable wind - and he submitted to it as soon as it made an appearance... With the immediate result that he found himself on the way back to solid ground and secure from spending the rest of the day in a no-man's-land of his own making.

And not long afterwards, he shook off his malaise entirely and came to his senses. To his great relief, he felt a new and all-embracing calm. As he retraced his footsteps, the young man with the Jack Russell was ushering his pet into a Porsche. On the Long Water, a peace deal had been entered into by feral nature. The petals of the wild cherry were still making up for those almost forgotten days when winter snowfall was a virtually annual event. And the sun, in an effort to oblige, had found an opening in the clouds from which the rain, mercifully light, had ceased falling altogether.

CRIMINAL RECORD CHECK

Not all that long ago, Mrs Evelyn Duckworth was sitting comfortably in an underground carriage en route home to Helmsfield after a tiring day's work in the office. It was nearing the end of October; but despite this circumstance, the weather was unseasonably muggy - something which inclined her more towards a nap than it did to the Evening Messenger which she'd grabbed on impulse before joining the crowds in Baker Street station who were likewise making for home.

To all intents and purposes, Evelyn was a single mum as the inevitable result of her husband's sudden desertion. And although investigations had revealed no evidence of a mishap, it remained true that he hadn't seen fit to resurface since his disappearance - none of which led her even to *consider* remarriage. Consequently, it was still a bona fide *Mrs* Evelyn Duckworth whose drift towards sleep was abruptly halted when she spotted a headline on page 2 of the Messenger which included the word 'Helmsfield.' This was a turn-up for the books that immediately galvanised her attention and persuaded her to read on in order to find out what sort of event, in her own back yard, had successfully wormed its way into a widely read evening paper.

In radically different situations, of course, what she discovered within the space of the first paragraph might have led to a healthy mixture of laughter and disparagement. But being already worn out at the end of a tedious day - and because it affected her personally - she was reduced firstly to stunned silence and a red face, and then (under her breath) to an outburst of angry protest.

The substance of the report which so infuriated Evelyn boiled down to the fact that Helmsfield Council had just introduced a regulation banning all parents from accompanying their children while in the local adventure playgrounds lest they (the kids) fall victim to adult sex offenders. Now, not only did this piece of high-handed nonsense affect Evelyn (and her two children) directly, but it also struck her as sufficiently counter-intuitive as to call the council's competence into question. After all, she argued, wouldn't it be more sensible to allow only those children into the playgrounds whose parents were there as well - thus providing by far the most effective protection from predators?

* * *

First things first, of course. And having picked up her children from a family friend who cared for them after school, Evelyn sat them down, once they reached home, with a plateful each of hamburgers and chips supplemented by an unbuttered, insufficiently drained pile of greens. This familiar set meal was followed by two helpings (per person) of the strawberry trifle she'd bought from the Helms-field branch of Tesco on her way back to the council house which, until two years previously, she'd shared with her husband. That very evening in fact, as she rounded the last bend and the front door came into view, she'd pictured her former heart-throb living it up (God alone knew where) with another woman.

Long after the clatter of knives and forks had come to an end, Evelyn, still on the warpath, remained profoundly ill-disposed towards Helmsfield Council's policy on children's playgrounds. And having left her two offspring, Jenny and Tim, to their own devices in the back garden, she went online and tracked down the email address which looked best suited to a successful spot of target practice; and having composed an unplanned, highly discourteous dressing-down, she sent it to the leader of Helmsfield Council without even bothering to check it over before angrily despatching it without further thought.

The core of Evelyn's argument was as follows. It goes without saying, of course, that it included many disparaging adjectives such as ridiculous, ill-considered, daft, inconvenient and undemocratic. But within the lively cut and thrust of some profoundly unfortunate remarks, there was another group of assertions with a great deal more substance attached to them.

For example, she laid emphasis on the Evening Messenger's disclosure that no similar ban concerning children's playgrounds was to be found anywhere else in the United Kingdom. Did that mean, enquired Evelyn after blowing her nose and gazing angrily at the mess it made of her handkerchief, that twenty-first century Helmsfield was populated by an exceptionally high number of paedophiles - in which case, she added, why wasn't something being done about it?

But this was neither the centrepiece nor the parting shot in the course of Evelyn's complaint. She upped the stakes further; and she upped them decisively by claiming that criminal record checks were already mandatory in almost every context affecting children. And in the light of that 'obviously sensible arrangement', she went on to ask whether Helmsfield Council would now act with greater con-sistency by imposing similar criminal record checks on all parents whose children frequented the local playgrounds. Otherwise, she asked, how could the safety of youngsters accompanied *to and from* a playground by their parents be ensured if, at one and the same time and involving exactly the same parents, it couldn't be ensured when they were on the *inside* of what amounted to a few rusty railings?

It goes without saying, of course, that no answer was ever received!

WHEN I RETURNED TO WINTERDALE

When I returned to Winterdale, I found that the estate had changed hands. Some of its finest features had been demolished. The folly, no longer safe, was marked 'out of bounds'; and the summer house was wide open to the sky, derelict, its doors swinging listlessly in a wind that seemed to blow from nowhere.

The gardener's cottage had been replaced by a featureless, off-the-peg bungalow designed by office juniors. A tangle of weeds competed for living space with the wallflowers that were once the sole occupants of well tended borders. Snapped from their moorings by springtime gales, twigs and small branches littered the lawn.

At the heart of its rolling acres, the great house, once the envy and inspiration of my childhood, gazed across at me with the cold, indifferent eye of a fallen hero; from peeling paint and flaking bricks, gloom spread through the air like a mild infection.

Then came the first spits of rain as the light grew dimmer. Even as I reached the forecourt, the crumbling remnants of my past life had withdrawn to another country. Like a ship out at sea, I altered course. I returned unhindered to the bus stop. I waited under the shelter. With the noise of a friendly engine in my ears, I was whisked away... And I never looked back. For death had come to Winterdale.

BIRTHDAY CELEBRATION

Pink as... even pinker than
the icing on a birthday cake,
the glorious flowering cherries stand:
still leafless by the riverside,
their early blossom prematurely
carries spring to
Twickenham.

Michael Hill

Sheltered by the boughs of a cherry tree in full bloom, he was seated close to the bend in a river where the waves, as they swerved, flashed like an avalanche of silver coins. This was the first spring-like day of the year; and in recognition not only of a milestone in the course of his life but also in tribute to the long-awaited end of winter, Arthur had set aside all tedious thoughts and obligations.

The grind of everyday activity and the cumulative effects arising from it lay at the root of so determined an effort; and he was there-fore more than happy to adopt the rôle of a dreamer as he sat there half awake, gazing at a stretch of water whose lifespan exceeded his own paltry middle age to such a vast degree. Flowing back and forth with the tides, he perceived its capacity for endurance whilst he himself, vulnerable to wear and tear, grew older by the minute. It was a realisation he couldn't readily dismiss. And although it was a day he'd set aside for celebrating his love affair with living, he was also subtly reminded that time was running out.

* * *

Notwithstanding the mesmerising effects of light and shade at the point where the river disappeared from view, Arthur never lost sight of his immediate environment: the footpath in front of him, for example, or the grass verge that sloped gently down to the water's edge. With the result that, despite the wealth of detail at his disposal, his attention was suddenly drawn to a beetle scuttling across the paving stones under his feet. Moreover, in the wake of this brief diversion, he was also reduced to a state of wonderment as he reflected on the presence of consciousness in so minute and insignificant a life form.

His thoughts up to and including that point had been uninterrupted and random; and yet, how completely and how suddenly his concentration was shattered by a group of children who, unmindful of a world of dissent and innuendo, scampered past with such carefree gusto. Preoccupied with the present, they were deaf even to the roar of an aircraft tearing through a sky from which the benevolent sun, shining down through a thin veil of cloud, ignited the river as it changed course and headed back towards the sea under the ebb-tide's influence. And so, for several hours with his mind adequately rested and relatively undisturbed, Arthur thought deeply about the relationship between permanence and change.

* * *

Behind the bench on which he was relaxing, scraps of discordant and disruptive sound escaped from the cars and buses plying the westbound road on their regular errands - sounds which, although slight, were beginning to impinge on the environmental influences that hitherto had so successfully answered a pressing need. But the river, despite its headlong retreat, preserved a significance of far greater moment which, in Arthur's case, had come very close to realisation. It was a theme to which the many passing strollers were wholly oblivious - an oblivion that also obscured nature's means of provoking the blossom of a cherry tree into a passion for renewal long before its leaves emerged from their buds.

AN ANXIOUS HALF HOUR
AT THE ROYAL BOTANIC GARDENS

It was hot and humid under the immense glass canopy. And it was there, for at least twenty minutes, that a middle-aged, tall and rather scrawny-looking man with his bulkier but much shorter spouse had been sharing a bench with Mr Timothy Fraser whose averted eyes pointedly ignored them. At length, however, the pair rose to their feet, ambled off rather unsteadily and continued their tour of the Princess of Wales Conservatory.

For Timothy, who was engrossed in a novel, similarly middle-aged but better endowed on top than the scrawny-looking husband of a rather dumpy wife, the sudden restoration of silence came as a relief because the couple's chatter, reminiscent of hyperactive parrots, had severely distracted him. Not only that, but the map of Kew Gardens they'd been fiddling with had made a noise like the scrunching of a crisp bag in the middle of a film. The result being that Timothy's discomfort had finally boiled over into irritation, culminating in an unspoken, but lengthy, catalogue of bad language.

Not long after the restoration of acceptable noise levels, and by that time happily re-immersed in his book, his reading was again interrupted, on this occasion by the words 'excuse me, sir' spoken directly in front of him. And when, somewhat startled, he looked up, he was once more presented with the same scrawny-looking, middle-aged man who had now returned with a noticeably anxious expression on his face. Timothy's initial response, of course, was renewed frustration.

Before the distraught-looking individual confronting him had had a chance to state his business, the beleaguered Timothy (by nature quick on the draw) had reached an unfounded, off-the-cuff conclusion about someone who, by any definition a total stranger, deserved a hearing. Nevertheless, he was unable to perceive anything other than one of those very ordinary people who, despite the absence of any striking hallmarks, are clearly honourable, pleasant but unremarkable human beings who are consequently written off as bores. But in fairness, it has to be said that Timothy was not without a conscience; and as soon as he heard what the matter was, he began to back-pedal.

'We seem to have lost our rather expensive camera,' he was told, 'and I was wondering whether we might have left it here.'

This information, which carried a moral imperative, led to a change of attitude on Timothy's part. Accordingly, he closed his book with a snap and joined in a thoroughgoing search both beneath and around the bench - after which, unfortunately, both parties were obliged to concede defeat. They also reached the same, starkly obvious conclusion when Timothy pointed out that he'd never once strayed from his seat during the relevant interval. And so, disconsolate and with a fretting wife awaiting him by the lily pond, the still nameless stranger made off for a second time with nothing to show for his efforts.

Timothy then retrieved his novel, flicked through till he found the right page, and resumed the story where he'd left off. But only ten short minutes after concluding that he'd seen the last of a couple for whom he now felt some sympathy, both husband and wife reappeared yet again, this time together - and in much brighter spirits. For the plain truth was this: that sod's law (acting for once without malicious intent) had conspired to help them recover their camera from an altogether different bench where they'd sat down to nibble a few snacks earlier that afternoon.

* * *

At this point in the narrative, a brief change of tack is required in order to reflect on the emergence of two elderly unknowns from obscurity into a state in which they have not only acquired value in the eyes of Mr Timothy Fraser but also names - names that deserve mention. And the fact that Sam Beckinshaw and his wife Shirley both bothered to return to tell a similarly obscure Timothy about their good fortune quickly and pleasurably disengaged the latter from the novel he'd been reading and released him from his exclusive focus on purely fictitious characters.

And so, we reach the end of a quietly eventful afternoon. With laudable immediacy, Timothy had responded to a prick of conscience which, to tell the truth, had begun its subtle campaign when his irritation was still at its height. And moreover, the directness and simplicity of the story's happy ending encouraged him to come down from his pedestal, allowing him to experience something like connectedness with people whom, in other circumstances, he would scarcely have noticed.

'All's well that ends well,' he joked as Sam and Shirley prepared for their final departure. 'I'm delighted to hear the good news. And I do hope you enjoy the rest of the afternoon.'

And then, suspecting that his turn of phrase was perilously close to something that might have sounded glib or even a little dismissive, he added, as an afterthought, a conclusion he'd reached on the basis of his own past experience.

'I often feel that a scare like yours is almost worth the discomfort,' he remarked. 'After all, once the crisis is over, it's such an amazing relief.'

CHARITY BEGINS AT HOME

Mr Roger Baldwin was invulnerable to jokes about the first syllable of his surname for the very good reason that what hair he had left was dark in colour and effectively dignified at intervals by lighter grey streaks. He also had a paunch that was modest enough to enhance rather than detract from a self-assured bearing which he emphasised with rather loud jackets purchased from charity shops sufficiently far from home to escape the eyes of his neighbours. And this, of course, however naïvely, encouraged associations with Savile Row rather than with the wrong end of a shopping parade on the outskirts of Croydon.

Now Roger Baldwin, a retired company director, was the sort of male human being frequently to be observed with a spaniel in any leafy avenue you care to name in the stockbroker belt dividing the loose ends of South London from the rolling hills of Surrey. And set against this background, he was as unexceptional in appearance (with due allowance for the jackets) as he was in reality. For precisely the same reason, of course, this meant that he conformed to a pattern; and such being the case, he was automatically regarded by local residents as 'a decent sort of chap.' And to tell the truth, he *was* a decent sort of chap - a decent sort of chap who, to be fair, showed great concern for the needs of others without necessarily disregarding his own.

* * *

With a sideways glance at his standing in the local community, and more or less out of the blue, Roger took a sudden, somewhat conspicuous interest in the well-being of an elderly woman by the name of Miss Brown. Miss Brown was an ailing spinster in her mid nineties of whose plight he was first made aware during a chat after morning communion at his parish church. To be absolutely truthful, it's worth adding that Roger attended church only twice a year: at

Christmas and Easter. And it was on Christmas Day 2018 that he first heard of a senior citizen known to be in need of a regular visitor with whom to share a cup of tea, a slice of cake and a pleasant conversation. And so, on the strength of seasonal good will, Roger had volunteered for a commitment that boiled down to a modest hour each week - an hour during which, as time wore on, it proved increasingly hard to find anything to talk about.

As a former man of affairs, of course, Roger was a skilled wheeler-dealer well able to paper over the cracks. Consequently, whenever the conversation began to dry up, he swiftly manufactured an amusing (and often irrelevant) aside at which both he and Miss Brown burst out laughing without quite knowing why. The result was that, without the slightest inkling of a difficulty, the old lady took a liking to Roger whose regard for her welfare, notwithstanding the stresses and strains, was entirely sincere. And although her frequent attempts to prolong his visits added to his discomfort, he was successful, at the expense of great effort, in concealing his frustration.

Unfortunately, his struggle to keep the ball rolling proved increasingly burdensome. At the same time, although his human nature differed very little from the ordinary man in the street, Roger was more resilient than the many other pensioners like himself for whom getting older was becoming a bind. Furthermore, as a sop to the growing awkwardness of his relations with Miss Brown, he had at his disposal another, less attractive characteristic known only to his wife: namely, a well-developed capacity for ambivalence. And it was this ambivalence alongside the early realisation that Miss Brown had grown fond of him that proved a vital tool when it came to stress management.

Consequently, whenever the prospect of the next weekly encounter at Ferndale Cottage provoked conflicting attitudes, his spirits were restored by an opposing force which went hand in hand, very inconveniently, with the voice of conscience. For it was here that the Roger Baldwin brand of ambivalence came dangerously close to double standards when (having sifted the evidence unhealthily often) he was reassured by the likelihood that Miss Alison Brown's Last Will and Testament would bestow benefits that were well worth waiting for.

UNDER THE SEAL OF CONFESSION

When Tom told Nicolas that he'd recently been to confession, it came as no great surprise. Throughout their long acquaintance, Nick had known very well that his friend was a regular churchgoer who stuck to the rules. But from the latter's tone of voice and turn of phrase, it was obvious that an amusing anecdote was about to emerge.

With a characteristic grin that confirmed expectation, Tom made no bones about what had happened. Apparently, he'd told the priest that his list of shortcomings was always exactly the same. The present instance was no exception; and among his many peccadillos, he mentioned that he'd been swearing quite a lot. He wisely qualified this by pointing out that he hadn't been swearing *directly* at the various individuals concerned. In other words, he hadn't been abusing them to their face.

* * *

He went on to explain that, given these mitigating circumstances, the priest (being of a clearly genial disposition) had seemed somewhat at a loss - which led to the following question.

'Then, what *precisely* is the problem?', he asked.

To which perfectly innocent query Tom had candidly replied that, although he hadn't been swearing at people point blank, he *had* been swearing rather volubly *about* them - either for the benefit of third parties during private conversations or under his breath when obstructed by a shopper ploughing through a supermarket with a trolley. Furthermore, with scrupulous honesty, he'd added that although none of those on the receiving end had ever actually *heard* what he said, they would have found no cause for jubilation if they had!

And according to Tom's consistently frank account, it was at this point, somewhere in the darkness on the opposite side of the grille that the venerable father, on catching the note of levity in the penitent's voice, had ventured a quiet chuckle.

A MARKED IMPROVEMENT

Tom and Nicolas had been friends for many years; and for this reason there wasn't much that either of them was unwilling to discuss with the other. For example, quite a lot of water had flowed under the bridge since Tom had given his friend a frank account of his experience in the confessional at his local church when the priest had reacted rather unexpectedly to the misdemeanours presented to him.

As a matter of fact, since that occasion, a full two years had slipped by almost unnoticed. And so, in the run-up to Christmas 2015, it happened that the same two friends were having a seasonal get-together in the Fox and Hounds which was just a stone's throw away from Tom's spacious, mock-tudor semi in Teddington. But before detailing the sequel to this matter-of-fact piece of information, it's worth pointing out that both men were married to women who were more than happy to steer clear of their husbands' racy conversations - on the firm understanding that when they were all together, both the language used and the topics covered would be subject to common decency.

Now in reality, the two gentlemen's conversations were seldom, if ever, 'indecent' - although they were frequently laced with strong language. It's also worth remembering that it was Tom's mention of swearing that had struck so particular a note with his parish priest - as it had also done with Nicolas himself when he was originally acquainted with the details. As a matter of fact, Tom still clearly recalled the occasion when he'd told the story in the first place - and he also looked back with satisfaction at the laughter it generated. With the result that, in the Fox and Hounds on the evening of 21 December, he was emboldened to relate another anecdote that likewise benefited from an ecclesiastical setting.

* * *

Nicolas immediately guessed the direction the conversation was likely to take; and sanctioned by the look on his face, Tom soon got into his stride. He could see the clear signs of a sympathetic hearing in his old friend's expression; and wagging his finger in the air in order to dramatise a suggestive grin, he therefore continued in a markedly jolly vein.

'Let me tell you about the cold I endured a few days before last Easter' he said 'which made me inexplicably giddy and liable to fall asleep at a moment's notice. The result was that I spent several hours for several days on end with my head on the arm of the sofa. What's more,' he added in a somewhat mocking tone of voice, 'even while fully awake, I got hopelessly muddled more than once as I tried to follow an exceptionally opaque piece of prose written - yes, you've guessed it - by an art critic!'

* * *

The ecclesiastical stage of the story then began to make its appearance.

'On the afternoon of Good Friday,' Tom continued, 'I put a brave face on things: and in accordance with my annual custom, I nipped into the parish church where my state of health reached its lowest ebb.' At this point, one of several more provocative smirks emphasised the way things were going before Tom resumed the narrative by reminding Nicolas how many times they'd discussed his (Tom's) book 'The Devil in the Detail.' This was a project he'd been working on for many years; it had a theological slant - and it's worth adding that Nicolas was only too well aware of those unforgettable conversations that had bored him so frequently.

Tom then returned to the central theme. 'Once settled in the church,' he said, 'my discomfort persuaded me to make solemn representations to the powers on high - including mention of the fact that 'The Devil in the Detail' (which I wanted to complete before I died) included a fundamentally ethical factor whose merits, I felt, might possibly carry weight.'

The next stage in the narrative was then delayed somewhat when Tom burst out laughing at his own flippancy - although Nicolas had no hesitation in following suit before his old friend finally brought the story to an unexpected conclusion.

'Whichever way you look at it' he said, 'it seemed to work. And that, I believe, is why, two days later, following attendance at divine worship on Easter morning, it wasn't so much the brandy I had after lunch but my prayers that led to a marked improvement in my condition.'

At which point, Nicholas, with a cryptic smile on his face, ventured to raise his eyebrows.

IT'S OFFICIAL

Summer having been officially declared this morning, there's reason to suspect that today is the first of June - with the result that tomorrow is likely to be the second. It therefore seems that we've reached a turning point: which suggests that at least some readers will be looking for more and further particulars. In which case, as a responsible member of the public, I'm ready to provide significantly more information. Everyone should be aware, for example, that the year is 2018, the location West London and the time 23.00 hrs.

Other interesting details include the fact that, through my bedroom window, I can see a clear half-moon floating unsupported in deep space from which no signals from extraterrestrials have so far reached my ears. As to whether this is because I lack suitable receptors or because there's no one out there, I have no means of knowing.

This deficiency brings me regrettably close to my limits - except to point out that the moon, still midway through its cycle, compares well with a fly whose shadow, cast by the bedside reading lamp, has just zapped across the counterpane like a shotgun pellet.

Understandably, I do not like *flies*; but I do like *moons*. In consideration of which, at this very moment, within minutes of midnight on the first day of summer 2018, I shall switch off the light and get some sleep. I also advise my readers to follow suit. I have given matters a lot of further thought; and I'm now in a position to confirm that, when the sun rises tomorrow, it will *definitely* be the second of June!

VAN WITH AN OPEN WINDOW

It was only to a few close friends that Winston was regularly known as Winnie. And on that particular day, it was Winston rather than Winnie who, having parked his car in a lay-by, was lounging on a bench in mid Surrey where he nervously adjusted his tie. Rather improbably close to a minor junction somewhere between Abinger Hammer and Peaslake, the bench in question was sited in a spot whose sole claim to fame centred on the deceased person to whom it was dedicated. This was a simple enough circumstance usefully clarified by the inscription which informed all comers that 'Jenny' had been 'a lover of the surrounding country where she'd lived throughout her life'. It was a touching little tribute; and yet, for Winston, it introduced an unexpectedly gloomy note that turned his thoughts inwards.

The fact that he was neatly dressed in keeping with the formal rather than the informal version of his name was no mere coincidence. Instead, it had a direct connection with his destination and with the well-meaning purpose he had in going there. To be precise, he was en route to see his Aunt Dora who, on top of being a long-term widow, had few neighbours and no other surviving relatives. Consequently, three or four times a year, Winston paid her a visit in an attempt to cheer her up in a way that he hoped was more mean-ingful than a routine, slightly awkward phone call during which his dependence on platitudes was an inevitable embarrassment.

Given that Winston, before taking early retirement, had been a professor of English literature at the University of East Anglia, it seemed very odd indeed to be tongue-tied in conversation with an easy-going, elderly woman. But academic circles are significantly different from family relations. And so, for this and a wide variety of other personal reasons, he found his goodwill trips somewhat gruelling - and this was the real reason why he'd stopped off for a breath of country air before fulfilling his good intentions that day. It's also worth adding that his wife, Yvonne, accompanied him only occasionally on such visits because, to be blunt, she was rather less keen on Aunt Dora than her husband was.

* * *

It was about half past ten on a warm but overcast May morning; and the public highway was not particularly busy: a few private cars followed by an occasional farm vehicle were as infrequent as they were unremarkable. By contrast, however, the sudden, noisy arrival of a gadget-laden, twenty-first century tractor reminded Winston of a space buggy he'd seen on the TV as it embarked on a triumphant (if short-lived) exploration of the Martian surface. For the few minutes before it disappeared, it held his interest - after which, familiar transport conditions were resumed and relative silence was re-established.

Before continuing his journey, the return of rustic tranquillity encouraged Winston to spend a few more minutes in a spot that had once given such pleasure to the individual in whose memory Surrey County Council had sanctioned the bench he was sitting on. The mild melancholy that stole over him when he first arrived reasserted itself - equally mildly. And it was while he was staring vacantly at the road in front of him - and thinking about nothing in particular - that a small van suddenly backfired as it approached from the direction of Abinger Hammer.

Given that he was dealing with an object in motion, Winston focussed his attention as best he could on the source of the disturbance. The first thing he observed was the most obvious: namely, that the van was white. It was also fairly small and not all that new. Further to which, the fact that the nearside window was wide open made it easy to see that the driver was male, approximately twenty-five and Caucasian with very little else to show by way of distinguishing marks.

Not long after the van had disappeared round the next bend in the road, Winston cast his mind back and considered how much the human eye can absorb in the briefest instant. For example, he'd been struck by the fact that as soon as he'd been spotted on the bench, the driver swung his head round almost ninety degrees to the left in order to take a look - on top of which, there was something about the snappy nature of this gesture that was strongly reminiscent of an owl rotating its head virtually full circle before focussing on whatever had grabbed its attention.

* * *

In the wake of these impressions, Winston persisted in exploring the why's and the wherefores of his recollections and of the contingencies that flowed from them. And yet, they amounted to an incident so brief that the word 'incident' seemed like an exaggeration. After all, it began and was over again in a flash - despite which, every detail remained clear. The result being that with the after-image of the driver's face still uppermost in his mind, Winston couldn't help wondering what sort of picture of his own head and shoulders had been carried away inside the skull of that youthful driver at the wheel of a nondescript van. Did it all boil down to some indeterminate, blood-soaked formulation in the soft tissue of his brain? Was it something he could conjure up at will out of nowhere in his mind's eye? Or was it just a case of one thing leading to another without any apparent reason?

And that prompted Winston's final speculation. It was a simple but very human impulse that he articulated under his breath. 'I'd like to know how the visual image he took away of *me*,' he murmured, 'compares with the visual image he left behind of *himself*. And I'd also like to know in what unlikely circumstances those images will reappear, at some indeterminate point in the future.'

And as he looked out from the darkness within at the face of the stranger he'd never see again, he got up from the bench and strolled thoughtfully back to the car - by which time he was more or less reconciled to the cup of tea and slice of apple tart that awaited him in the obscurity of a small Surrey village.

ABERCROMBIE HEIGHTS

Into my heart an air that kills
From yon far country blows:
What are those blue remembered hills,
What spires, what farms are those?

That is the land of lost content,
I see it shining plain,
The happy highways where I went
And cannot come again.

A. E Housman

There was nothing extraordinary about the fact that he was foot-ing it alone - alone and out of doors among the trees crowning the gentle slope of the heath with a sparse, straggling little clump that just about amounted to a wood. It was a wood, it should be added, that dwindled almost to nothing by comparison with the ancient forest outlining the downs a few grey miles away to the south.

Furthermore, given that it was the middle of winter and in England, the virtually week-long disappearance of the sun was by no means remarkable. There was, in consequence, a predictably dreary atmos-phere in which it seemed inconceivable that the barren mishmash of branches overhead had ever burst into leaf, thereby providing cover for the violets sheltering from the April sun. Even the secretive fungi, nurtured by a series of suitably damp Septembers, seemed more like illustrations in a child's storybook than genuine recollections.

Being alone and accustomed to soliloquy, Oscar felt a certain uneasiness and expressed it out loud - rather melodramatically, some might say. And he more or less realised this himself. 'After all, emotions are hard to get to grips with,' he muttered by way of dumbing down the embarrassment arising from his acute self-awareness. And finding this insufficient, he ended with a follow-up. 'Facts and feelings can so easily get out of proportion,' he whispered.

But discontent is unforgiving and gnaws away like a rodent at a slice of cheese; and under that persistent shadow, Oscar maundered on. His focus veered this way and that until he questioned whether it was being alive (just the simple fact of his existence) that was responsible for wearing him down. 'Not so much life itself, perhaps,' he concluded, 'but at least the continuance of it in a world where the star that keeps things going seems to be running out of hydrogen.'

* * *

To be absolutely clear, this self-pitying monologue by no means implied that Oscar felt suicidal. Instead, it formed part of a range of highly unrealistic fantasies (such as winning the lottery) that might help him, in another more convenient universe, to buy his way out of the hopeless entanglements with which his current lifestyle had seemingly lumbered him.

For example: he had a good job as an accountant; but economic circumstances were such that he couldn't afford a mortgage. With the result that, although a lover of outdoor pursuits, he was confined to a drab basement apartment and the noisy neighbours overhead. He was strongly attached to his girlfriend, but not to the signs of disaffection that her constant demands imposed on him. His mother had a long-term illness; and he did his best; but he could never adequately match his sister's devotion in that quarter. He longed to fly away like a bird; but like a lump of concrete, he was anchored to the ground.

Thus hamstrung, it was unsurprising that a torrent of regrets and anxieties pursued Oscar on his walk - each and all of them exacerbated by the weather which had improved very little since the winter solstice about three weeks previously. And it wasn't just the fog and low light levels - not even the cold - that depressed his spirits. Instead, it was the absence of all character and identity, day after day, when incoherent, repetitive bleakness made getting out of bed like trying to walk on water.

In the long run, the burden that relentlessly weighed Oscar down went hand in hand with the planet's rotation on its axis and its interminable orbit around the sun; it subjected him unavoidably to the corrosive effects of time and tide. And in that context, his fundamental problem was simply that the plainest of all the facts confronting him was the one he was least willing to concede: namely, that although he remained a youngish man with a viable future, he was also a youngish man still in thrall to the trout stream at the foot of Abercrombie Heights where an evening's fishing had once provided him with unalloyed (and uninterrupted) fulfilment after a tedious day at school.

Into my heart... A.E Housman, A Shropshire Lad, No XL.

Trying to walk on water... See Matthew 14, 28 - 31.

TOO GOOD TO BE TRUE

Marcel was distinguished by thick, brown, infrequently cut hair which was over-oiled and rather-too-youthfully brushed back. As a person who stood out somewhat from the generality, he was also known for the boundless confidence he had in his ability to manipulate everyone he encountered - a characteristic seldom looked on with favour.

In certain respects, of course, he could be regarded, in all honesty, as a type. Without a moment's hesitation or misgiving, he was ready with a perfectly tailored response to more or less any challenge that confronted him. It was a skill so regularly and so flawlessly exercised that, for those with sufficiently sharp antennae, his instant explanations or comebacks seemed too good to be true. Clearly, his self-assurance was his most prominent public attribute; and as such, it often provoked searching questions: for example, was he by some fluke of nature as genuine as he was ingenious - or was he perhaps (and more probably) as slippery as an eel?

Unfortunately for Marcel le Brun, this most conspicuous aspect of his personality occasionally backfired and marked him out as a humbug in the eyes of experienced observers. Even more to his cost, by letting him think he'd got away with one or other of his off-the-cuff fabrications, wary acquaintances had been able over time to build up a picture of their friend very much at odds with that gentleman's objectives when engaging, rather offhandedly, in a devious circumlocution intended (or so he hoped) to enhance his personal standing.

More damaging still, and in direct consequence of such duplicitous behaviour, there was an inevitable underlying tension in Marcel's dealings that was closely (but not wholly) associated with his greatest mistake of all. This boiled down to a failure to differentiate between intimates (who habitually breached his defences and smiled at what they found) and circles like those in which, as a company director, he'd thrown his weight about before his retirement.

As demonstrated by the latter example, the dichotomy between what amounted to two separate worlds with different rules was made bleakly apparent by the fact that, apart from glancing sideways and nudging each other at board meetings, his erstwhile subordinates had been severely handicapped by the fear of losing their influence - or even their jobs. Yet as far as his friends were concerned, he was neither more nor less than a source of amusement or mild ridicule that provoked very little lasting irritation.

Looked at dispassionately, this contrasting, rather unhappy state of affairs marked a watershed that consigned Marcel le Brun's one-time under-appreciated staff to a backwater that he barely remembered and no longer acknowledged - a place where his unprincipled tactics and dismissive attitudes had effectively suppressed almost everyone's individuality. At the same time, however, and to their credit, the nasty taste thus left in the mouths of his former underlings proved surprisingly durable.

* * *

As a consequence of the foregoing circumstances, it's worth repeating that, well after their own retirement, it was Marcel's virtually forgotten colleagues from days long consigned to the dustbin who continued to judge him most sternly - in particular those who felt they'd been singled out and treated like fools. On the other hand, those whom he'd known as friends for nearly half a century remained willing to regard him as someone whose dependence on imprecise truths or rapidly cobbled-together lies was more of a joke than a call to arms.

But the broad-mindedness of Marcel le Brun's friends was partly a product of the long history they shared with him; and for that reason, they were more or less blind to a particular element at the very heart of their joint relationship. It was a blindness, moreover, that consisted of one very significant fact that Marcel had concealed throughout their association, namely: he'd never told them how conscious he'd always been that they took him with a generous pinch of salt which (in their folly) they believed he didn't realise!

And so, from his ivory tower among the ups and downs of a self-imposed modus operandi, Marcel made certain that his defences were always in good repair. His principal means to this end comprised the single, simple deception unsuspected by his friends which he'd successfully kept to himself for so many years. It was the one most important factor that enabled him to laugh off the occasional damage to his good name in the firm conviction that it was not that bunch of naïve, happy-go-lucky friends who'd gained the upper hand. On the contrary, it was his own awareness of what they thought he didn't know that provided the vital reassurance. After all, he told himself, he always *had* been 'top dog...' and always would be!

SHORT, SHARP AND NOT ALL THAT SWEET

It was a pleasant July afternoon in St James's Park when Derek, having walked nearly a mile before reaching his favourite bench by the lake, was pipped at the post by a woman who, at the very last minute, noticed how he'd suddenly altered course. After which, being a person of sensibility, she quickly realised the awkwardness of what had happened and apologised profusely.

Derek, who deeply coveted the shady spot in question but wished to be alone, decided that a breezy response would be the best means of concealing his annoyance. He therefore wrapped his face in smiles, inhaled briefly and prepared to look casual.

'Not at all,' he answered, broadening his smile in support of his strategy. 'Don't give it a second thought.' After which, thinking he'd established a sufficiently positive rapport, he light-heartedly added 'First bum, first served, madam; fair's fair, after all.'

At this point, however, realising at once that his attempt at humour had fallen on deaf ears, he gestured dismissively with his right hand and walked on without looking back. But had he done so, he would have noticed a somewhat disorientated, middle-aged woman with a very red face who felt no desire to prolong the acquaintance of such a vulgar old man. A vulgar old man, by the way, who as soon as he spotted another empty bench, affected a show of deep unconcern as he buried his head in the Times Literary Supplement.

First come, first served. A proverb with variants first recorded in English in Chaucer's 'The Wife of Bath', c1386.

DOUGLAS AND VIOLET CARSDALE
IN MEMORIAM

With no obligations whatever in the offing, I was whiling away a few minutes, seated on a bench paid for by descendants of the late Douglas and Violet Carsdale. And as the inscription behind me made clear to anyone who cared to read it, Douglas and Violet Carsdale 'loved these gardens.'

Spring, it seemed, was in the air. And as I took advantage of the fine weather and removed my shoes, a brightness overhead, somewhat behind schedule, appeared unannounced and grew brighter by the minute. Indeed, according to the forecast, it was likely to be the warmest day so far that year. Consequently, with nothing much to disturb me, I felt pleasantly relaxed. 'Not a care in the world' you might have said to yourself if you could have seen me, at that precise moment, as I faced towards the sun and demolished a supermarket snack.

* * *

For no apparent reason and without warning, as if my brain had suddenly acquired a secondary will of its own, my attention was diverted from the immediate, untroubled present to the broader, longer-term sweep of reality as it affected the late Douglas and Violet Carsdale.

And not them alone. I was reminded, for example, of countless similar benches I'd seen, not all that far off, bearing entirely different names, yet exactly the same form of words. And this brought home to me the enormous number of those who, along with the Carsdales, had 'loved these gardens' during the course of their lives. I was conscious, too, of the many other names recorded in quiet spots throughout the country where the identical phrase was repeated in appreciation of so many public spaces that I'd never get the chance to see.

Despite which, as my thoughts sank into the shadows and I became more aware of the world's vulnerable underbelly, the same brilliant day that it was when I first arrived remained unaffected. I was still the same casual visitor and long-term familiar of that peaceful, cared-for environment with its catalogue of heartfelt recollections.

And yet, with the benefit of hindsight, I remembered how names, formerly cherished, were worn away all too soon by the action of lichen, bird droppings and wood rot. On the other hand, neither the location nor the weather conditions that day justified the negative trend that threatened to take hold of my mind. I therefore pulled myself together, looked ahead and changed direction. After all, I told myself, it was spring again; and with the winter aconites in retreat, warmer winds disturbed the giant redwoods. The last snowdrops were packing their bags. The crocuses, in timely order, were massing by the pond. And shortly, the first swallows would be spotted in the sky above the downs where eager souls and welcoming eyes (mine among them) would be waiting.

BUSINESS AS USUAL

It was in the middle of April 2019, not far off lunchtime on a bright and cheerful morning, when Anthony de Roos (well into his seventies) found himself occupying a stone bench on the south side of Oxford Street. He looked overwhelmed, almost shell-shocked, by the ferment of activity that engulfed him: in fact, so all-pervasive was the spectacle of people knocking into each other or getting in each other's way that, feeling in need of a break, he'd made for the bench he was sitting on as soon as he spotted it. This turned out to be a wise move, since it provided an opportunity not only to slow down but also to catch his breath whilst the bits and pieces of a discordant world rained down like shrapnel on every side.

But although intent on planning the day ahead in more detail, Anthony was simultaneously catapulted by the inner city turmoil into a series of inexplicably tenacious recollections from his childhood. In particular, he remembered the well looked-after allotment where his grandfather not only grew vegetables but also kept bees; and still vivid in his mind's eye was the constant coming and going of those insects (of which he'd obviously been reminded by the bustle of twenty-first century Oxford Street). On the other hand, as he admitted to himself when his concentration began to falter, there was one big difference between his experience now and in the past: for whereas, today, the busyness of London's West End boiled down to uncoordinated individualism, there was (in the toing-and-froing of his grandfather's bees), a positive and beneficial unity of purpose.

* * *

Inevitably, as the morning drew to a close, Anthony's daydreams were submerged beneath the hubbub of hastily applied brakes and motor horns (not to mention the expletives of a youth who made it to the kerb just in time to save his life). It was, after all, an unplanned, starkly practical interlude in the course of which this somewhat weary old man was suddenly and bleakly struck by the thought of his personal insignificance. Indistinguishable from the crowd, he could almost see himself as others undoubtedly saw him while he sat there dressed in a well-worn M&S jacket, a red, French-looking beret and a scarf conspicuously in need of replacement.

And yet, being precisely who he was and no one else, there was also an invisible reservoir of energy. As a result, although he felt rather like a pebble shunted this way and that by the tide, he was also buoyed up when he recognised in his own clear-headedness a means of holding the blues in check. With the following outcome: that while the traffic trundled past shopfronts on fire with neon vulgarity, he found he was gazing inwards at himself and examining his options head-on.

And so, with fresh determination, as he prepared to resume his walk, Anthony faced up to the one thing about which he'd long been uncomfortably aware: namely, that his life so far had been a succession of clear periods and showers. He also had to admit that, although he'd never thought of suicide, there had certainly been moments of discontent and frustration when he'd wondered if it was really worthwhile carrying on.

But despite all this, he rose from his seat and, for a second time, confronted the disorderly crowds whilst making uneven progress towards Marble Arch. Moreover, between colliding with a some-what bulky shopper and tripping up on a loose paving stone, he also reminded himself, perhaps as a defence against the buffeting, that he still had a number of friends who thought well of him. And of these, he concluded, there were one or two who would always be a mainstay.

Consoled by that optimistic view of his present state, and therefore less crestfallen than he might otherwise have been, Anthony de Roos brandished his walking stick, crossed Speakers' Corner into the relative stillness of Hyde Park and then strolled at an easy pace towards the Serpentine where he sat down again, more comfortably this time, and watched the sun, indifferent to its own fragmentation, in playful competition with the waves.

MR GODFREY BALLANTYNE
MANAGING DIRECTOR, BALLANTYNE & CO PLC

I knew Godfrey Ballantyne quite well. In fact, you *could* say that I knew him very well indeed. Consequently, on overhearing his excuses when called to the scene of an accident in the staff rest room, I grew more rather than less confident in my ability both to discern and dismiss a tall story.

Allow me to elucidate. My understanding, for what it's worth, was simply this: that Godfrey, by remaining at a safe distance from the incident, neatly avoided being observed in contact with any circumstantial evidence of which he might later wish to deny knowledge. After all, there could well be a situation in which such knowledge would be contrary to his interests. In other words, he was the sort of person whose primary instinct was always to be ready with an escape clause. And in due course, it did indeed turn out to have been a wise move on his part when the accident in question (involving spillage of a hot liquid) was described by the official enquiry as 'a regrettable example of negligence, wholly inadequate safety regulations and a lack of proper supervision.'

Now given that these functions were widely thought of as the responsibility of other people, Mr Godfrey Ballantyne (I assume) was hoping that his quick thinking would be enough to shield him from any personal blame. On the other hand, after giving some thought to the matter, I suspected he might find it particularly difficult, as managing director, to fend off the charge of 'wholly inadequate safety regulations.' Not, at least, without casting aspersions on genuinely innocent members of his team who, in such circumstances, might prove less willing than before to play along with his style of management.

THE BUS TO UPPER SYDENHAM

At a bus stop on a busy main road near Crystal Palace in South-East London, a young woman by the name of Heather Ogilvie was reading a satirical magazine whilst waiting for the 555 to Upper Sydenham. Unfortunately, it was late. To make matters worse, Upper Sydenham was dreary by comparison with the open green environment of nearby Norwood Park; and the object of her journey - namely, a goodwill mission to her aunt Edna - failed to rouse much enthusiasm.

It was, however, a pleasant sunny morning: a blackbird was singing in the overhanging horse chestnut tree; and the temperature, which was comfortable, fully justified the pink blouse and brown trousers she was wearing along with a white scarf hung loosely round her neck. Furthermore, she was enjoying the mildly adult humour of an edition of *Bouncy Castle* - a publication aimed mainly (but not wholly) at a youngish readership of more or less broad outlook.

It goes without saying that Bouncy Castle, whilst open to a fairly relaxed treatment of real-life events, was also well known for foxing its readers with fictitious reports of the type common on April Fools Day. In fact, it sometimes came dangerously close to what is now known as 'fake news.' And it was one such example that caught Heather's eye with a reference to *Penge* - a location where another elderly relative occupied a two-up, two-down terraced cottage.

* * *

At the age of eighteen (but looking more like sixteen), there was no way that Heather could have known that the article which so greatly amused her was based on a joke (of obscure origin) that did the rounds when her mother was still a girl. Indeed, she never seriously thought to stop and ask herself whether what she was reading was true. The simple fact was that she found the account hilarious; and after glancing through it several times, she was reduced to audible laughter. The text in question is given below.

It has been disclosed that a young tearaway was recently arrested on suspicion of insulting the monarch. According to the evidence of PC Norman French who was on duty at the opening of the new Penge Waterworks on 22 April 2015, the Queen had just declared 'The Duke and I are delighted...' when Mr Gary Winthrop, a dashing young road sweeper recently sacked for impropriety in a phone box, rather sneeringly completed the Queen's sentence with words ill-suited to a respectable magazine like Bouncy Castle!

Winthrop, who strongly denies slipping an abusive implication into the Queen's announcement, has been remanded in custody.

* * *

As a tailpiece to an otherwise light-hearted interlude that morning, there was just one minor flaw in the course of events that wiped the smile off Heather's face. For whilst she was still engrossed in the Bouncy Castle article, her concentration was interrupted by the loud honking of what she thought was a car horn (plainly directed at herself).

Unfortunately, when she looked up to find out who was responsible, she discovered it was the driver of the long overdue 555 bus who had driven straight past without stopping. And it didn't take her long to work out that, having briefly taken her eyes off the road, he'd assumed she was waiting for the single alternative service at that location - namely, the 403 to the Dulwich Picture Gallery. And of course, being on the inside of an enclosed space, he'd favoured the lonely figure at the bus stop with the only substitute for a wolf whistle he could think of!

THE LATE SÉAMUS O'HARA

I hadn't heard from Séamus for a very long time. And when I rang him up, I got the feeling he was holding something back. It all fell into place, of course, when he mentioned that he'd *died* a couple of months previously.

I responded by telling him how glad I was to hear the good news. 'I've always been on the lookout for evidence of an afterlife,' I said.

'Unfortunately, there's more than one sort of afterlife,' complained Séamus before slamming down the receiver, 'and in my own case, I'm afraid, I *cannot* recommend it!'

THE MANY WAYS OF LOOKING
AT EXACTLY THE SAME THING

*There are three pivotal elements, so far undisputed,
about the evolution of life on Planet Earth. In
the first place, evolution acts without foresight
or predetermined objectives. Secondly, how life began
is still unknown; and thirdly, according to the
genetic evidence, it has only begun once.*

Michael Hill

In his book 'The Big Mistake' first published in the nineteen eighties, Professor Jack Somerville describes how the evolution of new life forms on earth is driven by the transmission and natural selection of genetic mutations rather than by species behaviour - a distinction which is absolutely fundamental and now widely accepted.

During an interview on BBC Radio commemorating the thirtieth anniversary of the book's first appearance, Somerville persisted in maintaining, as of old, that the means by which evolution has taken place is now so well established that it eliminates, once and for all, any need to posit a designer, namely God.

But in fact, this hard-and-fast proclamation does nothing of the kind for the very good reason that it not only overlooks several significant snags, but also assumes that the only way a supreme being can create universes and promote life is by an endless series of separate, virtually magical commands like those set out in Genesis - a position no longer supported either by the Jews or the Christians.

And so, looking again at the 'well established means' by which evolution has taken place, it is perfectly plausible to suggest that these 'means' were devised by a deity at the outset as part of a universe whose workings were independent of his subsequent interference - a universe that he created directly or, alternatively, *indirectly* via one or more antecedents which he likewise created... and so on ad infinitum, as happens to be or *not* to be the case...

It is therefore possible to see a degree of resolution in what is an age-old argument by dismissing the assumption that the creative action of a cosmic designer must necessarily imply interference *after* the creation has taken place - whereas all that he, she or it need do is to determine suitable initial conditions, fire the starting pistol, and then get out of the way as quickly as possible! Irrespective of personal preference, therefore, this way of looking at things means there is no fundamental conflict between religious belief and scientific reality. And as to the professor's constant demands for (scientific) *evidence concerning the existence of a divine person*, this is precluded by the very nature of transcendent being, thus leaving the matter defiantly open.

Finally, there remains at least *one* indisputable fact: namely, that however convoluted and self-determining the evolutionary process has been, it has still achieved what we assume was the creator's original purpose by successfully producing human beings. And not least among these, God rest his soul, is the grey (and now somewhat greyer) eminence of Professor Somerville himself.

WHAT'S IN A NAME?

It was about a year before the road accident that tragically ended his life when, aged just over fifty and with a blank expression
on his face, he found himself sitting (and fidgeting) in front of his
AppleMac. At root, the problem confronting him was an addictive
relationship with computers unaccompanied, at the time in question, by anything that actually needed doing. This created an impasse
which in turn opened up the way for a degree of navel-gazing that
required a more organised approach than he could muster. And
so, with nothing better in the offing, he tapped out his name on
the keyboard and glanced, rather idly, at the words 'Gavin Paisley'
as the letters appeared, one after the other, on the screen. Then,
without much sense of direction, he stopped: he felt oddly listless;
and consequently, being at a loose end, he proceeded to drum his
fingertips on the desktop during an interval that gave him a chance
to clarify his thoughts.

'Gavin Paisley,' he mumbled to himself somewhat interrogatively,
'Gavin Paisley?' In fact, he repeated the words over and over again
whilst an air of strangeness gradually affected the syllables so that
their routine familiarity started to fade. 'Who or what is Gavin
Paisley?' he asked himself during what turned out to be a mere
prelude before he began casting off into even deeper waters. 'What
does being me really signify?' he wondered. 'And precisely what does
it boil down to when having a name contributes little or nothing in
terms of information?' But he remained untroubled by the direction
his thoughts were taking; and this was largely due to the fact that he
couldn't fully grasp the nature of whatever it was that was baffling
him. Nevertheless, he was edging closer to those profound, often
asked questions about the ultimate meaning of experience; but of
course, no material evidence was available from the past any more
than it was from the present on which to base simple answers. Nor

for that matter was there much chance of focussing his mind in a significantly clearer way.

If anyone had seen fit to state the obvious, it would have been easy enough to define the reality that was Gavin Paisley as the unforeseen outcome of an event involving a man and a woman that probably took place on the spur of the moment; and it would have been just as easy, if naïve, to conclude that the conscious being engendered by that act just *happened* to be a collection of cells later associated with the meaningless label 'Gavin Paisley.'

It goes without saying, of course, that if Gavin had encountered this bleak assertion of fact whilst he was still alive, it would have struck him as a very evasive response to a puzzling issue. But as things stood, at a young age, equipped with inadequate philosophical tools, he remained in exactly the same state of uncertainty until he drew his last breath.

To be truthful, death was an eventuality to which he had never given any thought at all whilst in good health; neither had he ever considered the possibility that his final end, premature or timely, might prove the gateway to another, quite different comfort zone where there are more answers than questions.

In the final analysis, therefore, perhaps the most enlightening way for former friends to think about the problem that Gavin failed to solve is to take his name simply as an allusive pointer to what was essentially a mystery - just one among countless similar yet unique mysteries that are forever buzzing about like a swarm of bees between the two poles of a planet which, for the time being, most of us are happy to call our home - at least until, possibly like Gavin, we discover whether or not it was only a staging post after all.

What's in a name? William Shakespeare: Romeo and Juliet, act 2, scene 2.

THOSE WAKEFUL HOURS

For Tanya, a retired maths teacher, these were the wakeful hours - hours of diminishing hope, too... or so she felt. It wasn't the first time, either; and it left her with little choice other than to defy the challenge and grit her teeth, even though the sun seemed destined never to rise again.

From the garden outside, she could hear the faint pitter-patter of raindrops striking the privet hedge. And the indistinct mass of the cloud cover, barely visible through the window, seemed even more dismal. Indeed, as she lay there in bed, virtually at her wits' end, she was reminded of the moors: boundless, featureless, uninhabited to the point of desolation... and far removed from the glare of street lights or the ringing of door bells.

That night, from the world outside, only a few sounds were audible; but they had a character all their own: muffled, delicate... and as smooth as wet seaweed. For Tanya they remained in the background; but whilst listening to them because she had to, she was unaccountably struck by the fact that the window through which she was staring at the sky was divided into rectangular panes by the silhouettes of the crossbars.

There was nothing new about this; it was a familiar enough sight. But somehow, it reminded her of the air vents that she'd seen from inside whilst laying flowers in the family vault after her father's death. It was an eerie recollection; and consequently, confronted by everything that was negative on a damp and sleepless night, she covered her head with the duvet, gaining relief from the rise in temperature. Despite which, as dawn approached, she was still as restless as she was exhausted; but after a brief struggle, she became embarrassed by her own self-pity. So she relented; and rather like a swimmer desperate to avoid drowning, she rallied and began to fight back.

'I shall switch on the light,' she muttered as she threw back the bedclothes. 'I shall venture a cup of hot chocolate. I shall resort to emergency measures.'

It was an encouraging show of defiance. And Tanya, as good as her word, persisted with her monologue while waiting for the kettle to boil. 'I shall have a shower,' she went on. 'I shall get dressed and turn on the radio. I shall listen to the news while I make breakfast. I shall do the shopping as soon as I feel like it. And whatever the weather throws at me, I shall make the best of it.'

THE LONG AND THE SHORT OF IT

Not far from Hammersmith Broadway in West London, Brook Green is a long and slender public space which, apart from the tennis courts and children's playground at one end, is almost entirely grass-covered. In addition, similarly conducive to a village-like atmosphere and despite contact with two main roads (one at each extreme), it is generously bordered by trees.

The twin highways that extend along both edges resemble in outline a rather wobbly, overstretched ellipse reminiscent of the enormous soap bubbles engineered by street performers on the South Bank, largely for the benefit of tourists. And furthermore, as if to safeguard its special identity, the area is surrounded by tall period dwellings that give ground at intervals to a pub, a Catholic church, a former Jewish synagogue and the classic grandeur of St Paul's Girls' School. Not forgetting, of course, that there's also a St. Paul's *Boys'* School situated about a mile away among playing fields on the opposite side of the river near Hammersmith Bridge.

Depending on which way you look at it, several leafy avenues lead into or out of Brook Green. And among them, to the east (with a block of redbrick flats on the corner), Aynhoe Road is a regular conduit for strollers making their way along its length to the point where it meets Blythe Road with which it forms a T-junction. And it's here that visitors, if they stop to look, will see facing them a parade of shops with regrettably little about it to arouse or retain their interest.

* * *

It's true to say that the foregoing description of the area as it is now confirms conditions surprisingly similar to those appertaining at the time of this story in the late nineteen eighties. With that in mind, it's also helpful to note that in those almost forgotten days, any person approaching the T-junction in Blythe Road might have spotted among the shops opposite a small general store whose owner, venturing outside when trade was slack, was often seen staring at the point where the far end of Aynhoe Road opened out (as it still does) on to Brook Green. Furthermore, if sufficiently alert, any such observer might have been struck by the wistful look on the face of this forlorn figure and by the accompanying haze of cigarette smoke surrounding his head. It's also worth explaining that the smoker himself was unaware of these inadvertent signs of what was, in reality, a longing for change... change, moreover, that he couldn't precisely identify in the absence of a clear view of the link between the longing itself and the village-like green he was gazing at in the distance.

On reflection, it can be no accident that the proprietor of this run-of-the-mill local store came from a rural background. He was born in Coalport (Shropshire) where he spent his earliest years. But to his dismay, not long after his twelfth birthday, he and his family moved to London where he never quite got used to what he regarded as the bleakness of urban living. Even so, he suppressed his demons and stayed put until, aged forty-two at the time of this narrative, he'd developed a conspicuous beer belly. On top of which, his once abundant blond hair, formerly ruffled by country breezes, was at the last stage of a losing battle with the march of time.

But Mother Nature took his part; and the loss of fair hair didn't deprive him of his fair complexion which, on one tedious morning twenty minutes after opening up the store, was noticeably flushed due to a staffing problem - a problem well known to customers on their way to the office whose features swiftly developed into smiles. In consequence, busy hands that were fondling pre-packed sandwiches acted in consort with an exchange of sidelong glances which (mercifully) the frustrated shopkeeper was too preoccupied to notice.

By now, events were approaching the climax that everyone was anticipating. In the end, it turned out to be an episode lasting little more than five minutes. All the same, in the course of that very short interval, the spotlight shone exclusively (and brightly) on the unfortunate retailer whose nickname, Sonny Jim, was occasionally used by impoverished customers hoping for a knock-down price. Furthermore, still on the 'sonny' side, impatience was mounting among the shoppers whose expectations of the final outcome produced an unnatural (and very indicative) stillness.

* * *

At this penultimate stage, Jim was holding a somewhat grimy black telephone very close to his ear. He was standing entirely alone behind the checkout - and his patience was evidently running short as his face grew redder and redder. For the painfully obvious fact was this: that (not for the first time) the person he was ringing was in no hurry to grab the receiver. And when at long last the familiar murmur of a woman's voice was heard at the other end of the line, eager listeners were rewarded with the latest version of a well-worn theme that never failed to amuse them.

'Oh good morning, darling,' said Jim whose tone of voice was as convincingly affectionate as it was provocatively insincere, 'were you considering coming to work this morning?'

THE AFTERMATH

Making sense of the underground map and working out the bus route had been a struggle. But at last, he'd finally reached his destination among the back streets of Stepney where he came to an abrupt halt. The smell of gas was still in the air. Moreover, standing outside the cordoned-off areas as he gazed at the remains of a once solid building, the photographs of countless missing persons, like pictures in a family album, stared back at him from every inch of wall and railing. Post-its and scraps of torn-up paper carried appeals for information. And candles of every description flickered on the footpath.

Given an event of such magnitude, it was inevitable that within minutes of the first pictures, it was front page news from one end of the country to the other. And two or three days later, close to where he was standing, open-mouthed onlookers (at a loss for words) were still staring across the road at the leftovers of what was once home to so many.

It was in the middle of June on a swelteringly hot day when Brendan (who was no spring chicken) had trudged almost a mile from the bus stop to reach the scene of the explosion. Under growing pressure, he'd consumed nearly a litre of juice since leaving his home in Twickenham; and as the minutes ticked by, it struck him ever more forcibly that age was catching up on him… The consequence was only to be expected; and as he dragged himself back to the bus stop after he'd absorbed as much of the scene as he could, he felt more like an ageing pop star on his last legs than the prolific artist he'd been all those years ago when he was younger.

* * *

It goes without saying that Brendan had little to complain of by comparison with those who died in that unprecedented disaster.

All the same, after he'd left the reality (but not the recollection) behind him, he interrupted his journey home and took time to reflect within the walls of a public garden where he sat down on a log among the coolest of green shadows. The foliage overhead was rustling in a breeze so gentle that he was completely unable to feel it. The twittering of birds he could barely hear was like the sound of gravel dropping into a pond. And although he realised he'd have to make a move in due course, he rejoiced for a short while in an environment fundamentally at odds with what he'd just witnessed in the East End of London.

Obscurely set apart in the shade of an oak tree, of course, and fresh from the scene of a great calamity, the change of circumstance was so glaring that he could hardly have failed to take account of it. On the other hand, he remained acutely aware of the everyday world and allowed his interest to focus on the many visitors as they strolled along the avenue of hollies just in front of him.

Meanwhile, as the mixed groups of day trippers continued strolling past at irregular intervals, he was also much taken by a party of school children as they topped up their water bottles from a drinking fountain. And despite his earlier experience that day, he was all ears listening intently to that disorderly crowd of youngsters as they pushed and shoved, chattering like budgerigars in a cage, oblivious to adversity and brimming with carefree laughter. For Brendan, it was music to his ears and a genuine sight for sore eyes.

* * *

The conflict he felt between open parkland and the disaster confronting him only an hour or so previously was a challenge. And it pointed to a lesson with a sting in its tail: namely, that under an impulse all its own, without any other external influence, life (like the motion of a wave) invariably carries on regardless. And carrying on *regardless*, it does so with complete indifference to whatever it sweeps aside. On that particular day, for example, notwithstanding birdsong and the buzz of insects on the wing, Brendan was mindful (and how could he *not* be) of those victims described in newspaper reports chiefly in terms of statistics - and this for the simple reason that, according to the police, few reliable means of identification had survived.

But perhaps just as much to the point, he also gave due consideration to the injured and bereaved who were still living and therefore compelled, in spite of their misfortune, to carry on... After all, the overwhelming truth that struck him was this: that despite any help they received or the number of years they carried on struggling, they could never hope, in the aftermath of what had happened, to carry on *regardless* - however much they might try.

A VERY TALL ORDER

Luke was reclining more or less comfortably. His head and shoulders were supported by a cluster of pillows; and the darkness beyond his bedroom window was softened by the glow of moonlight whose serenity, at least in part, had soothed his nerves and taken much of the sting out of sleeplessness.

In these circumstances, as a substitute for the dreams that eluded him, he allowed his imagination to run amok. The moon was clearly visible and, for a person who was naturally susceptible, it provoked colourful turns of phrase: for example, 'bright as the midday sun', 'white as powdered diamonds' and so on. In addition, there was another, perhaps more surprising contribution that came to mind consisting of the words 'the moon, a dish of beaten gold.' It was a particularly obscure fragment of verse; and he had no idea what went before or after. Moreover, it was the only line he could remember from a poem composed many years previously by a school friend who was now in his grave.

Lacking consistent direction, Luke's train of thought eventually strayed into somewhat more troubled waters which were all the more enticing by reason of their roots in contemporary science rather than in literary allusion. And this led on to an area of specu-lation which had always foxed him. Consequently, as he lay in bed, he pictured countless other human beings in a state of sleeplessness similar to his own whose 'observations', according to followers of the still widely held 'Copenhagen Interpretation', were critical in lending substance to the reality of absolutely everything that ex-isted - including the sun, the moon and the stars. It was a profound concept... and, for Luke, a very tall order!

* * *

It was certainly a fascinating idea; but as he continued looking up at the sky, although his underlying attitude was ambivalent, he felt no compulsion to think he was in any way responsible for what he saw. Neither did he experience a pressing need for supporting evidence from other stargazers when he could plainly see for himself that Planet Earth's only satellite was in orbit as usual - further to which, he also noticed that, compared with the night before, it had diminished slightly in size and was therefore on the wane.

And so, in the early hours of that particular morning, as he watched its gradual motion, the moon's face, rather like a battered coin chamfered along one of its edges, continued to descend into oblivion. Indeed, it was perfectly obvious that only a few more minutes remained before it would disappear entirely from view to the left of a small wood whose silhouette loomed darkly in the gradually diminishing glow.

* * *

What followed was more or less inevitable; and in those final moments of moonlight, it seemed natural enough for Luke to consider once again some of the fundamental conundrums to which there were either no answers at all - or alternatively, answers that were much too challenging to deliberate on when half asleep. On top of which, he was already well aware from past experience that the various questions weren't much clearer when he was fully awake.

'All in all,' he murmured under his breath, 'the problem is this: who and what am *I*, this maker of worlds, who lie here alone in the stillness, sure of his existence, acutely self-aware, all-too-certainly solid in the midst of his speculations... and yet himself unverified by anybody else's observation?' There was always 'cogito, ergo sum', he told himself by way of reassurance - but it hardly made the jigsaw any less puzzling.

* * *

In the end, it was at this juncture, in a state of ignorance common to everyone (and in Luke's case exacerbated by fatigue) that he abandoned his focus on the relationship - if there *was* one - between observation and reality. There was, of course, a modicum of relief in the fact that the dilemma was not his alone. Nevertheless, to his way of thinking, it left much food for thought in its wake - food, unfortunately, that was rather indigestible.

A final comment now seems appropriate. To this effect: that in Luke's case, describing the basic question and its possible answers as 'indigestible' is probably an understatement. Which makes it highly likely that some other word, with a note of caution attached, would have been more suitable. And this, of course, must be true not only for Luke but for anyone else, then or now, who wishes to penetrate that mysterious stronghold, marked with a 'no entry' sign, where there's just one and only *one* observer capable of assigning *reality* to everything.

Cogito, ergo sum (I think, therefore I am); René Descartes, 1641.

THE BOOKWORM

It was a very long way from the Tyneside of his youth when, once again, Geordie John left his sparsely furnished, gloomy abode comprising a riverside tent and occupied his accustomed chair in the elegant wood-panelled reference library where he pursued his special interest in warfare, arms and historic battles. Open before him was a colourful double-page spread illustrating medals and military insignia. Sadly, this had become his regular daily practice since becoming homeless when his former bosses withdrew the financial help to which he was entitled as an overseas war veteran. And unfortunately, the reason given for this decision was as blunt as it was brief: namely, that 'no further support' would be appropriate in respect of the shell shock he'd sustained under enemy fire.

* * *

But today, with laudable resilience, and having adopted a sensible routine from the start of his latest misfortune, Geordie John is again taking it easy in the congenial surroundings of the reference library. Beside him, his surviving kitbag and sundry ancillary packages contain all his worldly goods. Geordie John, now aged forty, has seen better times, as is evident from his appearance; and for hours on end (between naps) he still continues to bury himself in books about anything from munitions and army transport to World War II tanks and submarines.

Come rain come shine, Geordie John still sleeps rough, but has moved from his insecure tent into a sturdier, open brick shelter by the Thames near Kingston where he occupies a vacancy in a recess at the back. On the negative side, he gives off a faint smell which is not exactly the 'odour of sanctity.' And recently, this provoked an altercation with a member of the public on his way to a family party at Carluccio's where the size of the bill would have far exceeded Geordie John's monthly unemployment benefit.

THE DIGITAL IMAGE

I

Annabelle Pettigrew, a retired schoolteacher, had treated herself to a day off from domestic chores and was relaxing in a conservatory - a conservatory which, open to the public three days a week, was the centrepiece of the Ainsley Botanical Institute's gardens near Nottingham. She was comfortably seated; and it didn't take long before she noticed the unusually large number of people (mostly young) whose indifference to botany was plain to see as they traipsed along the paved walkways whilst barely glancing at the exotic vegetation all around them.

But fortunately, as things turned out, this disparate band of wanderers (some clearly bored, others chattering wildly) was accompanied by many other visitors who represented every shape, size and age group; and some of these, as demonstrated by the wide range of languages spoken, were from overseas. All the same, on that particular afternoon, the highest (and most disorganised) proportion of human traffic comprised children from local primary schools who, as far as Annabelle could judge, were under the care of teachers who contributed very little of value - educational or otherwise - to an excursion rich in lost opportunities to stimulate interest.

* * *

Annabelle continued to look on in silence whilst her mind probed beneath the surface. And inevitably, it soon became clear that, having no one to command or direct their attention, most of the youngsters were left to their own devices. And since, as a result, they made a great deal of noise, she closed the book she'd been hoping to read and cast her eyes with resignation over what amounted to the nation's future hell-bent on a level of toing-and-froing much like that of a teeming anthill in the middle of a summer's day.

Unsurprisingly, of course, the comparison with an anthill failed to present itself at the back of Annabelle's mind. Instead, more or less out of the blue, she was struck by the equivalence between the shilly-shallying of the children and the characteristically indecisive behaviour of butterflies going about their business in the middle of August. And as she'd found out from a lifetime's experience, this is a spectacle most easily observed among the commoner white varieties often seen flitting from a bush of purple buddleia to a clump of lavender and then on to a supine mass of pink sedum in a rock garden...Without a pause, they zigzag this way and that...or suddenly change course at a perfect right angle. And yet, throughout their disorderly flight path, and rather like the children, they never seem to settle down - apparently disdaining anything like a rational plan of action.

2

And so, coincidentally, in a perversely similar fashion, these very young and very inexperienced citizens of the world had been left rudderless by those in charge of them. Unfortunately, in that circumstance, they displayed no inclination to select, distinguish or concentrate... There was no impulse to pick out a detail or to be amazed by something like the flamingo flower whose scarlet spathes neither they nor their friends had ever seen before. Apparently, their curiosity had withered away in the classroom where it was conceivable they'd been poorly prepared for their visit - or never prepared at all.

In the event, both the immediate cause and its outcome was a simple matter of observation. But to be fair to the schools and the rôle they had or perhaps hadn't played, Annabelle concluded that both the teachers and the children that afternoon almost certainly reflected a broader social picture in which, on the one hand, the teachers were wary of current attitudes to 'control'; whereas the children, on the other hand, were addicted to must-have products like mobile phones whose built-in cameras flashed like machine-gun fire at the mere sight of a brightly coloured object to which no attention whatever was paid - not at least until, back at home, the pressers of buttons (in the presence of bored parents) scrolled through images that only became actual for those who did the scrolling when reproduced digitally on a battery-powered screen.

And sadly, there's one further point worth making: namely, that later on, after closing time in the Ainsley Botanical Institute's conservatory, the original hard realities were left unidentified, unremembered and consigned entirely to oblivion behind securely locked doors.

The commoner white varieties of butterfly: the small white and the (rarer) large white, Artogeia rapae and Pieris brassicae respectively.

Flamingo flower, Anthurium scherzerianum: a tropical American species.

THE FAITH THAT MOVES MOUNTAINS

I differ from a lifelong friend of mine called Angela in one particular respect. This boils down to the fact that although, speaking personally, I'm a religious believer, Angela, by contrast, is a convinced materialist.

On a pleasantly warm summer afternoon, seated together at a small table in my garden with a bottle of sparkling wine and two glasses, she once asked me (in a mildly challenging tone of voice) whether I'd ever requested a miraculous cure for my fear of driving. To which I answered rather lamely that contingent upon being delivered from the fear itself, I would also need a second, equally miraculous exemption from the risk of a road accident. I pointed out that this would almost certainly require a degree of trust equal to 'the faith that moves mountains' - something, I suggested, that was probably beyond me.

Being of an affable disposition, she understood what I was saying: namely, that in the long run, her idea was somewhat over the top. Nevertheless, setting aside our differences, I agreed that her request for another drink was almost as reasonable as it was irrelevant to the issue we'd been discussing. 'And a good way out of any further nonsense,' she replied as she raised the glass to her lips.

Faith that moves mountains: St Matthew 17, 20.

THAT NICE YOUNG MAN

The duke's trusted gamekeeper was a young man of quiet disposition blessed with a broad range of accomplishments and abilities. When at Aberystwyth University, during his gap year, he sailed with an international crew, made up mostly of teenagers, from Melbourne to Hobart. He held a valid firearms licence - and he could dig drains, lay fences and control foxes as well as any lifelong professional.

Less noised abroad was the knack he had of reining in poachers by persuading them that he was really on their side. And he did this with a flair for deception which was no less convincing when doing the rounds with the duke in conjunction with deferential body language and fawning agreement with every superior expression of opinion on the part of his employer. And with talents like these, he was of course well liked by the smallholders and villagers whom he greeted with a winsome smile supported by an impeccable intonation of the words 'sir' or 'madam.'

But the duke's trusted gamekeeper was better at eliciting admiration than he was at fulfilling longer-term undertakings - as his employer soon discovered when his protégé, with only a month's notice, suddenly left him in the lurch, hell-bent on pastures new where, after almost a year of assiduous scheming, he had at last secured an offer of a more interesting and better paid future.

MR COLIN BLAKETON
CANDIDATE FOR COULSDON CROSS

Crafty but collaborative in his style of political planning, Colin Blaketon knew precisely when to wear a necktie and when not to. And in terms of his career prospects, this was a very particular day, indeed a *necktie* day - and one that found him in a state of heartfelt fraternal union with the top brass as he paused to take stock in the waiting room at the local party headquarters. His euphoria arose mainly because, unassumingly but carefully dressed for the meeting, he'd just been chosen as the Conservative candidate in the forthcoming general election. The constituency was known as Coulsdon Cross; the successful nominee was all agog with excitement; and the big day, God save us, was just around the corner!

In the aftermath of his success, it should be added that Colin was seated alone in the party offices comprising a former World War II air raid shelter (with various health-and-safety innovations such as windows and fire exits). This faced the entrance to the railway station. It's also worth mentioning that the station itself had once contributed to an outburst of local colour, having made the headlines in the nineteen sixties due to an offence against public decency so lurid that no hint of the details is possible in the present (relatively innocuous) story. Colin was still a boy at the time, of course - and consequently innocent of any association with a very salacious event in a largely law-abiding community.

* * *

With his genius for hitting the nail on the head with a resonant platitude, Colin Blaketon was appointed primarily because it was assumed that the voters of Coulsdon Cross would fall hook, line and sinker for the manifesto he outlined to the selection committee members before they finally took the plunge. This strongly upheld the right of the local electorate to maintain the same (some might say 'boring') identity and lifestyle which they and their forebears had enjoyed since their mock-tudor semis were built in the nineteen thirties.

The thirties, by and large, was a period in British history when the privileged inhabitants of Coulsdon Cross shared the same values in a location where, crucially, every man's home was still thought of as his castle. Since then, of course, critical changes have occurred, not least among which is the policy of certain local councils that risk opposition from the many in order to resolve the grievances of the few. The Couldsdon Cross council was no exception to this; and unfortunately for some, it was actively supporting the conversion of what were once private flats into social housing. Added to which a new and overly downmarket name had been proposed. Unsurprisingly, this was a fact of life well known to Colin Blaketon. And he was more than eager to exploit it.

* * *

In the wake of his recent appointment, it was his shrewd insight into the constituency he intended to represent that explained why Colin Blaketon was so eager to get going. After all, undeclared aspects of his programme were already well advanced. For example, was he not planning to wear a blue tie when mustering support among the mock-tudor semis whilst parading open-necked on the existing Clement Attlee Estate accompanied by his wife dressed in a red Marks & Spencer trouser suit? Tactics such as these, of course, were merely symptomatic of the degree to which he was already immersed in the details of the task that lay ahead. And as a result, he was reasonably confident that a healthy majority would secure him a seat in the House of Commons (which it did).

Honesty, however - always the best policy - compels the addition of just one more vital factor. Alongside such evidence of his skill and determination, he was similarly hopeful that his election would provide him not only with an improved financial situation but also with enough spare time to prune the roses in the back garden of his family home (which was auspiciously sited in the neighbourhood of the Reigate Hill Golf Course). And so, as he looked ahead to those happy days from the vantage point of the local party headquarters, it was a picture guaranteed to soothe the nerves of any overworked and under-appreciated parliamentarian - not least among whom was the future Mr Colin Blaketon MP.

CLOSER TO A DAYDREAM

The warm October air, with manifest disregard for all fixed positions, played havoc with the patchwork of sunlight and shade wherever the wind's influence was felt. Resilient branches swayed; the patterns of leaf and twig flickered on the turf; and a charm of finches, dislodged from a flimsy perch, flew off in droves with their faithful doppelgangers scudding across the ground beneath them.

These trifling, randomly occurring events took place within a stone's throw of a young woman whose attention, for the most part, was focussed elsewhere. Without much by way of an alternative, she was listening to a mother and daughter who were deep in conversation as they strolled casually past. But it was the briefest of interludes; and as they receded arm-in-arm into the distance, their voices grew more and more indistinct before being drowned out entirely by the action of the wind among the leaves of a nearby poplar.

From the start, as a plain matter of fact, the woman's interest had been little more than incidental; and latterly, of course, she could no longer distinguish one word from another. At the same time, it scarcely seemed to matter: after all, they were mere passers-by. And in any case, her state of mind was much closer to a daydream than to anything else until, as if from nowhere, she was suddenly brought to her senses by an overflying aircraft whose arrival instantly wrecked the silence of an almost cloudless sky. The roar of the jet engines was reminiscent of a pneumatic drill digging up a motorway; it was not only deafening, it was also deeply confrontational. On the other hand, after reaching its peak, the disturbance gradually died away; and the former peace and quiet was soon restored.

* * *

In company with these and many other short-lived circumstances, the young woman (whose name was Helen), sat complacently on the trunk of a fallen tree - perfectly content, yet in a visibly thoughtful frame of mind. Indeed, as her friends well knew, she was naturally inclined to treat the world as a question mark... as something to be examined in depth. And under the spell of what seemed like a return to July or August, she felt as if the passage of time was in a state of suspended animation.

It was a perception she felt bound to articulate. 'Who could ever guess' she murmured, 'that this brilliant afternoon is October's contribution to the last days of summer?'

And by way of a helping hand, all the evidence around her confirmed the implication. For example, a wide range of bees, wasps and hoverflies, oblivious to what was in store, were making the best of things. Moreover, the wind that stroked her cheeks was still hot, blowing from the south. On the other hand, the leaves, whose seasonal colours were now evident, seemed far better adapted: and in their quiet conversation with the air, Helen could hear the first hints of lamentation as a shabby-looking brown butterfly, true to its woodland habitat, fluttered in and out of the shadows and then vanished.

'Gone for good,' Helen thought, as her mind fast-forwarded not only to spring of the following year but to the renewal of life in all its astonishing configurations. And it helped her realise it was a prospect on which she'd depended, whenever winter loomed large, for as long as she could remember.

Shabby-looking butterfly: the 'speckled wood' butterfly, Pararge aegeria, favours the dappled light and shade of wooded areas.

IN THE PINK OF HEALTH

One morning, during the summer heatwave of 2018, I attended the Royal Eye Unit at Kingston Hospital which is situated to the south-west of London. After arrival, there was the usual delay due to the number of people awaiting treatment. Things began to improve, however, as soon as a nurse summoned me for a sight test which was then followed by a field test. A field test, for those who don't know, is a five-minute procedure that involves gazing fixedly ahead into the pitch-dark, box-like interior of a machine. At the same time, while thus occupied, the patient is expected to press a button whenever a pinpoint of light is observed at various distances from the centre. The result is then printed out in the form of a diagram and reserved for analysis by a doctor at the end of the consultation.

This, for me, was an already familiar introductory routine after which, in preparation for a retinal scan, two different eye drops were administered in order to dilate my pupils; and apart from a mild stinging sensation, there were no adverse effects. In due course, after the drops had performed their function and the scan was complete, the doctor, having gathered all the results together, assured me that my sight had not deteriorated in any significant way since the previous examination. This was very good news indeed - and well worth waiting for.

* * *

The hospital, whose internal architecture was never likely to inspire an award, was nevertheless very effectively air-conditioned. On the other hand, when I finally put my glasses back on and emerged into the glare of the midday sun, I was met by a wall of heat which immediately took me back to the occasion when, on leaving a cinema many years previously in the Indian city of Chenai, I was bowled over by a similarly sudden rise in temperature.

Despite this distant recollection, of course, I was soon reminded that I was in Britain rather than South India by a very odd experience. To be more precise, I discovered that the drops I'd been given were having a completely unforeseen side effect which caused the visible world around me to abandon its familiar colour range in favour of a disconcertingly pervasive pink. It was as if some charmed vapour had entered the earth's atmosphere from outer space, staining the environment by means that were visible only in terms of their outcome.

This transformation was particularly marked in the case of the various white objects that happened to be within range; and among the first examples I noticed were the shorts rather inadvisedly worn by an elderly man waiting at the bus stop near the car park. To attribute reality to the obvious illusion that confronted me would have been absurd, of course; but with a more or less clear picture of what was going on, I had to chuckle at the sight of an ageing so-and-so with his rear end draped in a pair of pink shorts - shorts, by the way, that clearly hadn't been ironed since they last emerged from the washing machine.

As I strolled downhill towards the station, the drops continued to affect me and gave rise to a pair of curiously striking daydreams that I still clearly remember. In the first place, the reflection of the sun, repeated a thousand times over on the glossy leaves of a holly bush, evoked an image of the fairy lights glinting on an out-of-season Christmas tree. And secondly, the white (now pink) paintwork on the nearby properties suddenly brought to mind the well-remembered, multicoloured cluster of beach huts at Margate basking in the sun while the waves rolled lazily ashore from France.

* * *

In the end, after the novelty had begun to pall, I made up my mind that (pink or otherwise) the discolouration that confronted me was something of a damp squib by comparison with the subtlety and variety of Mother Nature's time-honoured inventiveness. And therefore, as I waited impatiently for the effect of the drops to wear off, I concluded that the world was *not* a better place when looked at through rose-tinted spectacles.

STRICTLY BETWEEN FRIENDS

Daniel Boothroyd was lying supine with his head and shoulders propped up on a heap of pillows. He was feeling rather groggy, and consequently somewhat sorry for himself. He'd also been fending off an unspoken suspicion, for which there was no actual evidence, that he was on his last legs.

A few moments earlier, with the object of cheering him up, a friend of his, Justin, had put in an unscheduled appearance. And before going on, it's worth mentioning that, by the time of this story, both parties (who were former school pals), had survived relatively unscathed into their early seventies.

* * *

Following some prefatory banter and a few light-hearted enquiries about the invalid's progress, Justin and Dan began to reminisce - as was their established custom after a month or so without seeing each other. Such retrospective interludes were often repetitious insofar as they covered similar ground - ground, moreover, that was usually concerned with the amusing or daredevil escapades of their youth. In addition to this, very occasionally, a cat was let out of the bag by one of the two friends that came as a surprise to the other. On this particular occasion, however, once the familiar routine showed signs of faltering without any 'unexpected surprises' to keep it going, Justin altered course and asked Dan how he regarded his past life in the wake of the long innings which they both shared. To which Dan made the following, somewhat disconcerting reply.

'Now and again,' came the answer, 'I suppose I've quite enjoyed my encounter with the world and his wife. But broadly speaking, and strictly between you and me, it's been a bit of a *bore* most of the time!'

There was then an impromptu hiatus - after which, by common consent, both parties concealed their embarrassment with the help of a somewhat artificial outbreak of laughter. This continued to rumble on rather awkwardly until sobriety was restored under the influence of tea and biscuits supplied by Dan's alter ego: namely, by his wife who returned to the kitchen without delay following a polite but rather flat exchange of pleasantries with Justin.

* * *

Before concluding this story, Dan's wife, whose name was Heather, deserves something more than a passing mention. She was, when all's said and done, a quiet, singularly composed woman who, at the same time, was shrewd enough to make herself scarce when her husband and Justin were engrossed in a bout of nostalgia from which she felt excluded. It was an unfortunate situation arising from lack of forethought to which neither Dan nor Justin had ever paid much attention. And this was for the very good reason, as simple as it was sad, that they were both completely unaware of it.

NORHAM CASTLE, SUNRISE

Bernadette Picoche, who commanded excellent English, was assiduously studying the caption alongside Turner's painting of Norham Castle - a mesmerising amalgam of yellow and blue light set in a dramatic Northumbrian landscape that seemed weightless and appeared to float. Without any question, it was one of the finest works of art then on show at London's Tate Britain gallery.

With great care, she was following the details provided, glancing occasionally at the picture itself so as to compare description and reality. Indeed, there was something like the doggedness of a metronome about the right-then-left-hand movements of her head.

All the same, it wasn't long before she took the briefest of concluding looks at the painting - a look she limited to under three seconds. The effect was reminiscent of a traveller, in the middle of saying goodbye, whose smile fades in an instant while making a dash for the last train to a remote destination.

* * *

It was almost certainly a case of actions speaking louder than words. And for Madame Picoche, who was close to fifty and very well informed, provenance and historical associations were extremely important. It was an attitude, unfortunately, that left the object itself in a state of limbo. And the reason was simply this: that, although an art lover, she'd long ago forgotten that commentary and information are not the only rewards for someone like her - a principle supported, for example, by Hiroshige's many images of Mount Fuji whose beauty in no way depends on the accompanying calligraphy which, for most Westerners, is as hard to understand as the physics of a Northumbrian sunrise.

Hiroshige: Japanese woodblock artist, 1787 - 1858.

SOD'S LAW

Having discovered through the usual channels that my private collection included works by a certain up-and-coming artist, Professor Robert Tremaine, director of a local but well regarded art gallery in the West of England, wrote to me at my London address to ask whether I would allow a selection of these works to feature in the next exhibition he had in mind. It was a tribute to my perspicacity and good fortune, he added, that I owned several paintings by the young man in question that were uniquely fine examples of his oeuvre. And on this account alone, he hoped I might be interested in raising awareness of so promising a talent in an area beyond the confines of London and the South East.

I replied, perhaps a little too bluntly, that I would happily consider his proposal subject to rock-solid insurance cover at the gallery's expense. I also mentioned that I would be looking to my solicitor for an opinion on the precise terms and conditions of the protection thereby offered. At the same time, I was at pains to point out that my cautious approach in no way implied lack of confidence either in the gallery or in its director. But as I went on to explain as succinctly as I could, it *did* imply a lack of confidence in a world where the risks associated with sod's law were common knowledge.

Robert Tremaine was obviously a dab hand at dealing with jittery art enthusiasts; and much to my surprise, my stipulations were taken on board virtually by return of post. This prompted me to act with similar speed and, in the form of a first class recorded delivery letter despatched on the following morning, I returned my carefully worded consent to the loan, adding that for the time being, at so early a stage in the negotiations, this was to be taken as a 'statement of intent' - and nothing more. But I had reservations; and fearing my turn of phrase might sound a little ominous, I toned it down by emphasising that I could foresee no prospect of a snag.

In jumping the gun by more or less giving the go-ahead before consulting my solicitor, I nevertheless refrained from mentioning my perception that any enlargement of the artist's reputation might well increase the value of his work. And as I look back, I think this thought (and its persuasive effect) is more than likely to have been at the back of the professor's mind when he referred to raising *awareness* of the young man's talent beyond London and the South East.

Whether or not any such outcome was consciously planned as a means to an end can never be known. But the conspiracy, if that's what it was, certainly bore fruit about six months after the exhibition drew to a close. There could be no doubt that, by chance or otherwise, I immediately remembered Professor Tremaine's words when, whilst browsing the internet, I noticed that a forth-coming sale at Sotheby's included two paintings by François de Ville - a discovery that was all the more exciting now that the five examples of the same artist's work had been safely returned to me after their resounding success in the West Country.

Given such a promising set of circumstances, of course, I was more than willing to concede that, for once, sod's law must have been working in my favour rather than against it. And on the strength of a powerful impulse, I decided that nothing would stop me from standing on the sidelines as the bids came in and the auctioneer's hammer came down. As a result, I immediately marked my diary in bold red letters to the effect that April 23 next was to be kept clear of all possible impediments to my presence, as a fly on the wall, at an event whose effect on my future might well be crucial.

LLYWELYN

Looking back to the early fifties, 'Old Grammarians' from a school in South London may possibly recall a fellow pupil by the name of Llywelyn. Llywelyn, who kept himself to himself, was (as the name indicates) of Welsh extraction.

He was also remarkably pale of feature, and known to be of an evangelical disposition.

* * *

One summer, there was a school trip to Belgium led by a master called Rabson - popularly known as Rab. Our accommodation was situated by the sea at Blankenberge which was within walking distance of the mediaeval city of Bruges.

The Flemish name for Bruges was Brugge which, with the hard g's and the voicing of the final e, naturally came in for a certain amount of mutilation on youthful lips.

* * *

An excursion by coach to Ghent was organised, the details of which I no longer recall. But on the way home to Blankenberge, a startling rumour was circulated as the coach rumbled on through unfamiliar territory.

It appeared that an unnamed party had offered a pornographic booklet for sale - something which in those days was a very rare commodity. More startling still were allegations concerning the purchaser.

And it was noised abroad with profound amusement that the quiet, withdrawn and evangelical Llywelyn must have had another side to his character!

PEACOCK BLUE

High up on the Marlborough Downs in Wiltshire and at some distance from the nearest large town, Maureen was strolling alone in the grounds of Ocklesham Manor. The surrounding landscape was regarded by many as being on the barren side; but Sir Desmond Northcliffe who owned the estate and was a keen horticulturalist, had managed to create a delightful and surprisingly diverse garden tucked away in a natural depression which, under the scrutiny of an all-weather sky, was overlooked by the elegant façade of Sir Desmond's stately home.

Maureen, it should be added, lived locally in a village that was roughly divided into two parts: the original, historic core and the mid-twentieth century redbrick addition scornfully described by its critics as 'the development.' Inevitably, the historic area was the only part of any interest to visitors. It consisted of a picturesque hotchpotch of properties dating variously from the eighteenth and nineteenth centuries with a surviving medieval church at its heart. By contrast, the modern section was respectable and neatly laid out; but unfortunately, it was made up mainly of bungalows and was of no interest at all to anyone other than those who lived there. Luckily for Maureen, however, she occupied a house that was neither a redbrick bungalow nor a cottage with ailing thatch from a bygone era - despite which, it was built in 1897 and securely situated on the traditional, long-established side of the borderline where the village of Westerly Green was now divided into two distinct communities.

* * *

As it happened, Maureen was a long-term lover of Ocklesham Manor; and because it was a regular 'open day', she'd taken advantage of her husband's absence on business and had made an early start. As a plain matter of fact, it's worth knowing that although she was born and bred in a South London suburb, she'd developed over time into an authentic countrywoman. And in keeping with this acquired characteristic, other visitors to Ocklesham Manor that day would have noticed a middle-aged woman of medium height with a brown headscarf supplemented by tweeds of matching colour. They would also have deduced the practical side to her nature from the threadbare carpet bag hoisted over her shoulders containing the day's refreshments.

Most of Maureen's friends and family were aware that, although she made no claims to expert knowledge, she was still a committed enthusiast when it came to landscape and wildlife. Furthermore, it was something she'd apparently been born with - a characteristic which worked in her special favour whenever her other half was away on one of his frequent business trips. It was also a bonus when a suitable opportunity coincided with favourable weather conditions - as was the present case at the beginning of yet another enjoyable trip to Ocklesham Manor where the colours of autumn were at their best and the sun still generous before the winter finally took charge.

Maureen was a naturally observant woman - always on the lookout. She was interested in everything that caught her eye; and conditions could not have been better that day. In the depression where the garden was situated, she was sheltered from the cutting edge of the wind she'd noticed at the top of the hill. And consequently, at that much lower level, it meant that the air was almost stationary and made no inroads into a prevailing stillness that bristled with sounds so faint that they reminded her of the scuttling feet of mice she'd once heard as a child in a dilapidated barn.

To Maureen, even the falling leaves left a positive impression: florid as newly minted coins, they tapped dryly on the hard foliage of a holly bush whose berries sparkled in the November light. It was a day when the sun transformed whatever it touched. Among the grass blades, for example, the overnight hoar frost had dissolved into a scatter of uncut diamonds that flipped from colour to colour as she strolled serenely on. Even the shadows glimmered; and reality, however impermanent, seemed to have achieved perfection.

* * *

Now, Maureen's favourites among the various animals and birds in the Ocklesham Manor gardens were the peacocks. And with luck on her side, it didn't take long before she spotted them in a sheltered suntrap on a bed of leaves. Indifferent to her arrival, they were preening the blue exuberance of their feathers. They were visibly content - content in a manner specific to time and place as they sprawled flat on their bellies in the unseasonal warmth of the sun.

Maureen derived great satisfaction from what was, for her, an eagerly awaited reunion with old friends. And so, in keeping with their evident euphoria, she sat down on a nearby log and watched them as they gradually dozed off in all their absurd loveliness. On the other hand, struck by an undercurrent of seasonal foreboding, she also felt sorry for them.

It was an understandable sentiment. And despite the idyllic environment, she couldn't brush the feeling aside. After all, she knew something the peacocks themselves were totally unaware of: namely, that winter was getting close. But she also reflected that each one of them would be soldiering obliviously on - blind to Mother Nature's indifference until the clouds gathered, the temperature dropped, and the custom-built woodland shelter became their life-saving wintertime home.

PROPYLEA 14-PUNCTATA

During a sunny afternoon walk in the picturesque Brookside Burial Ground, Myfanwy, conspicuous for her snow-white hair and a sturdy woollen jacket with matching skirt, noticed a ladybird on the lavender which was growing among the weeds on a nineteen-seventies grave. The woman who accompanied her, Alice, was dressed more casually than her friend and wore a frilly white blouse with a contrasting pair of bright red trousers - added to which was an imitation pearl necklace that glowed faintly in the May sunshine. She had known Myfanwy, who was also her neighbour, for a very long time; and so, when that rather grand lady came to a halt and began examining the ladybird, she prepared for what experience told her might prove a rather lengthy outpouring of supposition.

Alice was perfectly correct; and there was no shortage either of question marks or statements of the obvious. There was earnest comment, for example, on the insect's oddly unfamiliar spots which raised the question as to whether it was an alien or native species; and this uncertainty gained even greater force when Alice pointed out that, unlike the red colour commonly associated with ladybirds, the specimen before them was bright yellow with black markings that deviated decisively from the usual understanding of what a spot ought to look like.

Now it happened that a youngish-looking stranger called George had been tending a nearby grave during the course of this conversation - every word of which he'd overheard without the slightest difficulty. His curiosity was naturally aroused; and so, as soon as the coast was clear, he set aside his trowel and went to have a look. He noticed, of course, that the insect, although exactly like a ladybird in size and shape, was indeed a brilliant yellow rather than red. But like Alice and Myfanwy, he also noticed the particularly bizarre black markings that reminded him, on the one hand, of a wasp and, on the other hand, of certain geometrical patterns he remembered seeing some years previously at an exhibition of tribal fabrics. But he was no entomologist; and the matter remained as much a mystery for him as it had done for the two women who were now some way off. And so, mildly perplexed, he returned to the task of smartening up his father's grave.

Until then, the afternoon had been a pleasantly cloudless experience for everyone alike. But from that point onwards, it slowly subdivided into the distinctive, separate worlds of those who happened to be enjoying it. Myfanwy and Alice popped home for tea and a slice of chocolate sponge. George, the youngish-looking stranger in his mid thirties, finished clipping the overgrown rosemary and drove off to collect his children from school. Which meant that the ladybird, left to its own devices, was troubled no further by human curiosity.

Meanwhile, the broader environment went its own, characteristically quiet way. Loosened by the faintest of breezes, pink petals tumbled like snow from the flowering cherry trees. Pollinators of every description buzzed to and fro. And headstones, ancient and modern, many of them the sole surviving reminders of forgotten lives, bristled peacefully in the sun at divergent angles.

Yellow ladybird... with bizarre black markings: the fourteen-spot ladybird, Propylea 14-punctata.

TAKING STOCK

*The river flowed steadily on through
summer meadows. Trout, effortlessly
defying the current, hid among the rushes
at the water's edge. Brick-red and darkly
speckled, fritillaries glorified the thorny
brambles. Alone at last, but released from
constraint, she inhaled the pure air.*

Michael Hill

I

Geraldine and Martha were siblings with at least twelve years between them. And when Geraldine, the eldest, finally realised that she'd intruded too much and too long on Martha's future plans, private interests, work pressures and domestic tensions, something inside her snapped like a vital organ in the throes of a crisis.

Until that point, the dependent nature of Geraldine's association with her sister had been taken for granted by both parties. And in fact, any suspicion that the closeness of the connection was wearing thin had only come to light since Martha suddenly announced that, barely three years following what was still an all-too-recent divorce, she was on the brink of a second marriage. Indeed, it was clearly in the aftermath of this unexpected news that the worsening relations were rooted.

During that period, short though a three-year interval may seem when spelt out in black and white, the two children of Martha's first marriage had matured and were beginning to present the usual problems associated with teenagers. Far more disturbing and radical, however, were the increasingly frequent alterations to lifestyle introduced by Martha's latest heart-throb: namely, by Ralph who (in the belief that he'd damaged his reputation by marrying her) was determined to improve the visible marks of his newly acquired family by upgrading their previous, run-of-the-mill routine in pursuit of his own social aspirations - aspirations that (in practice) Geraldine considered not only pretentious but also unreasonably ostentatious and therefore a source of embarrassment and resentment.

Before going on, it's worth emphasising that, harsh though Geraldine's judgement may have been, there was no shortage of truth in it. And unfortunately, this gave rise to a feeling of alienation that strayed well beyond the bounds of her unspoken reflections. In other words, gradually and by some wholly indefinable means, it generated a dark, yet invisible cloud that overshadowed the once carefree atmosphere characteristic of the family as a whole.

2

For Geraldine, the progressive downturn in the course of events and the bleak conclusion it led to gave place to a depression compounded by growing anxiety. After all, until things became as clear as they now were, she'd spent almost as much time under Martha's roof as she had in her own modest cottage near the village green and the local shops. Moreover, as a widow, as a close relative and also as an extra pair of hands, she'd got used to staying overnight in her sister's house where, among other things, she'd enjoyed playing her part in caring for the children. And so, almost inevitably, Martha's pebble-dashed semi had become established in Geraldine's mind as a regular bolt-hole that she simply took for granted.

But in the end, of course, reality had to be faced - and this led to the recognition that Ralph's intrusive influence had turned everything upside down. This meant that, after many years of reliance on her

sister's support and companionship, Geraldine now regarded herself in the same light as she suspected she was regarded by others:
namely, as a worn-out piece of furniture which, in her own words,
had been 'consigned to the rubbish heap' - 'rubbish heap' being an
ironical and somewhat spiteful allusion to her own perfectly comfortable residence that both locals and casual day trippers looked
upon as 'that pretty little house by the green.'

* * *

It was a rather dramatic assessment which, at the same time, genuinely
summed up how Geraldine felt about her situation. And the final
upshot of the ongoing upheaval was this: that without any awkward excuses or ham-fisted manoeuvres, she ended up spending
much of her time alone in a cottage which, despite its picturesque
setting, seemed bleaker than it ever had in the past. Even more
worrying was the fact that she began to feel older. And added to
the stiffening of limbs and an upper lip that had never complained
about what had happened, she also began to feel the first genuine
pangs of loneliness. In the wake of these developments, two
significant responses arose: firstly, she lost the impulse to pick up
the telephone; and secondly, she found that, in any case, there was
little left to talk about. All of which, very unhelpfully for Geraldine,
created a degree of self-pity that trapped her in an unfamiliar
wilderness while the visits to her former home from home became
significantly fewer.

3

Nonetheless, despite adversity, she stood her ground. And in the
sheer barrenness of her predicament, she fought back. It was an act
of revenge directed more against change itself than against those
responsible for it. She defied the shadows that crept about like

ghosts in her modest home; and instead of giving in, she consented more readily than before to the cheerful conversations and casual chit-chat freely on offer in the village post office. The village shop-cum-post-office, of course, is a regular meeting place common to many rural communities; and in the present instance, as things turned out, it involved Geraldine in a welcome personal encounter and a consequent invitation to join a local history group - a group much given to exploring places of interest within easy reach of its members.

It was a well meant proposition made by friendly neighbours in full knowledge of the troubles which they'd gently persuaded her to disclose. But in response, at least to begin with, all she could manage was to smile vacantly for a week or so while she battled with the misgivings that came with what was, for her, a tempting but challenging opportunity.

In the end, however, with reluctance and curiosity in equal proportions, it was an offer she decided to go along with. And rather to her surprise, she was by no means disappointed. She enjoyed the visit to the abandoned Ravensbourne tin mine; the view from Highpoint Hill was amazing; and she was particularly taken by the idyllic little river near Talisman Wood which, as she instantly remembered, was the exact spot where she'd once watched her father landing a battle-weary trout.

* * *

It was an experience as revealing as it was refreshing; and although unforeseen, it was also a turning point that exposed reserves too long neglected. In addition, there was another inherent benefit that suited her needs more than any other: namely, clear proof from the monthly walkabouts with ordinary people that human warmth can be found beyond the confines of family relationships. She also rediscovered the highways and byways of her childhood which amounted to a great deal more than the riverside recollections near Talisman Wood which, along with so many others throughout her adult years, had been obscured by the passage of time.

And so, at some length, and keeping her qualms at bay as best she could, Geraldine began the long road to a destination that inevitably involved the risk associated with her new way of life; but lacking a viable alternative, it was also a risk she was genuinely willing to take. And wisely, despite the recurrent hankerings that pursued her, she never turned back.

Fritillaries: a colourful and profusely speckled group of related butterflies; family Nymphalidae.

IN A COUNTRY GARDEN

It was the first day of July 2018. And in the canopy of the oak just above where he was sitting, he could hear a series of sounds - each of which reminded him of a husky, rather fraught intake of breath reinforced by the croaking of a frog with a bad cold.

From past experience, of course, Evan was well aware of what was going on. And having briefly set aside the newspaper he was reading, he recognised that the call to arms among the leaves above his head was that of a grey squirrel warming up to a territorial challenge from a fellow member of its own species whose gender it shared and whose impending intrusion it was determined to thwart.

* * *

All of which, taken together within the confines of a beautiful afternoon, was being played out against the background of an otherwise overwhelming silence. This was a condition whose origin lay in the fields and forests; it was the welcome sign of a rural setting that stood defiantly apart from the forthcoming scene of battle. Not only that: if everything followed the usual pattern, the silence, so rudely interrupted, would return and hold good at the heart of a lasting peace. It was something about which Evan was quite certain. And the reason was simply this: that a host of similar incidents in the past had taught him that the minor skirmish he anticipated and the chase that followed it would soon be over and done with.

A PERFECTLY ORDINARY MORTAL

Sitting at his desk by the window, he was reaching the end of yet another day. The sky, which was partly obscured by the silhouette of an oak tree, had assumed the colour of damp grey flannel. And in the background, like the sound of a distant waterfall, the tyres of passing cars hissed and spluttered on the wet tarmac.

Scribbling away on a ruled notepad, his approach was rather disjointed. He was struggling to come up with ideas about the future and what it might hold for someone like himself whose recollection of youth was so faint that it seemed more like a mirage. But although he'd steeled himself against deviating from so vital an issue, he had to acknowledge that the glass beside his wrist (which he'd emptied twice within the hour) could be taken as a means of dodging the very problem he was trying to concentrate on. More-over, the imminent prospect of the next working week went hand in hand with a state of anxiety he was doing his best to overcome - which, as he well knew, meant that a third glass of wine would have to be tackled before long.

And yet, despite the gathering gloom outside the window, Duncan fought on in company with a proliferation of side issues, concerns and involvements that had little bearing on his future. He was quite clear - surprise, surprise - that the planet was still spinning. At the same time, he was struck by the silence of the birds whose voices he knew well from the dawn chorus and from his frequent strolls in the nearby woods. It was Sunday, of course! And the hubbub of everyday living was inevitably supplanted by an indefinable tran-quillity that encouraged him to take the coming week in his stride. At the same time, however, with characteristic ambivalence, he couldn't suppress his resistance.

* * *

In consequence of his dilemma, he found himself staring Monday in the face as if it had already come and gone. Tuesday (when similarly contemplated) looked no better. All the same, laying his notepad to one side along with his pen, Duncan retaliated by reeling off a few home truths directed, in hope rather than conviction, at himself.

'When push comes to shove,' he murmured, 'there's always a silver lining - or so they say. After all, I have *not* been diagnosed with cancer; I am *not* in pain; and I am *not* impoverished. On the contrary,' he went on, 'my wife is in good health; I am anticipating our evening meal together; and between us, we shall make light work of a bottle of Chateau Something-or-Other.'

At this point, Duncan paused in order to consolidate his progress before continuing. 'I'm well aware,' he said, 'that I'm a perfectly ordinary mortal - which amounts to a bonus in its own right. It's equally obvious that I'm not much of an improvement on the average man or woman... although I'm certainly no worse. But perhaps my best claim to fame is simply this: that I know I'm *different* only insofar as I realise that I'm *not* different.'

And on that approximation to an optimistic note, he poured his third glass of wine, drank it... and closed his notepad with a yawn.

LIGHTS OUT

Janice lay awake in bed, burdened (and not for the first time) by the imperatives of recollection. One by one, the lights of the seaside village where she lived were going out as a pale moon gained the ascendant and shone indifferently down on events from her past that would never be repeated. Vividly, but in no special order, she pictured the faces of departed friends who once rejoiced in a care-free present and looked ahead to the future as a beacon of hope. And yet, in the aftermath of those anticipated years which by now were themselves relics of a bygone era, prospects (once bright) had seemingly come to nothing; and great expectations (whether realised or not), might just as well never have been thought of. For Janice, therefore, if memories such as these could be said to have any reality at all, it was a reality akin to the cosmic microwave back-ground radiation that carries the birthmarks of a universe that is already middle-aged. It was a combination of regret and longing which, well into her seventies, had left her feeling relegated and forgotten long before yet another, all-too-recent disaster com-pounded her acquaintance with emptiness.

* * *

Her latest misfortune, as it happens, was a setback that differed from all the others not only because it was recent but because it was more than merely human - given that Janice, out of the two parties concerned, was the only representative of homo sapiens. In plainer words, what it amounted to was this: that one of her few remaining and most abiding friends had finally taken his leave... had enjoyed his last walk on the esplanade... had barked one last time at a passing rival and had chewed his last bone... A common enough experience for dog owners, you might perhaps say - brushing everything aside in a moment of thoughtlessness.

Nevertheless, in all its stark simplicity, this was the long and the short of something she could do very little about - although what little she *could* do she'd certainly done. Unsurprisingly, as she lay supine in the darkness of her bedroom, a single sob interrupted the silence as she thought things over. Never again, she concluded, would that faithful animal get wind of a scent and drag her towards its source as she struggled to keep hold of the leash.

It was a heartfelt memory that left her with a lump in her throat and just one consoling reflection as she pictured him now: secure from the risk of pain, and buried with honours in a familiar spot where at night he could still hear the sound of breakers pounding an invisible shore.

SPRING FESTIVAL

I was alone beneath uncertain skies on a hill in the middle of nowhere. Beyond the reach of claim, counterclaim, phone calls and final demands, my ears were open to far distant voices.

Forgotten centuries like ghosts murmured in the woods as the leaves sprang back to life. Anemones, tilting to the north in the warm Atlantic breeze, huddled in suspense. Day-owls, hidden out of sight, countered each other's moans at quickening intervals. Even the frogs, croaking in a silver pool, sounded a fanfare among the ripples as sudden thunder hedged me about and filled my heart with joy.

Day-owls: the short-eared owl (Asio flammeus), often vocal during the day.

RESTORATION

In the Lost Gardens there is reconstruction, reimposed order, renovated pathways and former vistas triumphantly reclaimed from once impenetrable undergrowth. At last, the wind blows peacefully down cared-for woodland alleys; streams that were clogged with debris laugh out loud at their deliverance; and borders, long concealed beneath nettle beds and rubble, are now ablaze with summer flowers.

Heligan that was lost is found. Its ancient face shines like a bride's on her wedding day. Trippers and daydreamers flock there by the coachload: and in broad daylight they walk in quiet colloquy with the lingering shadows.

The Lost Gardens of Heligan, 19th century. Near Mevagissey, Cornwall. Owned by the Tremayne family: neglected after WWI, restored in the 1990s.

OUT AND ABOUT

Ewen McAllister was a retired art historian whose wife, three years previously, had died from breast cancer. He'd never fully got over it; and in the wake of so devastating an event, he'd become prone to anxiety whenever the slightest internal symptom of illness presented itself. Inevitably, therefore, on his way to see his doctor for what he thought were perfectly sound reasons, he was feeling extremely apprehensive - although, despite the pressure, he'd tried hard to overcome it.

His problem boiled down to the fact that, for several months, he'd been suffering from increasingly acute symptoms of heartburn; and although Doctor Jenkins had not been unduly concerned, he guessed that Ewen was afraid he might be following in his wife's footsteps - with lung cancer, of course, rather than breast cancer. Consequently, a hospital appointment had been organised; and a fairly intrusive scan had been carried out on the Monday of the previous week.

For Ewen, it was a very long ten days before, late in the afternoon, he again found himself in Doctor Jenkins' surgery. By that time, the results of the tests had been received; and after closing the door behind him, it appeared quite natural when the doctor pointed to a chair and asked him to sit down. At the age of fifty-eight, however, Ewen's lifelong tendency to brood remained undiminished. With the result that he immediately began to suspect that the routine invitation to sit down was a preparation for bad news. And unfortunately, it was a suspicion by no means alleviated when the doctor caught his eye and smiled in a way which would have been a great deal more reassuring if it had been a little less mechanical.

'Don't look so concerned,' said the doctor as he leaned across the table towards his patient. 'No untoward symptoms have come to light. It's just good old-fashioned heartburn, after all. Nothing to worry about.'

A light-hearted but brief chat then ensued - after which the doctor made out a prescription. He then advised Ewen that the treatment was in the form of tablets and would be permanent but effective. The conversation then drew swiftly to a close and the two men shook hands.

* * *

Just after dawn the following morning, Doctor Jenkins would have been quite surprised if he'd been a fly on the wall in Ewen's bedroom at the precise moment when his patient of the day before glanced at the window, spotted a cloudless sky and instantly sat bolt upright. He would have been even more surprised as he watched him leap out of bed, uttering cries of delight on his way to the bathroom. After all, the plain fact of the matter was this: that Ewen was overwhelmed with relief at his deliverance from the fear of cancer. For which reason, after a refreshing shower, he continued wandering up and down like a five-year-old while he pottered about in the kitchen. And in circumstances such as these, of course, who could blame him for celebrating his good fortune in suitably exuberant language as he made plans for a day out?

'Today,' he muttered under his breath as he prepared breakfast, 'I shall make the devil dance for his dinner. I shall walk on air. I shall dawdle in wild places and tread the gravel of a shallow stream. There is no time for despond today. The sun has risen already; and stiff of limb but glad of heart, the younger man must be out and about.'

Designed and typeset by David Bloomfield
Cover illustration by Michael Hill